M

Cohen, Stephen Paul.

Island of steel

$17.45

ISLAND OF STEEL

ALSO BY STEPHEN PAUL COHEN

Heartless

Stephen Paul Cohen

ISLAND
—— OF ——
STEEL

William Morrow and Company, Inc.
New York

M

11-88 BT 1800

Copyright © 1988 by Stephen Paul Cohen

Grateful acknowledgment is made for permission to use the following:

"Welcome to the Working Week," by Elvis Costello
Copyright © 1977 Plangent Visions Music Inc.

Library of Congress Cataloging-in-Publication Data

Cohen, Stephen Paul.
    Island of steel/Stephen Paul Cohen.
    p. cm.
    ISBN 0-688-07548-7
    I. Title.
PS3553.0433I85 1988
813'.54—dc19   88-13090
                                                          CIP

Printed in the United States of America

First Edition

1   2   3   4   5   6   7   8   9   10

BOOK DESIGN BY KATHRYN PARISE

**For Susan, Lesle, David
and Ronnie**

ISLAND OF STEEL

CHAPTER
—1—

At ten minutes to nine on Monday morning I stepped out of
the elevator onto the thirty-fourth floor of the Fred French
Building in New York. I was wearing a gray pin-stripe suit,
a white shirt, a blue tie and a new pair of shoes that hurt like
hell. The hallway was clean and quiet and I listened to my
new heels clicking on the polished floor. The first office on
the left was a dentist's office, and the next office belonged to
Melvin & Melvin, Architects. The last office on the left had
a big wooden door with gold lettering announcing Charles
Murphy Detective Agency, Inc. The door was locked, and
no one answered when I rang the bell, so I put my hands in
my pants pockets and leaned against the wall.

After a short wait the elevator doors opened and a woman
came charging out into the hallway. She was large and
healthy looking, and she had a lot of black and gray hair that

did not seem to be in any particular order. She was wearing a beige raincoat that went down to her ankles and she was fishing around in her big pocketbook for keys. She did not seem to notice me until she was right in front of me, and then she took me in with one casual glance and turned her concentration to getting her keys in the door.

"I'm Eddie Margolis," I said to her back.

"Yeah, I figured," she said, pushing the door open, but not stepping inside. "I'm Kate, the secretary." She slid her hand along the inside wall and turned on the lights, and led me in. I had expected the office to look like Murphy's old office in the Narcotics Division at the Ninth Precinct, but instead I found a beautifully decorated reception room, with a plush carpet of blues and grays and a deep, comfortable-looking couch. A big glass coffee table was lined with glossy magazines.

Kate peeled her coat off and disappeared behind a closet door. "Charlie called me at home this morning," she said into the closet. "He won't be in today, but there's some meeting he wants you to go to."

"Where is he?" I asked.

She closed the door and looked down at her feet, as if making sure she was all there, and I had to give her the once over, two or three times. Her face was put together all wrong. Her chin and her mouth were too small for her cheeks and this exaggerated the peculiar lines that ran down both sides of her mouth from her nose. Her eyes were big and dark, but too close together. It wasn't a particularly pretty face, but it was interesting. Her body was another story. She wore a blue and black dress that fit her perfectly: pinning her big shoulders back, gracefully taking the long curve out over her breasts, gently tapering in at the waist and finally coming to a perfect stop about three inches above the knees. Her legs were in black stockings and she wore black shoes with heels that she did not really need.

"I know," she said. "Not much in the face department, but I've never had any complaints about the body. Don't get any ideas, though. I don't believe in fishing in the office pool. No coat?"

"No, no coat."

"He's in Poughkeepsie. He'll be back tonight and he wants to meet you here in the office around six. *My* hours are nine to five," she said, walking around to her desk, "with an hour for lunch, whenever I can take it. I won't work late, but if you give me enough notice, I can get someone who will." She sat at her desk and swung her chair around to face me. "Once you're settled in a little, I'll show you how to work the answering machine, for when I'm not here. The mail comes around eleven, and I open it right away, so don't be like him, asking me every ten minutes if the mail's come in yet." She stopped to catch her breath and put her fists dramatically on her hips. "So you're Eddie Margolis. We must have received a hundred résumés and done twenty interviews, and then suddenly Charlie goes out and hires some guy he says he found in the gutter. You're a little young, aren't you?"

"I've never been any older."

"Charlie says you were down in Florida."

"I was visiting my father."

"I heard you used to drink."

"What'd he do, show you my résumé?"

She laughed. "What was it like?"

"My résumé?"

"No, drinking."

"It wasn't like anything. What's Murphy doing in Poughkeepsie?"

"Did you have a job?"

"Is this an interview?"

"Oh, don't mind me. I've been like this ever since I left my husband. You ever been divorced?"

"No."

"Come on, I'll show you your desk. But then you're going to have to leave me alone, because I have a lot of work to do."

She got up from her desk and led me to the door that led off the reception room. We entered in the middle of a huge rectangular office. It had a shiny wood floor and potted plants. Directly across from us was a cozy little setup with a couch, a few arm chairs and a coffee table. Behind that a wall of windows presented a spectacular view of the west side of Manhattan. A large antique desk monopolized the far end of the room to the right, and to the left there was a wall of filing cabinets. In the near left corner there was a small desk with a chair.

"This is yours," Kate said, leading me over to the little desk. "There are some papers here for you to fill out. The Employee's Statement has to be completed and sent in today. The application for a pistol permit can be done whenever you get a chance. You'll need your fingerprints taken. I think you'll need three sets all together, and you'll need some photos. There's a place around the corner. Oh yeah, and every morning you have to give me your working memo from the day before, together with your time sheets and your expense sheets."

"*Working* memo?" I moved around in front of my desk and looked at the piles of papers and applications.

"Oh, well, maybe he better explain that to you. Here's the Dictaphone. And here's your keys. This is for the office door, right here. This one is to the outside door of the building, in case you need it. I think they lock up down there around ten. Listen, I've got to make some coffee, would you like some?"

"What's Murphy doing in Poughkeepsie?"

"How the hell should I know. You think he tells me anything?"

"You said there was a meeting I was supposed to go to?"

"Oh yeah, You're supposed to go see this guy George Walsh over at Fenner, Covington and Pine. It's a law firm that wants to hire us."

"What am I supposed to do?"

"Hey, if I knew that, Charlie could've hired me instead of you. Now do you want coffee or don't you?"

CHAPTER

—2—

Fenner, Covington & Pine was prominently perched on the top three floors of the Pan Am building. The main reception area was on the fifty-eighth floor and consisted of approximately two acres of Persian rugs and antique furniture. The only modern accent was an expansive view of twentieth-century downtown Manhattan. I approached the three women behind the large reception desk, feeling vaguely self-conscious in my suit and tie. A matronly woman, with a full body and big eyes, sat comfortably in the middle of the desk, her arms thrown out casually in front of her. Her relaxed posture and listless hands exuded an attitude that said, "I've been here forever. I belong here. Call me Mrs. Fenner, Covington and Pine." There was a young girl to her left who spent most of her time answering the telephone. The third woman, on the other side of Mrs. Fenner, Covington & Pine, seemed to have no purpose whatsoever.

Mrs. Fenner, Covington & Pine raised her eyebrows at me. It wasn't hard work, a far cry from the days when she used to have to smile.

"I'm here to see George Walsh," I said.

"Yes, and your name." It was a statement more than a question.

I tried to match the disinterest and forced patience in her voice. "Eddie Margolis," I said. "I'm from Charles Murphy Detective Agency."

Suddenly her hands clasped together. "Oh yes," she said, leaning forward and giving me a slight conspiratorial nod. "Please have a seat. I'm sure Mr. Walsh will be with you shortly."

I found a seat on a comfortable-looking couch. There was a big group of people, five men and three women, standing in a tight circle and arguing in loud whispers. I heard the words "jurisdiction" and "motion to dismiss." An old man in the corner seemed to be sleeping, and I wondered if he had just recently arrived or if he had grown old waiting. On the wall behind the sleeping man there were three gigantic, turn-of-the-century portraits of, respectively, James Fenner, Richard Covington, and William Pine. They stared out over the room like three Uncle Scrooges, wearing those big black vests with gold chains that seemed to be designed for protruding bellies. They all had small bow ties and big curly mustaches, and I couldn't help feeling like they were watching me.

As I studied the portraits, I listened to the telephone-answering girl at the reception desk, who had a remarkable talent for filling the empty seconds between telephone calls with chatter. "Okay, so Friday night she goes out with this guy she doesn't even know," she was saying, in her heavy

Brooklyn accent. Then into the telephone, "Fenner, Covington and Pine. Who shall I say is calling? One moment please. Mr. Green? Joe Serling on the line for you." And then, back to, "On Saturday morning she's not home. Now ' I say, what the hell's the matter with this girl? She's not even . . . Fenner, Covington and Pine. Who shall I say is calling? One moment please. Yes, Susan Bodine is on the line for him. Not even eighteen years old. If I had done that when I was eighteen I would have been walloped from here to . . . Fenner, Covington and Pine . . ."

I tried to imagine what Messrs. Fenner, Covington and Pine thought about all this, but my thoughts were interrupted by a little old plump lady with thick glasses, who came buzzing into the reception area: Mr. Walsh would see me now.

I was led down a wide hallway, neatly done with plush carpeting and handsome wallpaper. There was a nameplate outside each doorway leading off to the right, and even though the doors were all open, all I could see were the alcoves where the secretaries sat. Inner doors led to the attorneys' offices. The hallway took a series of turns to the left, and I watched the nameplates roll by. Mr. David. Mr. Stephens. Ms. Ronald. The left wall was lined with drawings and prints from the American Revolution and the Civil War. I noticed more than a few portraits of Abraham Lincoln. Finally we turned into Mr. Walsh's office and we walked through the alcove. The little plump lady stood halfway through the inner door signaling with her hand for me to walk past her, and I stepped into Walsh's office.

George Walsh stood up from beind his desk. He was a tall, good-looking man with big shoulders and long arms. He had a disarming combination of a baby face and gray hair, which made it impossible to determine his age. His wire-rim glasses could have been either old-fashioned or New Wave.

It was easy to imagine him as a young boy. He looked like his life had moved so quickly that only his hair had managed to keep up. He walked around his desk and held his hand out to me. "George Walsh," he said, without smiling.

We shook hands, and he waved me into a seat in front of his desk. His office was clean and sunny. The window faced downtown and east, a view dominated by the Chrysler Building. The bookshelves on the wall behind his desk were neatly lined with books and files. The piles of paper on the table, which ran along the back wall, were neatly stacked and held together with paper clips and rubber bands. His desk was mostly clear, except for a few neat piles of paper and the usual desk ornaments: a telephone, a lamp, a blotter. There didn't seem to be anything personal in the office, except for a framed photograph of him with two vaguely familiar-looking city politicians.

"I don't mind saying," he said, sitting down, "that I expected someone a little bit older." He straightened out an already neat pile of papers on his desk and then stared at me as if he hoped I might age in front of him. It struck me as an interesting comment coming from someone who might not be very old himself. "What happened to Mr. Murphy?" he asked.

"He's in Poughkeepsie today," I answered. "I'll be handling this initial interview, but he will be taking over from here."

"Good." He rested his arms on the arms of the chair and leaned back. The chair creaked. "Mr. Murphy has been highly recommended to us, and we're relying on his experience to make sure this matter is handled delicately." His emphasis on the word "experience" was slight but noticeable.

"What's the problem, Mr. Walsh?" I asked.

"Well, let me start off by telling you something about our

firm. We are one of the top ten law firms in the city. We pay top dollar and we attract the best lawyers. We're expensive. Our clients are banks, oil companies, insurance companies, *Fortune*-five-hundred companies, you name it. Get the picture?"

I nodded.

"We also represent a large number of foreign companies and individuals. Europeans, Asians, South Americans . . . Arabs. The funny thing about foreigners, Mr. Margolis, is how sensitive they are to publicity. They come to us because they know they can trust us. In this regard we are the number-one firm in New York. You would be amazed to hear the names of some of the internationals that we represent." He straightened another already neat pile of papers on his desk. "So when I say that this is a delicate matter, I am not just being a prude. We expect any matters that transpire between our firm and yours to be held in the strictest confidence."

"You have my assurances, Mr. Walsh." It sounded pretty good, and I added, "That's part of our job."

His phone rang and he looked at it, but made no move to answer it. "Good. I hope I have made myself clear, Mr. Margolis. For my sake, as well as yours. When will Mr. Murphy be back?"

"Tonight."

A young man appeared in the doorway. He was tall and blond, in his late twenties. "You wanted to see me?" He leaned his head in, but kept one foot tentatively planted outside the office.

Walsh looked up at him and bellowed, "Yeah, what the hell is this?" He held up a pile of papers stapled together.

"That's the report," the young man said. I thought he was smiling, but when I looked closely there was no trace of a smile on his face.

"What do you mean that's the report. Where's the rest of it?"

The young man took a few hesitant steps into Walsh's office. "That's all there is. They were going to handle the rest of it in Chicago."

Walsh slapped his palm down on the top of his desk. "Damn it, Baldwin! I told you I don't want those clowns in on this!"

Baldwin took a few more steps into the office. He looked at me briefly. It was as if he was playing a joke on Walsh and he wanted to make sure that I was appreciating it. "Leslie told me he wanted them to do it. I thought you knew."

"Shit. Look, call them up. Who do you deal with over there?"

"At the bank?"

"No, in Chicago."

"Dan Lewis, usually."

"Call Lewis. Get a copy of whatever they're working on. I'll have to call Leslie and get this straightened out. How come you didn't tell me?"

"I thought you knew."

"*You thought?* Baldwin, every time *you think,* we get fucked. Now get a copy from Lewis, and take this thing back. I don't want it on my desk." He picked up the report and handed it out to Baldwin. Walsh returned his attention to me before Baldwin had even taken the report out of his hands. "Okay, look, I'll give you a brief background on this, and then I'm going to turn you over to Alice Pinder, and she'll help you out with whatever you need. And have Mr. Murphy give me a call tonight when he gets in. I'll be here late. Baldwin, close the door on your way out."

He waited for the door to close and then proceeded. "Raymond Fidel is a fifth-year associate in our real estate department. Columbia Law School, I think. His personnel file, which I'll give you in a moment, indicates that his performance on the whole has been good. He has gotten the 'going rate' raise every year. That means his annual salary is at the going rate paid by top firms. Not above it, not below it." He leaned further back in his chair and brought his hands out in front of him, lightly tapping his fingertips together. "Let me explain how our raises work here. The raises, given every December, are the best indication to our associates of how they are doing. An 'over the going rate' raise means you're on the top of the list. If you keep it up, you have a decent shot at making partner. 'Going rate' means your performance is satisfactory and you have a chance of making partner. 'Less than going rate' means you're blowing it, and no raise means it's time to look for another job. Anyway, Fidel has been getting 'going rate' raises. He's a hard worker, he's competent and he's trustworthy. Worked on a lot of big deals by himself. His problem is that he's so goddamned disorganized. Personally, I always worry that with someone like that something big is going to fall through the cracks one day."

"Is this all in the file?" I asked.

He nodded. "Yes, here," and he handed me a thin manila folder with Fidel's name typed neatly on the cover. "Nobody sees these except the Personnel Committee. Nobody. Not associates. Not partners. I trust you'll keep it that way."

I took the file and placed it in the back of my notebook. "Of course."

"You can't begin to imagine the problems that would be created for us if an associate's personnel file ever got around."

"Mr. Walsh," I said, standing up. "I can assure you that everything will be handled discreetly. There will be no publicity. No one will see Raymond's file. If you trust me, then let's not discuss it anymore." I pulled Fidel's file from the notebook and handed it out to him. "If you don't trust me, that's fine too. Take the file back."

He sat there dumbly, looking at the file. Finally he took a deep breath and let the air out slowly through his lips, blowing out his cheeks in the process. "All right. Your point is well taken."

I pushed the file back into my notebook and suddenly a blood-pumping, breath-stopping nervousness knocked me back down into my seat. I had almost blown it. But there I was with the file in my hands, and the nervousness quickly gave way to a new sense of confidence.

"I was just being careful," he was saying. "I want to make sure you appreciate our concerns." A brief hint of a smile appeared on his face. "Raymond Fidel disappeared from the office last Wednesday afternoon and hasn't been seen or heard from since. He has been working on some sensitive projects and, in view of the Dorfman matter, we felt his disappearance had to be looked into professionally. Obviously we can't trust the police to keep the matter quiet."

"What's the Dorfman matter?"

He picked his head up suddenly, as if he were surprised to hear me mention it. "Oh. Michael Dorfman was a real estate partner at the firm Torens and Clarke. About two weeks ago he was working late and he was thrown out of his office window. They still don't know who did it."

"He was killed?"

Another hint of a smile appeared. "His office was on the thirty-second floor."

I found myself trying to imagine a thirty-two-story fall, but all I got was a feeling in the pit in my stomach.

"I'm not saying there's any connection here," Walsh was saying. "I'm just saying that we're all being a little bit more careful. Anyway, Fidel is single and lives by himself. He has a mother and sister, who live out in Long Beach. By last

Friday it had become obvious that he had disappeared and we consulted with his family. We have all agreed that a private investigation is the best way to go. I have arranged for the family to come in later this afternoon. I figured that Mr. Murphy . . . or you, might want to talk to them."

"When you say you consulted with Fidel's family, I take that to mean that they agreed not to go to the police if you initiated this private investigation."

His face turned a slight shade of red, and again he took a deep breath and let the air out slowly, puffing up his cheeks. "I'd like to think that we convinced his family that it might be in Raymond's best interest for the matter to be handled discreetly."

"Did they give you a time limit?"

The red deepened in his forehead and his cheeks, and I wondered if I was pushing him too far. "If there had been any such discussion, I would think that it would be between my firm and Raymond's family."

"I'm not sure about that. If you're operating under a deadline, I think it's only fair that I be told. Obviously, you can pull the rug out from our investigation any time you want to, but let's not play games. . . ."

"Mr. Margolis, please," he said, sitting up. "Let's just say that we have agreed to reconsider the issue of going to the police at the end of the week. Obviously, if by that time he shows up . . ."

". . . or I can show that his disappearance has nothing to do with his work here . . ."

I got a real smile this time. "You're up front, and I respect that. Of course we are all concerned here with Raymond's well-being, but we have to protect our professional interests as well. Today we have notified our clients that Raymond is missing, and that all of his work will be handled by another one of our associates, Alice Pinder. We'd like to be able to assure our clients that their affairs will not be disrupted by his disappearance. But most of all, we'd like you to find him."

"Fair enough. What can you tell me about the projects that Fidel was working on?"

"I'm afraid not much. You'll have to talk to Alice Pinder about that. I do know that he was working with several other attorneys here on a hotel deal for one of our Saudi Arabian clients."

"I'll need to see his office and have access to his papers and files."

"Of course. We've arranged for you to be set up in Raymond's office for as long as you need."

"Thank you."

"I assume that my partners have already worked out the fee arrangement with Mr. Murphy?"

"We'll both have to assume that," I said.

"Okay, then, let me get Alice Pinder down here. Unless you have any other questions for me?"

"Yes, one. What is your connection with Raymond Fidel?"

He looked confused. "I'm not sure I understand your question."

"I mean, if you don't know what Fidel was working on, why am I talking to you?"

"I'm a partner in the litigation department. I don't keep track of the deals in our real estate department. That is why I've arranged for Alice to be available to you. The reason you're talking to me is because I'm on the Personnel Committee. Anything else?"

"No, not at the moment."

He picked up his phone and said, "Tell Alice Pinder to come down, will you?" Then he hung up and looked at me. "Alice is one of the stars in our real estate department. She's only a third-year, but she can handle a partner's load. Her claim to fame is that as a first-year associate she outsmarted three partners from one of the big downtown firms in a contract negotiation. She saved our client close to ten million dollars. Beautiful woman, too, I might add," and he smiled. Now that he had started smiling he didn't seem to be able to stop. "She's got a real future."

The woman with the future showed up in Walsh's door, and she *was* beautiful, if you liked that stuffy, corporate look. Her mouth and her teeth were perfect. Her skin was clear and outlined by the straight blond hair that she wore down to her shoulders. She was wearing a black skirt and a white blouse that was silky but not prissy, and the blouse was open at the top to reveal a string of small pearls. She took a few steps into Walsh's office and let the door close behind her.

Walsh came around from his desk and introduced us. She gracefully held out her hand and I was surprised by its warmth. Her blue eyes met mine and held them a fraction of a second longer than I expected, but instead of winning me, like it was supposed to, her look hit me like a slap of cold steel. It was a gesture that had been used for too many years without feeling. Before I had much time to think about it, I was scuffled out of Walsh's office and was walking down the hall with Alice Pinder.

CHAPTER

—3—

"So what'd you think of The Wall?" Alice Pinder asked as soon as we were out of hearing distance from George Walsh's office.

"The Wall?"

"Yeah. First it was The Walsh. And then somehow it became The Wall. How'd you ever get him to smile, anyway?"

"A little verbal tap dancing."

"I'm surprised his face didn't crack. Somewhere underneath it all he's really a nice guy. Just a little uptight. He's a bitch to work for. Real belt-and-suspenders man."

"What's that mean?"

"Belt and suspenders? He's super careful. Never doing something once if he can do it twice. Probably puts double knots in his shoelaces. Know what I mean?"

We came to a wide staircase and I followed her up the steps, past more portraits of Abraham Lincoln.

"He had only good things to say about you," I said.

"Yeah, they like me here," she said. I glanced sideways and liked her just a little bit more for blushing. We got to the top of the stairs and turned left down a hallway that looked identical to the one downstairs.

"Where are we headed?"

"Raymond Fidel's office," she said. "All the partners are on fifty-eight. The associates are all on fifty-nine and sixty. Raymond's office is here on fifty-nine."

"Not a fun place if you don't like lawyers."

"We have about two hundred in New York. Then we have offices in D.C., L.A., London, Paris, and Cairo. Do you think Raymond's okay? Oh, and Hong Kong."

"I don't know. What do you think?"

"About Raymond? I don't know. I have a bad feeling about it. Raymond has sort of a different past. He took some time off before going back to school, and he never really fit in here too well."

"What about his social life?"

"As far as I knew, all he ever did was work, but that's all any of us do around here."

We came to an office that had Fidel's name outside the door. There was no secretary's alcove, and the office was smaller than Walsh's. The window faced uptown, with a view of Park Avenue and the Citicorp Center. There were no neat little piles of papers, like in Walsh's office. Just big mounds of it all over the desk, the chairs, the filing cabinet, and the floor.

"We call this the trash bin," Alice Pinder said. "It's the first place to look for missing files. You can imagine the time I'm having trying to pick up the pieces."

I followed her into the office and we stood in the crowded

space in front of the desk. For an instant her eyes closed and her face seemed to change. I tried to imagine what she would be like at home, or on a warm sunny beach. Then she looked at me, and the steel blue reminded me that Alice Pinder was a lawyer, and probably not much else.

"Who's been in here since he left?" I asked.

"I don't know. Just me and his secretary probably."

"What'd you do in here?"

She waved her hand at the mess of papers on the desk. "I went through some things."

"Did you take anything?"

"Yeah, I took some files."

"I'll need to look at them. Did you take anything from the desk?"

"I don't remember. I don't think so."

"Okay. What can you tell me about this Saudi Arabian deal he was working on."

"Did the The Wall tell you anything?" She walked slowly around the desk.

"Nope. Just that he was working on a hotel deal for some of your Saudi Arabian clients."

She was staring out the window with her back to me. "Saudi royalty, to be more exact."

"George Walsh seemed impressed with them."

"Yeah, he's impressed with himself too."

"And he's impressed with you."

She turned and looked at me over the desk, but she seemed to be distracted. She didn't smile, or blush. "I haven't done anything on the hotel deal yet. I can tell you what I've heard. There's about six attorneys working on it. Let's see," she counted on her fingers, "three corporate, one tax, and Raymond. Okay. Five attorneys."

"Is that normal?"

"Sure." She began looking over the papers on Raymond's

desk and then suddenly looked up at me again, as if remembering that I was there. "It's a hundred-and-fifty-million-dollar deal. And it's really a corporate deal, not real estate. The hotel is owned by a corporation called the Two Hundred Delta Corporation. Two Hundred Delta, in turn, is owned by Philo Investment, Inc. Our client is buying Two Hundred Delta from Philo Investment. See? Instead of buying the hotel, they buy the corporation that owns the hotel."

"Why do they do that?"

"Tax reasons usually."

"Doesn't your client end up getting everything else that the corporation owns?"

"The hotel is the Two Hundred Delta's only asset."

"Oh. What part does Raymond play in this?"

"Not much. Since they're doing it as a corporate acquisition, all the papers and negotiating are being done by the corporate department. Also, since the hotel is in Louisiana, our local counsel is doing more than the usual amount of work."

I held up a finger to stop her.

"Local counsel?"

I nodded.

"We always use local counsel. You need lawyers from the state where the property is located. We don't know anything about Louisiana real estate law, so we hire local counsel from New Orleans. Louisiana, for some reason or other, has very different laws from all of the other states, so local counsel is really important on this deal."

"If your client has local counsel on the deal, what do they need you for?"

She rested her hands on the back of Raymond's chair and gave me a half smile that for some reason made me feel like an idiot. "We're their lawyers. We hire local counsel to assist us and to consult on aspects of Louisiana law, but we still do most of the actual drafting and negotiating. Local counsel does a lot of the legwork. Title work, zoning research, stuff like that."

"Okay. So now, getting back to Raymond."

"So all Raymond has to do is look over documents to see if they look all right with respect to the real estate aspects. He's not actually in there drafting or negotiating. As far as I know, the only people he's had to deal with were people at our firm, and maybe local counsel. I don't think he's spoken to the client, or to any of Philo's lawyers."

"Whom does he report to?"

"Jim Hall, probably. He's the corporate partner in charge of the deal."

"Can you tell me exactly who the client is?"

She shook her head. "I don't really know, to tell you the truth. Officially, the client is Aman Coastal Corporation. We deal with the officers of the corporation, but they're just puppets. The real money comes from some Saudi bigwigs. I'm sure I could find out who they are, but the names probably wouldn't mean much to me. It's probably some government official married to somebody's niece, or something ridiculous like that."

"So what's the big secret?"

"There is no big secret. It's just a lot of paranoia."

"Does local counsel know who they are?"

"I doubt it."

"If Raymond knew exactly who the client was, what could he do with the information?"

She shrugged. "What could he do with it? I really can't imagine who would care, except maybe *The National Enquirer,* or someone like that."

We stared at each other over the messy desk. My eyes fell on her pearls but my thoughts were on Aman Coastal Corporation. Aman Coastal Corporation was a dead-end street.

There were too many other people at the firm, and in Louisiana, involved in the deal. Too many people had access to finding out who the client was, and there was no reason to think that anyone would really care. George Walsh probably cared, but that didn't mean that it was in any way connected to Raymond's disappearance. Unless Walsh knew something he wasn't telling me, and that seemed unlikely. I had to assume that I was getting all of the facts.

"Listen," Alice said at last. "I should talk to you about the other things that Raymond's working on, but I have a conference call coming in in about five minutes. Are you going to be around later? Can we meet this afternoon?"

"Yeah, sure." I looked around at all the paper. "It looks like I'll be here most of the day."

"Arnold Kaplan sits just down the hall, that way," she pointed in the opposite direction from where we'd come. "He knew Raymond better than anyone here. He said he'd have lunch with you if you wanted. You ought to do it just to meet him." She looked at her watch. "Okay, I gotta go. I'll see you later."

I sat down at Raymond Fidel's desk. The chair was big and comfortable, but I sank in to it so far that the desk came up almost to my chin. I swiveled the chair around a little bit and sat up and it was better, but not great. I took out my pad and scribbled some notes from my conversations with Walsh and with Alice Pinder. Then I looked more carefully at Fidel's desk. To my right, against the wall, there was a row of law books about real estate and taxes. A few of them had papers stuffed inside and some of them had little yellow index cards sticking out, like bookmarks. There was the telephone and next to that a Rolodex. In the middle of the desk, toward the back edge, there was a desk lamp. A clip on the metal shade of the lamp held a bunch of little pink slips of paper with telephone messages on them. There was one of those date books where each day is a new page, and there was a pencil holder filled with pens and pencils. A wooden tray in the left-hand corner of the desk was overflowing with mail.

And then there was the paper: letters and documents were piled haphazardly all over the desk. I looked through them casually, trying not to rearrange anything. There was a letter from Philo Investment, Inc., and there was a document called Amendment to Third Deed of Trust. Underneath some of the papers there was a big yellow legal pad filled with doodling that had names and numbers scribbled all over it. I turned to a new page in my notebook and made a list of all things that I had to look at. Then I ventured down the hall to find Arnold Kaplan.

His office was the same size as Fidel's but fairly neat. He looked up from his desk and smiled. "You must be the detective."

"And you're Arnold Kaplan."

"Hey, how'd you know? That's pretty good! What'd you do, read the name outside the door?"

"Sorry, I can't give away all my secrets."

He laughed and stood up with his hand outstretched. "Call me Arnie." He was much taller than he had looked slumped behind his desk, but it was an uncoordinated sort of height, all arms and legs. He had a neatly trimmed beard, but his skin was a pasty green.

"Say hello to Uncle Bill," he said, pointing to a small portrait on the wall to my right. William Pine was wearing a big black top hat that made him look even more like Scrooge than he had in the portrait out in the reception area. "I stole it from one of the conference rooms. Look at the inscription."

I leaned closer and at the bottom of the picture there was a little piece of white paper taped over the glass. It was a quote that said, "Didn't I let you have a vacation day just last year?"

Arnie laughed, as if it were the first time he had seen it. "Listen," he said, still smiling. "There's a cafeteria downstairs. It isn't The Four Seasons, but it's pretty quick. Join me for lunch?"

I agreed and he led me through a maze of hallways and stairs to the cafeteria on the fifty-eighth floor. "They had to put the cafeteria down here with the partners," Arnie Kaplan explained as he picked up a tray and some silverware. "We'd lose too many of them if they had to climb the stairs everyday to fifty-nine or sixty. You know," he said, tapping his chest with his fingers and lowering his voice, "ticker problems."

We joined the short line at the sandwich counter. "Hey, Bobby," Arnie called up to an older man who was ahead of us on line. "Bobby, what's happening?"

"Hey, Arnie!"

Arnie leaned over to me and said, "Bobby's one of our top messengers. Hey, Bobby, where are my Yankees tickets?"

Bobby laughed. "The season's been over for a month already."

"Yeah, but you said you were going to get me tickets."

Bobby the messenger turned away from us to give his sandwich order over the counter.

Arnie leaned closer to me and whispered, "He's gonna promise me box seats for next year. Watch this."

"Hey, Bobby."

Bobby turned around from the counter again. "The season's over, Arnie. But I can get 'em for you next year if you want. I promise. Box seats. You want 'em?"

"You know I do."

"Okay. Next year. I promise."

Arnie whispered to me again. "Every year it's the same thing. Hey, Sandy! How's my favorite sandwich maker?"

We got to the counter and he ordered a roast beef sandwich and I ordered tuna fish.

"Sandy, how's your cat?"

"He's fine, Arnie. He says hello. What do you want on your roast beef?"

"Sandy's got a cat that's seventeen years old. Can you believe it? Is that right, Sandy? Seventeen, right? Just some lettuce and tomato. Are you sure that cat is still alive?"

"Arnie! I love that cat. I can't believe you said that!"

"Oh, don't listen to me. Hey, hey, hey. Not so much mustard!"

When we had gotten our sandwiches and coffee, I followed big, gawky Arnie Kaplan to a table in the back. There were comfortable leather seats and the tables had been set with tablecloths and cloth napkins.

Arnie Kaplan took a few big bites of his roast beef sandwich and then a few quick gulps of coffee. Then he put his napkin on his lap and seemed to relax. "I'm in a bad mood today. I just found out that I'm not going to be able to take my vacation before the end of the year. That means I lose it. Gone. Two weeks down the drain. My wife is gonna kill me."

"Didn't Uncle Bill let you have a vacation day just last year?"

He laughed. "Can I tell you something, Eddie? Partnership track at a firm like this is like a pie-eating contest, where the prize is more pie."

"What'd Raymond think of it?"

He drank some more coffee and rolled his eyes. "He didn't like it any more than I do. The truth is, Eddie, nobody likes it."

"So why do you all keep doing it?"

He shrugged. "Who knows? Maybe we're all idiots."

"Alice told me that you and Raymond were friends."

He chewed on his roast beef for a while, thinking. "Yeah, I guess you could say that. We're in the same class, and we went to law school together. I've known Raymond for eight years. God, I must be getting old. How old are you?

"Twenty-seven."

"Shit. I'm thirty-two. Margolis. What kind of name is that, anyway. Russian, isn't it?"

"My father's Jewish." And then, so he wouldn't have to ask, I said, "My mother was Cuban."

"No shit. A Cuban Jew. Wait till I tell my wife about this. I thought you looked a little bit—"

"Ethnic?"

"Yeah," and he laughed. "Ethnic. Anyway, I don't think it would be fair to say that Raymond and I were friends. I don't think I ever saw him outside of the firm, except for firm functions. Actually, that may not be true. I guess when we were first-year associates we used to hang out a little, you know, go see movies and stuff. But then I got married, and well, I don't know. I didn't see him much. We ate lunch together a lot, and last year we went to Denver together on a deal. Let me tell you something. Raymond is a neat guy. He's quiet and he never talks much about himself, but he's smart. People don't know what to make of him, but I think he's neat."

We both munched away on our sandwiches.

"Alice said that he didn't have much of a social life."

"She's dynamite, isn't she?" Another one for the Alice Pinder fan club. "I'll tell you something, Eddie. People think that because a guy spends all his time in the office and doesn't have any friends, that that's his choice and that he doesn't want friends. But I think Raymond was lonely."

"Okay, so he was lonely. Where'd he go?"

Arnie shook his head and smiled. "Hey, if any of us knew that, they wouldn't have hired you."

"Yeah, but if you had to guess."

He looked up at the ceiling, inspired by the challenge, the forgotten sandwich suspended in midair above his plate. Finally he put the sandwich down on his plate without taking a bite, and he looked at me, dead serious. "Jesus, Eddie. I think that's what really scares me. I come up with a great big blank."

CHAPTER

—4—

After lunch I spent a few hours going through Raymond Fidel's office. First I gathered the top layer of paper from the desk and made a pile in front of me. I would have to check with Alice Pinder to find out how much she had removed or rearranged in taking over Fidel's work, but I had what I thought were, roughly, the last things that Fidel had worked on before he disappeared.

Then I picked up all the old newspapers, law journals and junk mail and piled them on top of the filing cabinet. I sorted everything else into separate piles as best I could and I stacked them on the floor beneath the window. One pile was for a project with Norco Construction Company for the development of something called the Hudson Harbor Office Complex. Another pile held letters and documents relating to Travis Realty Corp. There was a big stack of documents relating to Aman Coastal Corporation's purchase of the hotel in New Orleans. The fourth and the biggest pile was all the things that I could not identify.

I went through the date book and made a list of all the names and telephone numbers I could find. Then I went through the legal pad I had found among the papers. I checked the desk drawers and rummaged through the ad hoc collection of office supplies, blank legal forms, such personal belongings as a shoehorn and a nail clipper, and business cards. There was a small hand-held Dictaphone with a tape on it, and I put the Dictaphone and tape with the pile of papers on my desk.

By three o'clock I had made a preliminary search of the office. Murphy might have handled it differently. Somehow, I couldn't imagine him wading through piles of paper, and I worried that I had wasted my time. I looked at the piles and felt overwhelmed and depressed. I was never going to find Raymond Fidel.

I picked up the telephone and buzzed Raymond Fidel's secretary. She was a young woman named Debbie with bright red hair and lots of freckles, and when she came into the office she sat on the edge of the chair with her back straight, as if it would be presumptuous of her to make herself comfortable.

I could have told her to relax, but instead I asked her a question. "Did you see Raymond before he left on Wednesday?"

She bit her lower lip and then said, "Yeah, he stopped in to tell me that he was going down to the concession stand, down in the lobby, for some cough drops." Then she bit her lower lip some more.

"Stopped in where?"

"Where I sit. Across the hall."

I leaned back in my seat. "Does he usually tell you things like that, where he's going?"

"Always. Some of the others don't. But Raymond always does."

"What time was it? Do you remember?"

"Right about four o'clock."

"Did he have a cold?"

She bit her lip again and moved a few inches back into the chair. "What do you mean?"

"You said he went to get cough drops. Was he coughing?"

Her face lit up like a pinball machine. "Oh gosh! No! I hadn't thought of that!"

"Are you sure?"

"Yes! I'm positive! Oh, what do you think that means?"

"Probably nothing." She slumped down in the back of the seat.

"Did he have a coat with him?"

"Not when he told me he was going downstairs. But the closet's on the way out. He could have picked it up."

"Do you know if he was wearing a coat on Wednesday?"

"Sure. I mean, I didn't see it, but it's been pretty cold. He always wears it."

"Do you know what his coat looks like?"

"Sure," her back straightening again, her enthusiasm rising. "It's one of those London Fog coats or whatever they are. You know, like a raincoat, but it's got a plaid lining."

"Have you checked the closet to see if it's there?"

Her face lit up again. "No! I didn't think of that! Do you want me to check now?"

"In a minute." I held out the pink telephone messages. "Did you take these?"

She leaned forward and looked at them, and pulled three of them out. Her hands were pudgy and had freckles all over them. "These three I took. That's my initials at the bottom. The other one was taken by Nancy. She sits next to me and answers my phone if I'm not there."

"Do you keep copies of messages?"

"Sure."

"Who else takes messages for Raymond besides you and Nancy?"

"Just the receptionist."

That would be the mouthpiece with the Brooklyn accent in the reception area. "Okay. I'm going to need copies of all of the messages Raymond got for the last two weeks. Can you get me that?"

"I guess so."

"Now, how can I find out what calls Raymond made in the last two weeks?"

"Jeez, that's harder. I don't make his calls for him, so I wouldn't know. Let's see. There'll be a printout of all of his long-distance calls. It's all on the computer for billing purposes. But it's only for long distance."

"Can you get me a copy of that?"

"It usually comes out at the beginning of each month, but I'll see if I can get one now."

"Okay. Let me know. Do you remember what you did for Raymond last Wednesday?"

"Mmmmm, let me think. I don't really remember. I think just a few phone messages and maybe a couple of letters. I could check if you want."

"Yes, please. Do you have any idea what Raymond was doing just before he left?"

"No. I mean, I can't see in here from where I sit, but I think he was on the telephone."

"How do you know?"

"His light goes on on my extension."

"How long was he on for?"

"Mmmmm, I think probably about a half an hour. It

could've been more than one call, but he seemed to be on every time I checked."

"Do you know who he was talking to?"

"No."

"Okay." I pushed myself further away from the desk and put my hands behind my head in a pose that I hoped said that the interview was over. Anything from here on was purely social. "How long have you worked here, Debbie?"

She seemed to relax into her seat. "Two years."

"Like it?"

"It's okay."

"You like working for Raymond?"

"Yeah. He's nice."

"Were you friendly with him?"

"No, not really. We got along okay."

I brought my hands down and lowered my voice. "Did you notice anything unusual about him in the last few weeks?"

"No."

"Anything unusual last Wednesday?"

"No."

"Okay. Is there a key to this office?"

"Yeah. All the attorneys' offices have keys."

"Who would have a key?"

"Well, Raymond had one. And I think the mail room keeps one."

"Can you get me the mail room key?"

"I don't know if they'll give it to me."

"Tell them to check with George Walsh if there's a problem."

"Okay. Anything else?"

"No. Thanks, Debbie."

"Let's see. The key. Phone messages. Printout of long-distance calls. Letters. And . . . wasn't there something else?"

"Check the closet for his coat."

"Oh, right. His coat."

Debbie left and I thought about the coat. I let myself assume that Debbie had been right and that Raymond always wore his coat, even though *I* knew some people who didn't always wear coats in November. If he had left the coat in the closet, then that would mean that he did not intend to go outside and that he had intended to come back. Or he could have left it there on purpose, to make it look like he intended to come back. If he had taken the coat with him, then, at least, he intended to do more than get cough drops. In that case, since he had lied about the purpose of his departure, it was fair to assume that his actual purpose had something to do with his disappearance. Of course, he could have intended to come back in an hour, but in that case he would have used a better lie than running downstairs to get cough drops. The excuse that he used for leaving the office meant that either he thought he was coming right back up or he knew he wasn't coming back at all. Still, it was possible that he had not worn his coat at all on Wednesday. I felt myself starting to get confused. Where was Murphy when you needed him? I called my office, and Kate answered the phone.

"Hi, Eddie. I hadn't heard from you so I told Murphy you quit. I have some messages for you. Listen, you have to get me those photos and your fingerprints for the Employee's Statement."

"I have them with me, but I can't leave yet. I'll try to get them over to you soon."

"Want me to send a messenger to pick them up?"

"Yeah, maybe you better."

"Okay. Let's see. Murphy called. He says he won't be back tonight. Maybe tomorrow morning. He says to handle everything as best you can and if you need anything, you can call him later at his hotel."

"Damn."

"And there's another message here. Marty Margolis called. Who would that be?"

"My father."

"He gave me a message. Wait a minute. Here it is. It says, 'Knock 'em dead.' He was funny. I liked him. Is he single?"

"He's too old for you, Kate. Look, can you call Murphy for me and leave a message at his hotel that he has to call George Walsh tonight at the office? And leave him the number in case he needs it."

"Sure. How's it going over there?"

"I'm having a blast."

CHAPTER
—5—

Raymond Fidel's mother was a big, fat woman with flabby arms and short, stubby fingers. She just barely fit into the chair across from me. Despite her size, she was a pleasant-looking woman, with deep-set eyes and a warm face. Her daughter, Andrea, was thinner, though still bulky. She had more prominent cheekbones and a stronger chin than her mother, which gave her a tougher, colder-looking face. Andrea wore her hair in a bun, like her mother, and she wore clothes that made her look older and heavier than I imagined she really was. It was unfortunate because she could have been pretty.

They sat across from me, filling Raymond Fidel's office with that pungent blend of perfume and outdoors that I have always associated with Long Island commuters. I imagined that the perfume came from the mother, who was focusing her big, heavy eyes on me. "I can't tell you how worried we are, Mr. Margolis," she said. "This isn't like Raymond to just disappear. He's always so responsible. I can't imagine what has happened to him."

"I'm sure he's all right, Mrs. Fidel." Andrea's eyes wandered casually around the room, as if her brother might be hidden somewhere in the corners. I turned back to the mother. "How often did you see Raymond?"

"Oh, maybe once or twice a month. But I talked to him every week, at least once. Andrea talked to him a lot."

Andrea's eyes were still wandering.

"How often did you talk to him, Andrea?"

Slowly her eyes drifted down from the ceiling and settled on me. "Almost every day. We were very close." Her voice was slow and strange.

"Did you talk to him last Wednesday?"

She nodded. "Yes. I spoke to him in the morning. I had just brought my car in to be fixed and they told me I needed a ring job. I called Raymond to see what he thought." Somehow I got the feeling that there was something wrong with her. She was too slow.

"Did you notice anything unusual when you talked to him? Did he say anything or imply anything? Was his voice any different?"

"No. He was the same as always."

"Mrs. Fidel, had you noticed anything unusual about Raymond in the last few weeks?"

She shook her head. "Mr. Margolis, we have been asking ourselves these questions for a week now and we have come up with nothing. What are we going to do?"

"We're going to find him," I said, surprised by the confidence in my voice. "Do you have a picture of him?"

"I do," Andrea said and she reached into her purse and pulled out a small snapshot of her and Raymond standing arm-in-arm on a beach. "That was taken out in front of our apartment in Long Beach," she said. "It's about a year old, but he looks the same." I looked briefly at the snapshot and decided that Raymond had his mother's features without the family fat.

"Mrs. Fidel, can I ask you what you do?"

"We have a furniture store in Brooklyn. It was my husband's. I took it over when he passed away and I've kept it up. Andrea works with me." She spoke her daughter's name as if Andrea weren't there, the way people sometimes refer to children, and it confirmed my feeling that something was wrong.

"Any problems with the store?"

"Only the usual."

"Such as?"

"Oh, you know. Problems with the help. A slow summer. Things like that."

"Did Raymond grow up in Long Beach?"

"No, in Canarsie. We moved to Long Beach when Raymond was a senior in high school."

"And after high school?"

"Raymond got into a lot of trouble in school. Especially after his father died." Andrea's eyes started wandering again, as if she wanted no part of this conversation. Her mother continued, "He just barely finished high school. Then he worked at the store for a year. And then he just sort of drifted for a few years. He went to California like the rest of them. Then he worked running ski lifts in Colorado and he worked as a bartender in Florida. Suddenly he decided to go to college, and from there he went to law school. I was so proud of him. Andrea too. He's been so good to us."

"What about his friends. Did he have any friends that might know where he went?"

She shrugged. "No. Raymond was always a loner. He had

a girl friend when he was in law school. Julie. A nice girl. You know how a mother hopes." Andrea's eyes were drilling holes in the ceiling. "But he broke off with her. Or she with him. He never told me what happened. Just said it wasn't working. I think she's in Dallas now, or someplace."

"Fort Worth," Andrea said. "He doesn't keep in touch with her, though. He doesn't keep in touch with anybody. Just us."

"Did he ever discuss his finances with you?" I asked, trying to ignore the hint of hostility I detected in Andrea's voice.

"No, not really," Mrs. Fidel answered. "But he didn't have any problems. They pay him well here. And all he has is a little apartment in the Village. He always offers to help us out if we need anything, but we do all right with the store."

"I'm going to want to take a look at Raymond's apartment. Will one of you be available tomorrow to come with me?"

"Andrea can go," Mrs. Fidel said.

I looked at Mrs. Fidel. If there was anything wrong with Andrea, there was no hint in her eyes that she wanted to discuss it with me. "Okay. Now, listen to me for a minute. What I want you to do is go home and make a list of everybody that Raymond knew. Anybody you can think of. And give me their telephone numbers, addresses, and who they are. You know, neighbors, relatives. Anybody. Can you do that for me? And Andrea, I want you to bring that list tomorrow. Okay?"

They both nodded. Mrs. Fidel was taking me very seriously. I was her only hope of finding her son. "Mrs. Fidel, I don't want you to worry about him. We will do everything we can. We'll find him."

Debbie showed them out and then stopped back into the office to give me a key and copies of Raymond's telephone messages. She also told me that Raymond's coat was not in the closet. Okay, so he knew that he was going outside.

The telephone rang and startled me. It was Alice Pinder, saying that she was stuck in a meeting and wouldn't be able to meet with me until later. I agreed to have dinner with her. Then a messenger came in and I gave him my photos and fingerprints to bring back to Kate.

Then I picked up the photograph of Raymond and Andrea and studied it more carefully. Raymond and Andrea were bundled up in coats and scarves, and there was snow on the beach behind them. Andrea wore a wool pullover cap, but her hair stuck out from underneath it and the wind had blown a few strands across her chin. She looked perfectly normal, but I shivered when I thought about that strange voice and her slow, plodding speech. I had to force myself to stop looking at Andrea and to look at Raymond. He wasn't wearing a hat. His hair was short and his ears looked red from the cold. Still, there was the same warmth I had seen in his mother's face and I remembered what Arnie Kaplan had said. "Raymond's a neat guy." Raymond and Andrea were obviously posing and yet, their smiles seemed genuine and there was something natural about the way they were standing. They were probably in the habit of walking around with their arms around each other. Maybe all brothers and sisters did that. I wouldn't know.

I turned and put my feet up on the low windowsill and looked out over the city. The sun was gone and a late-afternoon grayness, the kind that only Novembers can make, packed itself neatly among the buildings on Park Avenue. I wondered what my mother had been like. My only memories of her were faded and were influenced by things I had heard about her after her death. I had never really missed having a big family. My father had always been more than enough for me. But now I wondered what it would have been like to have had a brother or a sister.

"Mr. Margolis?"

I swung around in my seat and found a short and nervous-looking woman in the doorway.

"Are you Mr. Margolis?"

"Yes."

"My name is Jane. I work for . . . I'm Bill Bryant's secretary. Someone told me that you were hired to find Raymond Fidel."

"That's right. Come on in, Jane."

She took a few steps into the office, but not too many. "I don't know if this is important . . . I just . . . They told me that you were looking for Raymond and I thought you should know. . . ." She was holding one of those pink message slips in her hand.

I reached my hand out for it and she stepped in closer.

"Raymond called Mr. Bryant last Wednesday afternoon. Mr. Bryant was out of town, so I . . . here's the slip . . . I didn't know if it was important or not."

I took the slip out of her hand and looked at it. It was a message for Bill Bryant from Raymond Fidel marked "Urgent." The time was 3:50 P.M. "Who is Bill Bryant?"

"Oh, he's . . . he's the head of the real estate department here."

"Has Mr. Bryant seen this message?"

"Oh, yes, of course. I showed it to him right away. I just . . . when they told me that there was a detective . . . I just thought maybe it would help."

"Thanks, Jane. Maybe it will."

Jane left and I scribbled Bill Bryant's name on my list of things to do. Then I swung back around and looked out the window. The *Newsweek* clock said that it was five-thirty and fifty-one degrees. It occurred to me that my shoes didn't hurt anymore, and I wiggled my toes around just to make sure that they were still there. I heard my father's voice saying, "Knock 'em dead." And then I heard my own voice, soft and steady. "I'm going to find you, Raymond Fidel."

CHAPTER

——6——

Alice Pinder took me to a small English pub on Lexington Avenue called Great Expectations. A neon sign outside advertised "Spirits," and from the beaming and jocular red faces crowded around the bar in the front it was clear that the sign was not referring to the kind of spirits that hung out in graveyards. We managed to find a quiet table against the wall in the back, and Alice sipped a Johnnie Walker Black while we perused the menu. Apparently, the dishes were all named for Charles Dickens characters, although I recognized only a few, like the David Copperfield Sandwich and the Oliver Twist Salad.

A waitress called us each "love" and gently touched my shoulder as we ordered, as if listening with her fingertips. Alice got something called Pasta Pickwick, and I decided on the Uncle Scrooge Burger, in honor of William Pine. When we were left alone again, I took a few sips of coffee and looked up to see Alice staring at me. "You don't drink, Eddie?"

"Nope."

"Don't meet too many of those anymore these days."

"I had a problem with it."

"Oh, I'm sorry."

A disjointed silence suddenly hung over the table. Alice Pinder was from a world of contract negotiations and conference calls. While I had been carrying on my love affair with the Scotch bottle, she had gone through college and law school. I had never really talked to a lawyer, never mind had dinner with one. And now, here I was, in a suit and tie, having dinner with a lawyer in midtown Manhattan. Alice Pinder was totally at home. It was me who was out of place, and thinking about my drinking days just made it worse.

Fortunately, it didn't seem to bother her. "God bless Raymond Fidel," she was saying. "His files are such a mess that I sometimes think it would be easier to dump them and start all over again. I spent the whole day negotiating a mortgage from a draft that was a week old because Raymond had the new draft stuffed into the back of the file with the title materials. I didn't find it until five o'clock this afternoon. God knows what else is in that file."

"Keep looking. Maybe you'll find Raymond."

She smiled politely, like a lawyer, and I decided that it was time to talk business. "I'm going to need to take a look at his files and anything else that you took out of his office. Is that all right?"

"Sure. That's no problem."

"I also have a pile of things in Raymond's office that I couldn't make sense of. Would you be able to go through it?"

"Of course."

"Good. Now, what else, besides the hotel deal, was Raymond working on? Start with this Norco Construction Company."

She took her hands off her Scotch and rubbed her temples. "Ever hear of Norco?"

"Nope."

"I'm surprised. They're one of the biggest contractors in the city." She dropped her hands onto the red-and-white-checkered tablecloth. "It's owned by a guy named Alfred Norens. Norens is pretty well connected in the city. He's always speaking at banquets and dinners. He's good friends with the mayor and a lot of the big developers in town. Has his fingers in a lot of things. I actually met Norens once at a seminar. He's this really short, little eccentric guy, who loves to talk. He cornered me for fifteen minutes, and told me all about how he got started and how he had built his first building by the time he was twenty years old. He interested me, actually. He seemed like a little kid somehow. Anyway, we represent them on this big project they're doing downtown on the river. You heard of the Hudson Harbor Office Complex?"

"I saw things about it on Raymond's desk."

"Well, we represent Norco on that. It's mostly contract work, with the subcontractors and consultants. Stuff like that. We represented them on the contract with the city as well."

"How's the city involved?"

"The city owns the property and is acting as the developer."

The waitress put a basket of warm rolls and a dish of butter on our table. I offered the basket to Alice and she declined. I chose a small roll and picked up a slab of butter with my knife. I never understood restaurants that served frozen pads of butter on ice. Trying to spread frozen butter is like trying to spread a brick. "So what does Raymond have to do?" I asked, dropping the butter on my plate and munching away on the plain roll.

"Well, he drafts and negotiates the contracts and, I guess, he attends any of the meetings where there are legal problems. There's a guy over at Norco, Allen Crane. He's the guy we usually work with over there."

"Yeah, I saw his name all over Raymond's desk."

"I talked to him today and told him that we had someone looking into Raymond's disappearance. He told me that he'd be happy to talk to you if you needed him."

"Yeah, I think I might. And what about Norens?"

"Norens would be a little bit harder to get to. I think we'd have to set that up through Bill Bryant."

"He's the head of the real estate department?"

"Yeah. Norco is his client. He's old buddies with Norens."

"Can you think of any reason that Raymond would try to call Bryant last Wednesday?"

"Could be lots of reasons. Did he?"

"Yeah. About ten minutes before he left. Bryant was out of town and Raymond left a message for Bryant to call him back. Raymond said it was urgent."

She shook her head. "I don't know. Did you ask Bill?"

"No. Not yet."

"Well, Bill might be able to tell you. And you can ask him about Norens. Bill could also get you in to see Sam Pulaski."

The waitress arrived with our dinners and Alice ordered another Scotch. Her pasta was green and it had big red chunks of tomatoes and peppers on it. My hamburger was hefty and juicy and after my first bite I realized how hungry I was.

"Who's Sam Pulaski?" I asked between bites.

"He's the president of Travis Realty Corp."

"Oh, yeah, I saw his name too. Tell me about that deal."

She spun some pasta around her fork. "Sam Pulaski is one of the owners of the Travis Building. You know that building up on Madison Avenue with the weird stairs that come out onto the sidewalk?"

"No, I don't think so."

"Anyway, the Travis Building is currently mortgaged to some offshore bank, and the loan comes due in a few months, so Pulaski's refinancing the loan. Raymond's working on the new loan from National Bank of New York."

"The new loan to pay off the old loan?"

"That's right. That's what I've been working on all day. Negotiating the loan documents for that deal."

"With Sam Pulaski?"

"Well, no. Sam Pulaski is the client. I've been negotiating with the lawyers from National Bank of New York. Anyway, I'm sure Bill can arrange for you to see Pulaski, but I'll warn you right now, he's not a fun person."

"Why not?"

"Because he's an asshole."

I laughed.

"I'm not kidding. The guy is a real asshole. He's known throughout the real estate industry as a 'screamer.'"

"A screamer?"

"Yeah. Some people get ahead by being good at what they do, like Norens, or by just being lucky—"

"Like the Saudis?"

"Like the Saudis. And then there's a bunch of people who scream their way to the top. Pulaski's not the only one. There's a handful of them."

"Screaming?"

"He doesn't have the intelligence to argue reasonably, so he tries to intimidate people into giving him what he wants."

"And if that doesn't work, what does he do? Break their kneecaps?"

She laughed. "You have to meet him to believe him. It's really sick, but you'd be amazed at what he gets away with because people are afraid of him."

"That's your client?"

"It doesn't stop him from yelling at us. Sometimes he doesn't understand what Raymond is doing and he chases Raymond around the room screaming at him. I mean, we're his lawyers. We're looking out for his interests, and he's just too stupid and insecure to understand."

"Well, I guess I should go see him too. See what he screams. Is there anything else Raymond's working on?"

"No. That's really it. I mean, there's always little things popping up now and then, but I think those three are the major deals he's got now. I just got back from vacation last week and I didn't have much to do, so when Raymond disappeared they gave me his caseload."

"Do you think Raymond is a good lawyer?"

She frowned. "It would be presumptuous of me to say, really, since he's two years ahead of me. But, I think he's a good lawyer. Not a great lawyer, but a good lawyer."

"What's the difference?"

She frowned some more and then leaned forward over her empty plate. "You go to these meetings on these really big deals, like the Bermuda deal I was on last month. There'll be thirty lawyers with their clients stuffed into this giant conference room. Big people in the industry, bankers, developers, you know, the top of the list. You figure the collective billing rate of all the lawyers in that room is something like five thousand dollars an hour. Think about it. The meeting runs all day and it costs fifty grand."

"Just for the lawyers?"

"Now you know why it costs so much to do anything in this town. Anyway, it never fails that of the thirty or fifty people in the room, only one or two will control the meeting. Not the most important people, or the richest, but the best. The Bill Bryants of the world. You have no idea how lawyers, supposedly good lawyers, can ramble on and on without having any idea of what the real issues are, of what they're saying, or of what they're trying to accomplish. A great lawyer never rambles. A great lawyer says what he has to say and then shuts up."

"You've thought about this, haven't you?"

She leaned back in her seat. "You bet I have."

"And Bill Bryant is a great lawyer?"

"One of the best."

"And you? Are you a great lawyer?"

"No. But I will be. I don't have enough experience yet. I've only been at it for three years. I will be a great lawyer, though. I don't mean to brag. It's just something I know."

The waitress cleared the table and Alice ordered another Scotch. The Scotch must have been getting to her because she rambled on. "There's a price to pay, though, I'll admit. Last year I billed twenty-eight hundred hours. This year I'll break three thousand. That's billable hours. That means that with meals and office stuff I have to do, I'm there on the average twelve hours a day, seven days a week. That wreaks havoc on your personal life, let me tell you. I bought a co-op last summer. Really nice place up on Sixty-fifth Street, with a terrace and a fireplace. I lucked into it. I've been there six months, and I still don't have the place fixed up." Her new Scotch came and she grabbed it eagerly. "So where do you live, Eddie?"

"On Christie Street. The Lower East Side."

"Near Sammy's?"

"Right down the street."

"Oh, I've been out there."

" 'Out there'? You make it sound like the Bronx Zoo."

"Well it is, sort of. Isn't it?"

There was nothing on the surface to indicate whether she was teasing me or not. "No, most of the animals in the Bronx Zoo are tame," I said.

She laughed. It was a fun laugh, full of hiccups and gasps, and then she took another big gulp of Scotch. "You ever been to a place called The Pyramid?"

"Sure, I used to go there all the time."

"I went there once. What an adventure!"

I had to laugh. The Lower East Side was "out there" and The Pyramid was "an adventure." I watched her guzzling her Scotch and tried to remember if it was her third or fourth. Then I felt restless and I tried to get the waitress's attention.

"Hey, you know what I'd like to do?" Alice said suddenly. "Let's go to The Pyramid!"

"Now?"

"Yeah. Let's go to The Pyramid, right now."

The idea of going to The Pyramid struck me as absolutely ludicrous. I could walk in, wearing my gray suit and blue tie, and order a cup of coffee and watch all my old friends in their varying states of inebriation. Then I could take Alice next door to The Pit to watch Leon and Billy and Lazy Bob, draped over their stools and drinking, laughing and getting crazy. Leon and Lazy Bob would be drinking Scotch. Billy would be continuing his personal campaign to subsidize the makers of Jack Daniel's. When he really got going we used to call him Billy Jack.

"What do you say?" Alice asked.

I shook my head, but it took a while to get the words out. "I don't think I'm ready to go back to those places."

Alice needed some files from Raymond's office, so we walked back to the Pan Am Building. It was late, and midtown had grown cold and quiet. There was still plenty of traffic racing down Lexington Avenue, but the sidewalks were empty and the "Walk" and "Don't Walk" signs blinked for nobody, like gurus without disciples. Alice surprised me by taking my arm, and I surprised myself by talking about the days when I used to hang out in the clubs. I told her about my long stint of unemployment and how I had met Murphy and had been offered a job. Her hand on my arm felt good, but there was something mechanical about it, like the gaze she'd used when we first met in George Walsh's office. It was as if she had read about such gestures in a self-help book: "Take his arm while you walk to make him feel closer to you, but never squeeze too hard. No man wants to feel like his date plays for the NFL."

Grand Central Station had emptied out considerably, and as we walked in through the doors from Forty-second Street, we were accosted by a young bum with long scraggly hair and a dirty beard. He was wrapped up in blankets and had a wool hat pulled over his ears, like the hat that Andrea Fidel had worn in the photograph. He held out his hand and mumbled, and I put some change into it.

Alice let go of me as we boarded the escalators that led up to the Pan Am Building. We signed in at the security desk at the top of the second set of escalators and then rode up by ourselves in the elevator to the fifty-ninth floor. The big wooden doors to Fenner, Covington & Pine were locked, and Alice cursed and rummaged through her pocketbook for her keys. Inside, the office was quiet and only partly lit. A few cleaning ladies in blue smocks were vacuuming the halls. I didn't see any attorneys, but Alice assured me that there would still be some about. She stopped off in the ladies' room, no doubt because of all the Scotch, and I found my way to Raymond Fidel's office.

Only after I had stepped into Raymond's office and flipped the light on did I realize that the door had been open. I automatically reached in my pocket and pulled out the key. I was positive that I had locked the door before I left. Raymond's secretary had said that only Raymond and the mail room had keys. If I had the mail room key, then that meant that Raymond had come back.

Or that someone had come back with Raymond's key.

Or that someone had broken in.

I checked the door. It had one of those little button locks built into the inside doorknob. The keyhole was on the outside doorknob. The door itself was not damaged or marked up, but this kind of lock was easy to pick.

When I looked back into the office again, I knew that something was wrong. I walked around the desk and stared out the window at the lights on Park Avenue. The clock on the Newsweek Building said that it was 10:48 P.M. and forty degrees. I turned around slowly and looked carefully around the office. The neat piles of paper I had made were all there. The desk, the chairs and the filing cabinet were all there. Everything was there. I sat down at the desk, and Alice showed up in the door.

"Oh, my god! What happened to this place? It's so clean!"

Something from the desk was missing. I studied the objects in front of me. The light, the phone, the date book, the pile of papers.

"What's the matter?"

"Something's missing. Wait a minute." I looked over the desk again. The light, the phone, the date book, the pile of papers.

"What's missing?"

The light, the phone, the . . . "The Rolodex," I said. "The Rolodex is gone."

"I'm not surprised. It's probably in with the title materials from Travis." And she laughed.

"I'm telling you, it's gone."

She sat down in one of the chairs across the desk from me. "I've never seen this office so clean." She pounded her fist on the desk. "Look, Eddie! There's a desk over here!" And she laughed some more. "What's the matter with you?"

"Somebody broke in and stole the Rolodex."

"Why would anyone steal the Rolodex? How do you know they broke in?"

"The door was open. Raymond and I have the only keys. Do the cleaning ladies have keys?"

"No. Hey! Maybe Raymond's back!"

"No. Someone broke in and stole the Rolodex."

"Who would want Raymond's Rolodex?"

"Somebody who wants to find him."

She looked at me, and her eyes were suddenly soft and real. Then she announced it was time to go home.

I hailed a taxicab outside Grand Central. Alice reached for my hand, but instead of shaking it she just held on to it tightly. More from the self-help book.

"It was nice to meet you, Eddie," she said, opening the taxi door.

"Yeah, it was nice meeting you too."

She slipped into the back of the cab and without looking at me she said, "I'll bet we could get past all this." She could almost have been talking to the driver. Then she slammed the door and I watched the taxi take off down Forty-second Street.

I got another taxi for myself and we went straight down Second Avenue, past the bars and restaurants in Murray Hill and into the East Village. When one part of the city goes to bed, another part wakes up. As we got down below Fourteenth Street, the sidewalks became alive again. Second Avenue was dazzled with colors from the theaters and the new restaurants, and punks and hippies crowded the streets. We cruised past the whores near Houston Street, and out of habit and nostalgia I looked for my old friend, Holly, the same way I sometimes looked for Scotch when I got home. Change is something that happens to people. I've always known that. But who the hell ever thought it was going to happen to me?

And as I rode the elevator up to my apartment the words to an Elvis Costello song came to me:

> *Welcome to the working week,*
> *I know it won't thrill you,*
> *I hope it don't kill you,*
> *Welcome to the working week.*

CHAPTER
—7—

I was dreaming of a toy city where the streets were littered with paper and the people had no souls. I was wandering aimlessly, looking for someone, when the telephone rang.

"Hello?"

"Margolis, get up."

"What?"

"Get up, you're going to be late for work. Your boss'll kill you."

"Who is this?"

"It's Murphy. Who the hell do you think it is?"

His voice seemed different. It was tight and full of energy, but it still reminded me of that hot summer morning when he first stormed into my life, sweating and smirking and accusing me of killing my friend, Tony Santucci. He stole my booze, he laughed at me, and he called me a drunk, but he became the first law enforcement official, other than my father, that I ever trusted.

I sat up and looked at the clock. It was seven-thirty and I had a nasty hangover.

"Margolis, are you there?"

"Yeah."

"Okay, listen to me. How'd it go yesterday?"

"It went fine." I didn't drink anything. How could I be hung over?

"Margolis, what the hell is the matter with you?"

"I need coffee."

"Well, get some for Christ's sake."

"I don't have any."

"Listen to me. I spoke to Walsh. And I spoke to Cadell."

Walsh and Cadell. Walsh I was supposed to know. I could figure that out later. But who the hell was Cadell? Nothing like poetry at seven-thirty in the morning. Who the hell was Cadell? Ring a bell for Cadell. "Who the hell is Cadell?"

"He's one of the senior partners there. He's the one who hired us. He said he was going to chew Walsh out for giving you a hard time. So don't worry about anything. Now tell me about this guy Fidel."

Who the hell is Cadell, tell me about this guy Fidel. Ring a bell and go to hell. . . .

"Margolis, are you all right?"

"Fidel's missing."

"Jesus, Margolis. It's like pulling teeth with you in the morning. What'd you find out yesterday?"

"Can you hold on a minute?" I walked to the bathroom and splashed some cold water on my face and looked at my sleepy eyes in the mirror. I wondered if the mornings were always going to be this bad. I went back to the telephone and managed to tell Murphy briefly about my first day of work. I left out a lot of the details.

"You did all right, Margolis."

"Thanks."

"Don't forget to fill out an expense voucher for dinner. Kate'll give it to you. What are you going to do today?"

"Recover."

"Jesus! Margolis! Have you been drinking?"

"No."

"Christ! You're tough in the morning."

"Buy me some coffee."

"Margolis, I'm in fucking Poughkeepsie." He pronounced it Po-KEEP-see.

"Federal Express it, then."

"Jesus. Okay, listen. I'm going to tell you what to do today, okay?"

"Why not?"

"Okay. One. Go to the office and do a working memo for yesterday."

"What's a working memo?"

"Two. Call George Walsh and tell him about the Rolodex. Find out if anyone else besides you and Fidel have keys. Three. Go to Fidel's apartment and see what you can dig up. Four—"

"Can I ask you something?"

"Four. Call that real estate guy and see if you can meet with those other clients."

"Can I just ask—"

"Five. Get his Rolodex, or see if you can find a telephone book in his apartment and start making calls. Call everyone you can—"

"Hey! Stop!"

"What's the matter?"

"I don't know what I'm doing!"

"Of course you don't know what you're doing. That's why I'm going over this. Call everyone you—"

"Listen to me!"

"Margolis, what's wrong?"

"I'm telling you what's wrong! I spent all day yesterday faking it every inch of the way. I told Walsh that you would be handling this from—"

"Yeah, I know. And I told you not to worry about Walsh."

"You don't understand."

"Look, Margolis. You're doing fine. Just make it up as you go along. I'll be back in the city tonight. We'll meet at the office around five. Do the best you can."

He hung up. I scratched my head and cursed out loud and then the telephone rang again.

"Hello?"

"Six. Check in with Kate later this morning. I'm going to have her check with some people to make sure that Fidel isn't sleeping at the morgue."

"Walsh said he didn't want any publicity."

"Relax, Margolis. Who said anything about publicity? You think my friends downtown have no discretion?"

"I don't think anything."

"Great. You'll make a fine detective. Get some coffee." And he hung up.

I got to the office at nine o'clock. Kate was already there, gabbing away on the telephone, and I nodded to her and slipped into the inner office and shut the door. I pulled out the pile of papers I had brought from Raymond Fidel's office and put them on my desk. Then I sat down and put my feet up and stared at the ceiling. This was my second day of work, and I still had no idea what I was doing. Murphy had told me to make it up as I went along. Fine. It was his office. His client. His reputation. What the hell did I care? The worst thing that could happen to me would be that I would get fired. So what?

So I called George Walsh and told him about the Rolodex. He assured me that there were only two keys to each office door, and he told me that he would check with building security to see if there had been any unwarranted visitors last night. Then I called Bill Bryant and left a message with his secretary, Jane, for him to call me back.

With those two phone calls out of the way, I began going through Raymond Fidel's papers. Now that I knew what the deals were and who some of the players were, it was a little bit easier to figure out what was what. There were some contracts and letters relating to Norco Construction Company, but it seemed like most of the papers related to the new loan on the Travis Building. I was trying to read a draft of a promissory note for twenty million dollars when my telephone started beeping.

I pushed the flashing button and got Kate.

"Good morning. There's a Mr. Bill Bryant on line two. Says he's returning your call. You owe me a working memo."

"Yeah. One of these days someone will tell me what the hell a working memo is. Line two?" I pushed the button for line two. "Hello?"

"Hello, Mr. Margolis. Bill Bryant. What can I do for you?"

"Your firm hired me to—"

"Yes, of course. I know. I was on the committee that hired you."

"It was brought to my attention that Raymond called you last Wednesday, approximately ten minutes before he left the office."

"Yes, and I wish I had been here to take the call. Tell you the truth, I haven't the foggiest notion what was on his mind. Did Alice go over everything he was working on with you?"

"Yeah."

"You know, Raymond's always been a little bit prone to

panic. It's not unusual for me to get urgent messages from him. I wouldn't worry about it."

"Alice told me you would be able to get me in to see Alfred Norens and Sam Pulaski."

"Wow. What do you want to see them for?"

"Well, I'd like to talk to all the clients that Raymond was working for."

"Well, Pulaski is no problem. I'm sure you'll enjoy that. But Norens I'll have to call. He's pretty busy these days, and to tell you the truth, I'm not sure he's going to be able to tell you much. I don't think Raymond had much contact with him. You'd probably be better off talking to Allen Crane. I'll see what I can do."

"I'd appreciate that."

"Anything else?"

"Not at the moment."

"George tells me we have a missing Rolodex."

"Looks that way."

"Well, let's not make a federal case of this if we don't have to. You know what I mean?"

"Of course," I said. And as we hung up, I wondered what he did mean.

CHAPTER

—8—

When it gets to Tribeca the West Side Highway, or whatever it's called down there, has no real boundaries. A wide no-man's-land of broken concrete and mud puddles that separated the flow of traffic from the landfill in the Hudson River was being used as a parking lot by construction workers. A chain link fence encircled the project, and a large sign on the fence announced the development of the Hudson Harbor Office Complex, owned by the City of New York and being built by Norco Construction Company. In smaller print the sign listed the names of the architects, a couple of banks, and a slew of city and state politicians, including the mayor and governor. The sign also proclaimed that the City of New York and Norco Construction Company were both equal opportunity employers. Who was I to argue?

A mud road through the parking area and a gate in the

fence served as an entrance to the project. There was a small security booth just inside the gate, where a guard sat reading *The Post* with his legs up. He gave no indication that he planned to prevent me from entering the premises, but I stopped outside the booth anyway and he brought his legs down and closed the paper. "Can I help you, sir?" He was an older black man with some peach-fuzz hair around his lip and chin.

"I'm looking for Allen Crane," I said.

"Mr. Crane? He expecting you?"

"Yes. I spoke to him this morning."

He turned around and looked through the dirty windows at a line of trailers behind the booth, as if Allen Crane might suddenly appear. Then he turned back to me. "Check the Norco trailer down here." He pointed toward the trailers. "Third one down. If he ain't there, then he'd be up with Mr. Norens."

"Up where?"

He showed me all of his clean white teeth. "Up there," and he pointed with his thumb toward the top of the building under construction. "Hope you ain't afraid of heights, now."

"No, I don't think so."

"No one thinks so, till they get up there."

"Thanks." I started to walk away.

"Hey, wait a minute!" He leaned out of the booth, holding on to the door frame with one hand, *The Post* dangling by his side. He was still smiling. "This is a hard-hat area. Get someone at that Norco trailer to give you a hat."

I carefully navigated with my new shoes, along the muddy path that led to the trailers. Boards had been laid out like sidewalks, but the mud oozed up around them and made them wet and slippery. The trailers were old and dirty, and little signs announced the names of the company that each belonged to. The Norco Construction Company trailer was painted a dull green and was slightly bigger than the other trailers. I climbed the makeshift wooden stairway and knocked once before entering.

A long empty wooden table sat solidly in the middle of the floor. Behind the table, to the right, a gigantic calendar for the month of November took up one whole wall. A small window let in some gray light, which obviously had not been enough for the dead plant that hung from the ceiling. To my left there were four metal desks and a wall of shelves and filing cabinets.

There were two women at the front two desks. They looked exactly alike and they were both buried under piles of yellow invoices. "Delivery?" one of them asked, without looking up.

"No. I'm here to see Allen Crane."

"Talk to Mitch," she said, still without looking at me.

The only other person in the room was a two-hundred fifty-pound monster sitting behind one of the desks in the back. He might have been made of cement and steel. He talked into the telephone, which he clutched as if it were a pencil that could snap in his hands. "Ya called 'em? Did ya call 'em? What'd he say?" His voice was so deep that I expected to feel the floor vibrate. "Greg, talk to me. What'd he say? . . . That's too long. You can't have fifty guys standing around. Can they do sometin' else? Greg, hold on a sec." He nodded his concrete head at me, "Yeah, what d'ya want?"

"Allen Crane."

"Who are you?"

"Eddie Margolis. I have an appointment."

He spoke into the telephone. "Greg, he's gonna hit the roof. Can't ya do nothing? What's wrong with the fucking thing? . . . Okay. Look, I gotta bring a guy up there now. I'll tell him. He's gonna wanna come out there. . . . I know, I know. I'm just telling ya . . . Okay. Okay. Right."

He hung up the telephone and without a word he threw me a hard hat and led me out of the trailer and down the muddy path. We came to another muddy path that ran between some small sheds. The sheds like the trailers, were labeled with names of companies and they were locked up with big chains and padlocks.

"Where are we going?" I asked.

He didn't answer. The trailers and sheds gave way to a field of mud, and suddenly the building loomed up in front of us, a dazzling mass of grays and greens, dominating the November sky with a princely arrogance. The bottom floors had walls of sparkling granite and lots of large tinted windows, which reflected the shimmering grayness of the Hudson River. The upper floors were incomplete, but the skeleton was there, a grid of black and red iron girders.

A temporary elevator ran up along the outside of the building on the southeast corner, and a few men were hanging around drinking coffee and smoking cigarettes. The relaxed atmosphere dissipated quickly as we approached, and one of the men nodded to the monster. "Hiya, Mitch." The rest of them joined in as a chorus, "Hiya, Mitch."

The monster said nothing as we walked into the elevator, and he pulled the door shut and threw down the throttle as if it were something that should have been done yesterday. He didn't look at me as we raced up into the sky, and although there was nothing to indicate how high we were going, I knew we were going to the top.

The elevator door opened onto a concrete floor that stretched out in a big square to the edges of the building. The girders went up for about ten more floors, but there were no more ceilings or walls. You could see out over Manhattan and into Brooklyn and you could see straight up the Hudson River to the George Washington Bridge. Large support beams grew out of the floor in even rows like trees in an orchard, and wires and pipes sprouted randomly across the floor like weeds. The wind off the river was strong, so I closed the top button of my coat and put my collar up. Men were working all over the floor to the high-pitched whirling sound of drills being operated at different speeds and in different places. The floor was littered with plastic coffee cups, cigarette butts, and brown paper lunch bags.

"What floor is this?" I asked.

Again the monster did not answer. Our destination was obviously the far corner, where a group of men were huddled in a small semicircle. As we got closer I could see through the semicircle and I caught a glimpse of a man sitting behind a desk. He was wearing a bright red tie and red suspenders and he was drinking a mug of coffee. It was Alfred Norens. The desk was about five feet from the edge of the floor and he kept leaning back on the two back legs of his chair, so that if he had looked over his shoulder, he would probably have seen down the side of the building.

If this was a test to find out who was afraid of heights, I failed. My stomach gaped as wide as the Hudson River and my knees wobbled so badly that I had to hold on to the outer part of the desk for support. I could hardly look at Norens without feeling like I was going to vomit. And for some reason, I thought of Michael Dorfman, whoever he was, falling thirty-two floors to his death.

"I can't believe this," Norens was saying. "How could this happen? Allen, who ordered them?"

The man called Allen dropped his fists onto the outer rim of Norens's desk. He was wearing a pair of clean blue jeans and underneath his leather jacket there was a white shirt and tie. His face had that steady look of an old-time sailor, and his skin was thick and rough from years of being out-doors. "We did. We ordered them according to the specs."

"So the specs were wrong. That's what you're telling me?"

"That's what the inspector's telling us."

"Well, goddamn it. What does Sperry and Sperry have to say about this?"

"They say the inspector's wrong. The inspector says they're wrong."

Norens came forward on his chair and leaned his elbows on the desk. He had dark wiry hair that was blowing around in the wind, and his jacket was draped over the back of his chair as if it were the middle of summer. He had a little face with big, puffy cheeks. The corners of his lips turned slightly upward, as if he were playing a joke on the world and was ready to laugh with anyone who caught on. "Okay," he said, "so they have to fight it out. What are we going to do in the meantime? How many floors do we have in so far?"

"Fifteen."

"Great. So if we bet on the inspector, then we rip out fifteen floors of panel boxes. If we bet on Sperry, then in two months we rip out seventy-two floors of panel boxes. No, that's no good. We wait until they make their decision."

"Yeah, but the electrical subs are waiting around. They can't do anything."

"Okay. So Sperry and the inspector have to make a decision. This afternoon. I want a decision by five o'clock. To-morrow I want the subs working, one way or the other."

"What if we can't get the inspector?"

"You can get him. Call the mayor's office if you have to. This is ridiculous. He can't say we're not up to code and then disappear." He looked up at me and then turned to the concrete monster. "Who's this?"

Based on the monster's track record for answering questions, I decided to field this one myself. "I'm Eddie

Margolis," I said, "I had an appointment to meet with Allen Crane."

The man called Allen held his hand out. "Hiya. I'll be with you in a few minutes."

"Yeah, but who is he?" Norens persisted.

Allen Crane answered. "He's a detective working for Fenner, Covington and Pine. You know, they're looking for Fidel."

Norens pushed his chair back so that the back legs were but inches from the edge of the floor and he put his feet up on the desk. He handled himself with an absurd mixture of a child's reckless obstinancy and a despot's self-confidence. "No shit," he said.

"No shit," I answered.

Then he stood up and held out a hand for me. He was no more than five feet two inches tall. "Alfred Norens," he said as we shook hands. "Bill Bryant called me this morning and said you'd be stopping by."

"And here I am."

"Great, let's talk. Okay, so you guys know what you're doing now? What's everybody standing around for? Allen, get that meeting set up. All right?"

"What about Mr. Margolis, here?"

"I'll talk to him. You take care of the panel boxes. Mitch, you look worried. What's the matter?"

"They got problems in Jersey."

"What kind of problems?"

"The generator is down and they can't get it fixed until after two."

"So?"

"They got no power. They can't cut wood for the frame. They got guys sitting around."

"What do you mean they got guys sitting around?"

"There's no power."

"Power my fucking ass. What about handsaws?"

"He says they need power."

"Shit. Let's go over there."

"He said he doesn't need you."

"He always says that. Let's go." He turned to me. "I'm sorry, what's your name again?"

"Margolis. Eddie Margolis."

"Okay. You call me Al, I call you Eddie. Right? Listen, you got some time?"

"Do you?"

"Come on, I gotta go to New Jersey. We'll take my new bird. You'll like it. We'll talk."

His new bird was a Spitfire Taurus helicopter that was sitting on the smooth dirt landing field between the building and the river. On the way down in the elevator Norens introduced the monster to me as Mitchell Dougherty. "Mitchell's my right arm, so to speak," Norens said. The top of Norens's head didn't even reach Dougherty's shoulders, and I marveled at the obviousness of a man so short surrounding himself with such big buildings and big men.

We climbed into the helicopter, where a pilot was already strapped in and waiting for us. The deafening roar of the engine and the propellers was suddenly dulled when Dougherty closed the door behind us. There were two seats up front for the pilot and a copilot, or extra passenger. Then there were two rows of three seats each, facing each other. Norens sat across from me by the window, facing the front, and Dougherty sat by himself near the other window, facing the rear.

"What do you think of my new baby?" Norens asked me as we settled into our seats.

"Pretty nice."

"Pretty nice," he imitated me. "That's cause you don't know shit about helicopters."

"You're right."

"Listen to how quiet it is in here. This thing has twin 250C-20B turbine engines. Four hundred twenty horsepower. It cruises at one hundred forty miles an hour. This is the executive version. Seats six plus look at the storage space." He stood up and showed me the compartments overhead. "I'm telling you, this thing is a beauty. Look, see that one?" He pointed out the window to another helicopter sitting in the mud. "That's my old Hiller. I haven't used it once since I got this one. This was a birthday present from my wife. I turned fifty last month."

"Congratulations," I said, wondering if his wife was six feet four.

"I don't know what to do with the Hiller. Maybe I'll sell it. Who knows? Maybe it'll come in handy yet."

Suddenly we began to rise and, although the cars and trucks and trailers shrank as they dropped away below us, the building itself seemed to grow, tirelessly revealing one floor after another of granite and steel. As we moved out over the Hudson River, the building gradually took its place among the other buildings on the Manhattan skyline, and although it was not as tall as the twin towers of the World Trade Center, its grandeur was still awesome.

"Seventy-two floors when it's finished," Norens said, looking out the window with me. "I got my desk up on sixty, but by Thanksgiving I should be up to sixty-three. I figure about a floor a week. Fantastic, isn't it?"

"Yes," I admitted.

"So what'd you want to see me about?"

I looked in from the window. "I've been hired by Fenner, Covington and Pine to find Raymond Fidel. He's been missing for almost a week."

"So I've heard."

"I was hoping that you or Mr. Crane might be able to give me some information on the things Raymond was working on."

Norens smiled. "Well, I can do that for you, but I'll tell you right now, it's not going to help you find him."

"Why do you say that?"

He shrugged. "I just can't see how what he was doing for us here could have anything to do with it."

"Anything to do with what?"

"His . . . disappearance."

"What *does* have to do with it?"

He shrugged and looked out the window. A man like Norens would have more to say, but I wasn't going to push him. Dougherty was looking out the other window. Unless we were in trouble, the pilot was looking out the front window. I looked up at the ceiling and waited.

Finally Norens turned back and looked at me. "He was a good lawyer, that Fidel."

"That's what I've been told."

"You never met him, did you?"

"No."

He looked out the window some more. "There's the Statue of Liberty," he pointed.

There she was, standing out in the middle of the bay, little, green and lonely. In my five years in New York I had never visited the Statue of Liberty, and a warm feeling came over my insides as I stared at her. I vowed to visit her that coming weekend.

"The thing about Fidel," Norens continued, "was that he worried too much. He was good at explaining to us what our risks were and why we should do something one way instead of another, but I think he took things a little bit too seriously. Always giving us what he called his 'worst-case scenario.' It was like he was walking around with world's problems around his neck. I think it was Herbert Hoover who once said that if you're walking down the street and you see ten troubles up ahead of you, don't run to them. Chances are nine of them will bounce off to the side by the time you get there. I think Raymond had a bad habit of running to trouble."

"My American history was never very good, but wasn't Hoover president when the stock market crashed?"

He smiled at me. "That wasn't trouble, Eddie. That was disaster."

"So what kind of trouble did Raymond run to?"

"Could've been anything. We've always liked Raymond. I sit on a few boards with Bill Bryant, and I've told him that I like Raymond. I know Allen really likes him too."

"I've been told that everybody liked him."

He frowned. "A guy like Fidel," he said, turning to the window, "he's the kind of guy that everybody loves until they find out he's wanted for mass murder in some northwestern state." When he looked back at me he started to laugh. "Just kidding, Eddie! I'm just saying that I have the feeling the guy's been carrying around a few secrets. Or do you have motion sickness?"

"No, I'm fine."

"Okay. So what did Raymond do for us? Let's see. Right now we're in the process of lining up our subcontractors to do the interior. We got electric, bathrooms, windows. You know. That kind of thing. So there's about thirty subs altogether and Raymond's doing the contracts for us. Eddie, he's a good lawyer, but it's not like we have to have Raymond Fidel. Any lawyer could do it. It's pretty mechanical at this point. They got a girl over at Fenner, Covington named Alice Pinder who's working for us now. Quite a gal."

We were over land now, row after row of little wood frame houses, and I watched a line of tiny cars follow the turns of a narrow strip of highway. "Staten Island," Norens said. "What a pit."

"Looks okay from up here," I said.

"Everything looks okay from up here. I'm from Staten Island. It's a pit."

"Oh."

"Where are you from, Eddie?"

"Florida. A town called Homestead."

"You're actually from Florida? I thought people only went to Florida. I didn't think anybody actually *came* from there."

"That's okay. I didn't know anybody ever came from Staten Island."

He laughed. "Yeah, and nobody goes there either. But there's some good opportunities there. That's where I started, you know. Building two-family houses in Staten Island, not that it needed any more than it already had. But it was a good place to start. There's nothing like the real estate business."

"So I've been told."

"You ought to get into it. You're young enough. There's money to be made."

"I don't know anything about it."

"You'll learn. What do you want to be a detective for? Snooping around people's shit. You could be making money!"

I used to think that I had some kind of a mental deficiency because I had no burning desire to be rich. Slowly I grew to realize that money was like food: you need it to live, but too much makes you fat. "I wouldn't know what to do with it."

"Buy a helicopter!"

"I wouldn't have any place to land it."

He laughed. "Buy a landing pad."

We flew over another river and then over the New Jersey marshlands. What once had been useless swamp now supported a multitude of bridges, train yards, office buildings, and gas refineries. My friend Leon, or ex-friend Leon, had grown up in New Jersey and he used to tell me about hunting for snapping turtles in the Hackensack meadowlands.

"Welcome to the Garden State," Norens said.

We landed in a giant open field, and a few men came up to greet us as we climbed out of the helicopter. One of them was screaming something at Norens, and as we got out of range of the helicopter, I could hear him explaining, "I got some guys working on it now, but they don't know what the fuck they're doing. They don't fucking care either. Their buddies just sitting on their asses smoking cigarettes."

"Who'd we rent from?" Norens screamed back.

"Jersey firm called Gayford."

"And they can't get somebody out here?"

The man shook his head. The engines of the helicopter stopped and suddenly everything was quiet. "Not until after two," the man said in a normal voice.

"Did you tell them we'll rent from somebody else?"

"They don't care. They can't fill the orders they got."

We got to a big van with a large gas generator in the back. The back doors were open and few men were in the van working on the generator. "What's the problem?" Norens called up to them. They all stood up inside the van and turned around to face Norens.

"It keeps conking out on us," one of the men explained.

"Can you start it?"

"Sometimes."

"Try it. Let me see."

They flipped a few switches and then turned a key and the motor roared into action. Thick gray smoke poured out from the back of it and the engine idled fast and then slow and then fast and then slow, as if someone were taking his foot on and off the accelerator of a car. It was a sound I had heard before, the sound an outboard motor makes when you run bad gas through it. The thick gray smoke was another indication of bad gas. The motor slowed down and then choked itself off.

"You see?" The man in the van held his hands out like a magician trying to show that he had no tricks up his sleeves. "We won't be able to start her for about ten minutes. And then it'll just do the same thing."

Norens shook his head in disgust, and I touched his elbow. "It's got bad gas."

He looked at me. "How do you know?"

"That's what happens when you have bad gas. Pour some dry gas in the tank and clean out the gas filter and it'll be fine."

He raised his eyebrows at me. "You a mechanic?"

"No, but I know a motor with bad gas."

Norens looked at the man who had met us at the helicopter. "Get some dry gas and try it. Come over here, Eddie. I want to show you around."

We walked around the outside of a great square-shaped pit. One side of the pit sloped up gently so that trucks and tractors could get in and out, but no one was in the pit now.

"We got another two months in the hole," Norens said, looking into the pit. "At least. Then once we get to ground we go a floor a week, just like Hudson Harbor."

"What's it gonna be?"

"An office building. Twenty-five floors. I only do office buildings. They make the most money." Then we walked a little bit further. Dougherty was about ten paces behind us.

"You checking with all of Fidel's client's?" Norens asked.

"Most of them, I guess."

"You gonna see Sam Pulaski?"

"Do you know him?"

"Who doesn't?"

"I hear he's a barrel of laughs."

"He's a moron. Don't tell him I said so, but you'll see for yourself. He's not gonna help you."

Suddenly the generator started. It idled fast and then slow and slid up into a fast idle and stayed there. We stopped and Norens looked up into the air, waiting to see if it would knock off, but it didn't. Finally he smiled. "Congratulations! You just saved me a lot of money," and he shook my hand. "Now I'm gonna save you a lot of time."

"How's that?"

"If I were you, I wouldn't go snooping around talking to Fidel's clients." There was hostility in his voice.

"No? What would you do?"

"I'd try to figure out where he went. I'd go look up all the people he knows and find out where he's hiding."

"What makes you think he's hiding?"

He shrugged. "Because nobody can find him."

"Who else is looking?" I asked.

He looked at me quickly and smiled. "Just you, Eddie. Just you."

CHAPTER
—9—

We are all prisoners of our own lives.

At twelve-thirty on another sunless November afternoon, I walked the midtown streets, feeling frustrated and stuck. Little things reminded me of a life that wasn't mine. Somebody selling fresh fruits and vegetables, a girl with a pretty dress, an advertisement for good Scotch, a travel poster for Hawaii. On the corner of Third Avenue and Fifty-ninth Street I stood with twenty fellow prisoners, waiting for the light to change. Somebody behind me talked about her daughter's wedding. Somebody else, or maybe the same person, smelled of cheap perfume. A male model on a bus shelter advertisement showed us his white jockey shorts. The light changed and we walked.

Norens had dropped me off at the East Side heliport at noon, which left me an hour to kill before my appointment with Sam Pulaski. I wandered the streets and tried to think about Florida and New York City, and why people live where they do, and why they do what they do for a living, but my mind kept coming back to Raymond Fidel.

Somebody else was looking for him.

First there was the missing Rolodex. Then there was Alfred Norens. He had said nobody could find Fidel. He had not said nobody knew where Fidel was. He had said that nobody could find him, which meant somebody was looking for him. Somebody besides me. It wasn't anyone from his office or his family. It wasn't the police. It was somebody else. Mr. X.

My stomach growled and I bought a hot dog and a ginger ale from a street vendor on Fifty-fifth Street. The question, then, was who was Mr. X? Norens? Someone Norens knew? Sam Pulaski? Or was I just making all of this up? I bought another hot dog on Fifty-second Street. Make it up as you go along.

Pulaski Enterprises was on the twenty-ninth floor of a new high-rise office building on Third Avenue. A pair of big smoked-glass doors greeted me when I got off the elevator. I searched the names of companies listed under Pulaski Enterprises and found Travis Realty Limited Partnership and Travis Realty Corp. Despite their size, the doors opened easily and I found myself in a bright, sparsely furnished reception area that had probably once been ultra modern. A receptionist had her head down and her eyes buried deep in the paperback on her lap. She had not heard me come in.

"Hi," I said.

She quickly jerked her head up. "Good morn . . . afternoon," and she gave me a little it's-been-one-of-those-days smiles. She had an exquisite face, with dark, beautiful eyes and light chocolate brown skin. Her mouth was big, but not too big, and her smile didn't fade, but hung around as if she were in a constant state of amusement. Maybe she was. "Can I help you?"

"Yes, I'm Eddie Margolis. I'm here to see Sam Pulaski."

"You're the detective." Her lips came together, puckered in curiosity.

"That's right."

"I never met a real detective."

I held my hand out. "Eddie Margolis. Real detective."

She shook my hand gently and with a mock formality said, "Pleased to meet you, Mr. Margolis. My name is Hope."

"Pleased to meet you, Hope."

"Let me tell Mr. Pulaski that you're here."

I sank into one of the big couches and began reading an article about decorating the second home. It was a fascinating article and about five minutes later, when Hope told me that Mr. Pulaski would see me, I had made it all the way into the second sentence.

A secretary led me down a long hallway with open doors leading off to empty offices and conference rooms. I did not see any people. She left me at the door to Pulaski's office at the end of the hall. It was a long room with a full wall of windows overlooking the East River and an odd assortment of shabby furniture that looked like it had been left where the moving man had dropped it. There were lots of photographs and trophies and little knickknacks for the man who has everything, the kind that grandchildren always buy Grandpa for his office. Pulaski was nowhere in sight, and I took a few hesitant steps into the room. Then Sam Pulaski came in behind me.

He was a fat, grubby-looking man, and if he had grandchildren, then I felt sorry for them. His cheeks and his chin were big globs of skin that hung down from his face, and his chest sloped outward to his stomach and made him look like a mountain with legs. There was nothing pleasant about him.

"Eddie Margolis," I said, and I held my hand out.

"Yeah, yeah, yeah, I know," he said, and he sat down at his desk without taking my hand. He picked up a pile of papers and studied them one page at a time. I stood in front of his desk and waited. "Well, what do you want?" he asked finally without looking up.

"I've been hired by Fenner, Covington and Pine to find Raymond Fidel."

"Bill told me already. What do you want?" He still didn't look up at me.

"I wanted to talk to you about what Fidel was working on for you."

He put on a pair of glasses with big black frames and studied the page in front of him. He creased his forehead as if he was trying to concentrate on something, but I had to believe that the only thing he was concentrating on was trying to intimidate me. After a while he looked up at me. "Well, okay. You want to talk to me. Talk to me. I'm listening."

But before I could say anything his eyes were back down on his desk. "I understand he was working on a refinancing of the Travis Building," I said to the bald spot on the top of his head.

"So?"

"Could you tell me a little bit about it?"

He looked up at me. "Listen, why don't you have somebody at Fenner, Covington tell you about it. Maybe they have nothing better to do with their time. I'm busy." And his head went back down.

To hell with him. I walked up to the desk and sat in one of the big chairs directly across from him. I put my hands behind my head and crossed my legs with my ankles up on the corner of his desk. "Alfred Norens told me you were a moron."

I made sure I was smiling when he looked up. His eyes darted back and forth between my face and my feet, as if he couldn't decide which offended him more. His head shook nervously as he tried to get some words out. "Norens?" he finally managed to scream.

"That's right."

"What the fuck do I care what Norens has to say about me?" he screamed. "Who the fuck is Norens to call me names? That little fucking bastard. And who the hell do you think you are? Get your goddamned feet off my desk!"

I left my feet where they were. "Would you mind answering some questions for me?"

"No. I won't answer any of your questions. Go to hell. I had enough of you."

"Where's Raymond Fidel?"

"How the hell should I know?"

"I think you do know."

He threw the papers down on his desk and pushed his chair back to look at me across the desk. "Look, punk. I've had forty-five years in the business. Nobody talks to me like this! Now, you got something specific on your mind, spit it out. Otherwise, get the fuck out of here!"

"Who owns the Travis Building?"

He took a deep breath. "Look. I'm gonna give it to you once, okay. No questions. You got questions, you talk to Bill Bryant or that Pinder girl. Then you leave me alone."

"That's all I ever wanted."

"Get your feet off my desk."

I let my feet down. They had served their purpose.

He pushed his seat back and stared out the window while he spoke. "Travis Realty Limited Partnership owns the building. It's a limited partnership. Ninety-five percent of the partnership is owned by investors. They buy their interests for twenty thousand a shot. All they do is invest their money. It's like buying stock. Okay? So they own ninety-five percent of the partnership. The other five percent is owned by Travis Realty Corp. Travis Realty Corp. is the general partner. The general partner is responsible for managing the building and is liable for all the partnership's debts. Travis Realty Corp. is my corporation, set up to act as managing general partner."

"So you own five percent of the building."

"You don't listen too good, do you?" He turned in from the window and looked at me. "I own a corporation which owns five percent of a partnership which owns the building. If you can't follow that, I don't know how the hell you're ever going to find Fidel. Fidel's helping us with a refinancing. We're getting a twenty-million-dollar loan from National Bank of New York. It's no big deal. No problems. You lawyers and detectives want to make trouble where there is none. Why bother me? What can I do?"

"Who are the limited partners?"

"What d'ya mean who are they? They're investors. You want their names? I can get you their names."

"Yes, I'd like their names. Who is the present loan from?"

He was very calm. "Ocron S.A. It's a Panamanian company."

"How come you don't like Alfred Norens?"

"Norens? What does Norens have to do with this? Look. What's your name?"

"Dick Tracy."

"Look, Tray . . . Ah, you fucking wiseguy. What's your name?"

"Eddie Margolis."

"Look, Margolis. I don't know what your fucking problem is. Some stupid-ass lawyer from Fenner, Covington and Pine disappears. He's probably in Tahiti by now. You go snooping around talking to Norens and me. Don't you have anything better to do? Why don't you hang it up? The guy's gone. Maybe he don't want to be found."

I put on a confused look. "I didn't see Norens."

"The hell you didn't."

"What makes you think I saw Norens?"

He was quick, but not quick enough. "You . . . you said he told you I was a moron."

"He called you."

"He did not! Why would he do that? Now I got to go to my meeting, if you'll excuse me . . ." He headed toward the door.

"What exactly is your relationship with Norens?" I called out to his back.

He stopped at the door. "You fucking bug me, you know that? You want to know *exactly* what my relationship with Norens is? He thinks I'm a prick and I think he's an asshole."

"Do you want me to find Raymond Fidel?"

"Why should I care if you find him or not?"

"Maybe because he's your lawyer."

"Look, wiseguy. Lawyers are a dime a dozen in this town. There was nothing special about Fidel. The guy takes off two weeks before my closing and leaves everything in the air. So maybe I'm pissed off at him. And maybe this Pinder girl can do a better job. I don't fucking care if you find him. I don't fucking care what you do. I got a meeting to go to." And he stormed past me and out of the office.

I sat still for a few minutes to see if he would come back. Then I walked around his desk and looked through the papers and phone messages, but couldn't find anything interesting. I went back down the hallway to the reception area and found Hope with her nose in her book.

"Hi, Hope."

"Hi," she said, looking up and smiling again. "Did he leave you in his office?"

"Yup."

"He always does that to people. Goes out and leaves them sitting there. Don't take it personally. He does it to everyone."

I walked up closer to her desk and looked down at her. It was a face that I would never get tired of looking at. "Who answers the telephone around here?"

"Me."

"All the time?"

"All the time. Except when I'm at lunch."

"When's that?"

Her smile got bigger. "Fifteen minutes."

She was like the Hawaii travel poster: beautiful, tempting and totally unreachable. Under ordinary circumstances I would have asked her out to lunch. But things were different today. I had a job. And Andrea Fidel was waiting for me downtown.

"Well, so long, Hope," I said, heading for the door.

"So long, Mr. Detective."

When I got to the door I remembered the question that I had meant to ask her and I turned around again. "Hey, Hope. Did Al Norens call for Mr. Pulaski this morning?"

"Sure did."

"Yeah, when was that?"

"About noon."

"Thanks."

About noon. That was just when Norens had dropped me off at the heliport. He probably called from his helicopter before they had even taken off again. I rode down in the elevator thinking about it. Something about Alfred Norens made Sam Pulaski nervous. And Pulaski didn't hide it very well.

CHAPTER
—10—

Cornelia Street is one block long and runs between West Fourth and Bleecker streets, just west of Sixth Avenue. It is home to a score of apartment buildings, a muddy parking lot with a smashed-in wire fence, a few ever-changing storefronts, a realtor's office, the famous cheese shop called This Is Murray's, a restaurant or two, and, of course, The Cornelia Street Café. The café, with its solid woodwork and big picture windows, anchors this anomalous sliver of a street to the rest of Greenwich Village.

The café was quiet at three o'clock in the afternoon, and I found Andrea Fidel sitting by herself at a small table with a cup of espresso and an empty dessert plate. She was wearing blue jeans and a navy blue sweater, but her hair was still in a bun, and she still did not look like anybody's younger sister. She looked more like somebody's aunt.

"Hi, Andrea."

"Hi."

I was surprised to see her smile and I made myself comfortable in the seat across from her. "Sorry, I'm late."

"That's okay. I like this place." Her voice was still slow and strange and it made me feel uncomfortable to hear it again. "I don't get to come here much during the week," she said, "and it's nice and quiet. On weekends I come here with Ray sometimes, but it's always busy then. I like it like this. You going to have something?"

"I don't think so."

Neither of us said anything for a while. She sipped her espresso and I watched a couple drinking Bloody Marys at the bar. The woman had her fur coat draped over the stool next to her, and the man stood in front of his stool, leaning his arms on the bar and smoking a cigarette. They were laughing and having a good time.

Andrea was gazing intently at a spot about six inches from the left side of my head. "Andrea?"

Her eyes moved slowly toward me.

"Andrea, I got the feeling that there was something you wanted to tell me yesterday but didn't want to say in front of your mother. Am I right?"

She shrugged and took a sip of espresso, but didn't say anything. Then she went back to studying that spot next to my head. I tried another approach. "You know, I think that you know where Raymond is."

She began nodding very slowly, but her eyes didn't move. "Andrea?"

"I do know where he is," she said, suddenly shifting her eyes onto me.

"You do?" I couldn't hide the surprise in my voice.

She nodded.

"Where is he?"

She studied me as if I was a menu, or a piece of art, or a slab of meat at the butcher shop.

"Andrea," I said carefully. "If you know where Raymond is, I think you should tell me."

"Why?"

"There's a lot of people who are worried about him. How about your mother? Does she know where he is?"

"No. Only me."

"And you don't want to tell me?"

"I can't."

"Why not?"

"Because . . . because, I don't want to."

I turned my head and looked at the couple at the bar. A week ago at this time I had been fishing out over the reef with my father. Now here I was in The Cornelia Street Café playing child-psychology games with a woman older than myself. The woman at the bar held out a cigarette and the bartender lit it with infinite grace. It was like a scene from a movie and I wondered if the woman was somebody famous. When I turned back toward Andrea, she was staring down at her empty espresso cup. "Andrea, is Raymond in trouble?"

"I don't know."

She was not looking at me, but I continued. "Listen, Raymond might be in trouble. I want to help him. If you know where he is, then we can help him together. Don't you want to help him?"

"He doesn't need our help."

"How do you know?"

She shrugged but wouldn't answer.

"I take it, then, that you don't want me to find him."

"No," she said quickly, cutting me off. Then softer, "I want to find him."

I took a deep breath and decided that it would be easier

for me to find Raymond myself than to figure out what the hell Andrea had on her mind. And I was tired of being polite. "Well," I said, staring off at the couple at the bar, "I wouldn't think that it would be too hard to find him if you already know where he is."

"Well maybe . . . maybe, I don't." Then before I could say anything, "Do you still want to see his apartment?"

Raymond's apartment was in an old brick building across the street from the café. There were eight mailboxes inside the tiny foyer, and I tried to look inside Raymond's box, but I could not tell if there was anything in it. Andrea did not have a mailbox key. She opened the inside door and I followed her up the old wooden staircase to the third floor. Yellow paint was peeling from the walls, and the brown rubber mat that ran up the stairs had been worn through in a few places. Still, the building was a lot nicer than most of the buildings in my part of town. There was no graffiti and there were banisters, and the lights worked.

Raymond's apartment was on the third floor, in the front. We entered into a kitchen that was old and dirty, even by my standards. There were piles of dirty dishes in the sink and on top of the stove, and the counter was covered with empty beer bottles and cardboard cartons from Chinese takeout. The cockroaches paid no attention to us when I turned on the light. There was a handful of menus from Chinese restaurants stuck to the refrigerator door, and inside the refrigerator there was lots of beer and soda, but not much else.

The living room was open and spacious and there were two big windows that looked out onto The Cornelia Street Café. There were a sofa and a few chairs scattered about, but the room was otherwise pretty empty.

The real mess was in the bedroom. There was a desk and a dresser and a lot of bookcases and there was stuff piled all over everything. The bed, unmade, was in the far corner and there were clothes hanging off all four bed posts. There were a couple of places where I could see the floor, but mostly it was covered by dirty clothes, newspapers and books, and more dirty dishes. It occurred to me that Raymond Fidel might have been running away from his own mess.

Andrea made herself comfortable on the sofa in the living room while I went through Raymond's belongings. There were jackets and slacks and shirts and ties all over the place, some of them on hangers and some of them thrown on the floor with the socks and shoes. There were more clothes tangled up in the sheets of the bed, and at the foot of the bed there was a telephone and a remote control for the television and the VCR. On the night table near the bed there was a clock radio, a pile of books, a carton of Chinese food with chopsticks sticking out of it (it looked like some kind of beef or pork, but I was not about to try it), and a few empty beer bottles. There was also a mug of something that probably used to be coffee and an ashtray with half a joint and a few roaches in it.

I went through his desk pretty carefully and found a lot of bills and junk mail. His bills did not seem out of the ordinary. There was a Visa card bill for two hundred and some odd dollars, an American Express bill for about three hundred dollars, and a telephone bill that was under fifty dollars. I looked at the listings for long-distance calls on the telephone bill. Long Beach, Long Beach, Long Beach. I read the number out loud and Andrea confirmed that it was her and her mother's number. That was it. There was a bank book that showed a balance of $3,548, and I could not find a checkbook or a telephone book.

The bedroom closet was another disaster area. Clothes hung from every possible place, and a pile of dirty stuff was thrown on the floor. There were a few boxes up on the top shelf. One of them was marked "Law School," and I decided it was not worth the climb to check it out. On top of the boxes there were old suitcases. I asked Andrea if she knew what kind of bag Raymond usually traveled with and she came in and found his overnight bag, hanging from a hook in the back of the closet. She did not know his luggage well enough to know if anything else was missing.

I spent a little bit of time looking through the books near his bed and in the bookcases. There were a lot of books about Lenin and revolution, and there were books about apartheid and socialism. There were a few law books and there were a few books that even people like me had heard of, such as *The Electric Kool-Aid Acid Test, All the President's Men,* and *Catch-22.* Andrea told me that Raymond had majored in political science in college. So Raymond Fidel smoked pot and was a closet rebel. Maybe that was why he didn't fit in at Fenner, Covington & Pine.

I was going through a small cabinet in the living room when there was a knock on the door. I looked up at Andrea on the couch, and she looked back at me, but neither of us moved. "You expecting anyone?" I asked.

She shook her head.

The knock came again and I got up and opened the door. It was an older man, probably in his sixties. He was tall and big-boned, but he was slouched over. He was smoking a cigarette. His flannel shirt had holes in the elbows, and a stained undershirt showed underneath where the flannel shirt was unbuttoned in the front. We stared at each other for a minute before he looked past me and saw Andrea on the couch.

"You looking for Raymond?" he asked her, talking right through me.

"Yeah."

"You're Raymond's sister, aren't you?"

"Yeah."

"Yeah, I thought I'd seen you around. You know where that bastard brother of yours is hiding himself?" he asked, still looking past me.

"No."

"Figures." Then he looked at me. "You a friend of his?"

"Yeah. We're kind of worried about him."

He dropped his cigarette on the floor in the hallway and smashed it with his big black shoe. "Well," he said, squeezing past me into the kitchen, "tell you the truth, I'm kind of worried about him myself." He walked over to the kitchen sink and put the water on. He turned it off and on a bunch of times and stared at the faucet. "Damn son of a bitch still leaks," he said without turning around. "Replaced the washers and everything. I must of told Mrs. Lyndale a hundred times these sinks gotta be replaced. She just don't wanna listen to me. Close that door, would you?"

I closed the door and he turned around and faced me and then looked in at Andrea, still sitting on the couch, and then he lit another cigarette.

"Yeah, I'm afraid Raymond might of got himself in some trouble."

"Why do you think that?"

"Hard to figure a guy like Raymond, being a lawyer and everything. He used to come down and drink a beer with me every once and a while."

Nobody said anything for a while, so I asked again. "What happened?"

"Friday, I guess it was," he said, turning and flicking his cigarette ash into the dirty dishes in the sink. "Yeah, it was Friday. Couple of cops were here, lookin' for him. Ringing his bell and shit. They rang my bell and I talked to them a little bit, you know, being the super and all, but I ain't told them nothing really. Fucking sons of bitches never did nothing for me except cause me trouble. Those two on Friday wanted me to let them into Raymond's apartment. No warrant, nothing. Just wanted to come in here and snoop around. They told me they thought he was in some kind of trouble. Shit. I know better than that. You don't have to be no lawyer to know they gotta have a warrant to go into someone's apartment. Even I know that, and I told those sons of bitches that I ain't opening any doors till I see me a warrant."

He turned around again and flicked his cigarette ash into the sink. "Now, I ain't the kind to be sticking my nose around where it don't belong, see, but those sons of bitches got me scared, wondering if Raymond was in some sort of trouble. So I started worrying and after they left, I came up here just to make sure everything was all right. I didn't think Raymond would mind, see, 'specially if he was in some kind of trouble. You ain't seen him, huh?"

"No," Andrea answered, not moving from her spot on the couch.

He puffed on his cigarette. "Yeah, I'm worried Raymond might of gotten himself in some trouble. Damned sons of bitches were back here again this morning too. And this time they had themselves a warrant."

"They were here?" I asked.

"Sure as hell. About ten this morning, the same two sons of bitches knock on my door, giving *me* all kinds of shit just for sticking up for my rights. Acting like it's my goddamned fault that they had to get a warrant. Now, I ain't no lawyer like Raymond, but I know my rights. You a lawyer?" he asked me.

"No."

"You don't look like a lawyer, but Raymond never looked much like a lawyer either. I never cared much for lawyers. Sons of bitches never did nothing for me. Raymond was all right, though. Like I said, he didn't look like no lawyer."

"Did you let them in?"

"This morning? I had to. They had a goddamned warrant. Like I said, they were all over me like it was my goddamned fault or something. Now I know a little something about the law, see, having had my own problems, see, and I know that if I had let them in here without a warrant, sure as hell, Raymond could of sued me. Now, I ain't saying Raymond would of done that or nothing, but I got a right to protect my ass. Sons of bitches." He backed off to the sink again to flick another ash.

"Did they say why they were looking for Raymond?"

"Nah. They wouldn't tell me a goddamned thing. Showed me the warrant, gave me some shit, and then to top it all off, they wouldn't let me come into the apartment with them. God knows what they did in here, though everything looks all right. Look okay to you?" he asked Andrea.

"Fine," she said.

Then he looked at me. "Understand now, I wouldn't of let them if I didn't have to. But I been out of trouble for a lot of years now, ever since I lost my wife, see, and I can't afford to be messing with those sons of bitches no more. But I waited right out there in the hall the whole time they were here. Yes, sir. Waited right outside. Everything looks okay in here, don't it?"

I looked at Andrea, but she didn't say anything, and the old man answered himself. "Yeah. They didn't do nothing but snoop around. I'd of heard it if they were doing anything they wasn't supposed to. Sons of bitches."

"How long were they here?"

"About a half an hour. And then, when they're done

snooping around in here they come out and tell me they need to get into the mailbox to check his mail. So I says to them that I have no problem with that, so long as the warrant says that I'm supposed to open the mailbox. Well, of course, there ain't nothing in the warrant about no mailbox, so I tell them where they can get off. Those sons of bitches threatened to haul me in as an accomplice, to what I'll never know. Now, like I said, I been out of trouble for some time now, and I can't afford to be messing with those sons of bitches. I know what my rights are, see, but like I said, I can't afford to be messing with those sons of bitches. Well, Charlie, the mailman's been delivering here for almost fifteen years. He knows me pretty good, and knows I keep an eye on things around here. So when Raymond stops picking up his mail, see, the box gets too full. So Charlie knows that I always hold Raymond's mail for him when he goes away, so Charlie starts giving me Raymond's mail, see. I got a pile of it downstairs. Those sons of bitches were never going to see it. I went and opened Raymond's box, knowing damn well there wouldn't be a thing in it. Them sons of bitches threatening me. Now I ask you. If that warrant don't say nothing about the mailbox, then I'd be breaking the goddamned law for opening it. Wouldn't I?"

"You still have the mail?" I asked.

"Sure as hell. Got it right downstairs. I'll give it to you if you want. I know she's Raymond's sister, and I know you're a friend of his. Somebody ought to be looking through it."

"Yeah, I guess we'll take it."

"Sure as hell, I'll get it right now," and he left, leaving the door open as a sign of how quickly he would return.

I paced around the living room while we waited for him. There was no way for me to tell what the police had done in the apartment. There was no way for me to know why they had been there. It did not make sense that the police had been looking for Raymond on Friday. If they had been looking for him, they would have contacted Fenner, Covington & Pine. But Fenner, Covington & Pine had contacted us because they did not want the police. They would not be using us if the police were already on the case. Which meant that the police had not been to Fenner, Covington & Pine, or that someone at Fenner, Covington & Pine was lying. Neither case explained why the police were looking for Raymond in the first place. Could it have been that my Mr. X was the police? I found myself staring at Andrea sitting quietly on the couch.

My thoughts were interrupted by the super, who came back in with a big pile of mail. "Here you go," he said handing me the pile. "That's everything right through today. I'll keep holding it, I suppose, until someone tells me to do otherwise. Just hope those sons of bitches don't come back. They ain't likely to believe that Raymond never gets any mail."

"Thanks," I said, dropping the mail onto the table. "Were you around here last Wednesday, around four o'clock?"

He laughed to himself. "Shit. I'm around everyday around four o'clock. 'Less of course I'm up at the hall or something."

"You happen to see Raymond last Wednesday?"

"Shit. The only time I ever see Raymond during the week is when he goes to work in the morning and when he comes home at night. Last Wednesday's the right day, though," he said nodding his head. "Yeah, he went off to work in the morning like always, and he just never came back. You think of checking with his place of employment?"

"Yeah. They don't know where he is either. Do you have any idea where he might be?"

He shook his head. "No way. Your guess'd be good as mine, at this point. Just hope he ain't in too much trouble. I don't like to see the cops lookin' for nobody. But Raymond didn't seem like the type to get in no trouble. Being a lawyer and everything. I guess Mrs. Lyndale's gonna be wanting some rent at the first of next month. Suppose we'll be knowing something by then. Like I said, Raymond was always nice to me. Used to come down and drink a beer every once and a while. Yeah, I hope he ain't in too much trouble."

The super finally shuffled out, leaving the apartment full of cigarette smoke and confusion. I closed the door again and looked back at Andrea, still sitting on the couch. "Did you know the cops were looking for Raymond?"

She shook her head. "No."

"You were at the meeting at Fenner, Covington and Pine last Friday, weren't you?"

"Yes."

"Did they know the police were looking for him?"

She shook her head. "My mother wanted to go to the police, but they said they wanted to hire a private investigator."

"How about you? Did you want to go to the police?"

"No. I knew Raymond wouldn't want the police looking for him. Just like he wouldn't want you looking for him."

"Keep it up, Andrea. You're being real helpful," I said and started looking through Raymond's mail. Bills, junk mail, catalogs, newsletters. Nothing interesting. Nothing personal.

"I know you don't like me," Andrea said softly from the couch.

I turned around and looked at her. "I like you fine, Andrea. You're just not helping me."

"I don't want to help you."

"Yeah, I figured that out. Why do you think Raymond doesn't want our help?"

She looked up at the ceiling and spoke even slower than usual. "I know Ray better than anyone in the world."

"I'll bet you do."

"He wouldn't disappear unless he wanted to."

"You don't know where he is?"

"Maybe."

"Maybe what?"

"Maybe I don't know where he is."

"And maybe you do?"

She looked at her watch. "I want to catch the four-twenty train. Are you finished?"

"No. Not yet."

The bathroom was the only room in the house that I had not yet explored. It was in pretty bad shape. The tile wall was caving in in some places, and the tiles on the floor were chipped and dirty. I looked in the medicine cabinet and found the usual stuff. There was a toothbrush and toothpaste on the sink, as well as a razor and shaving cream. In the cabinet under the sink there was one of those leather travel bags. The "Week in Review" section of the Sunday *Times* was on the floor in front of the toilet.

There were three postcards stuck to the wall over the toilet and I looked at them carefully. One was of a beach, one was of dramatic seaside cliffs, and one was of a snow-peaked mountain. Florida, California, and Colorado. The two bottom ones were curled and warped from the constant exposure to bathroom steam and heat. The one from Florida seemed brand-new, and I pulled it gently off the wall.

It was addressed in childish handwriting, and I read it quickly:

Dear Ray,
   *Finally got out of the tank and am working at the Beach House.
Not bad. Got a girl who's dynamite and trying to stay clean. Come
visit sometime.*
   Scott

I couldn't read the postmark because the Scotch tape had
ripped it off. I stuck the postcard in my pocket. It was time
to put lovely Andrea on her train back to Long Island.

CHAPTER
—11—

Kate was gone by the time I got back to the office, and there was no sign of Murphy. I was greeted instead by a cold and empty darkness. I switched on the lights and hunted around in the stark silence of the reception area for a thermostat, but I could not find one. Then I hung my coat up in the closet and kept my jacket on. I did not like being in the office when it was like this, but I guessed that it was better than being home, so I grabbed my message slips from Kate's desk and walked into the inner office.

I had been vaguely aware of the nagging identity crisis that had been following me around for the last two days, but I was not prepared for the shock of seeing my own reflection in the big windows on the far wall. In the reflection I saw a man in a business suit, with message slips in his hand. He had a job and an office, and he didn't drink. He didn't hang out in the downtown clubs, but he liked being in his office because it was better than going home. I flopped down in the chair at my desk and stared at the reflection. Where had I gone wrong?

I turned away from the windows and looked through the messages in my hand. Murphy had called to say he would be late. George Walsh had called. And there was a small typed note from Kate saying that Raymond Fidel had not shown up in the city morgue. I put the messages on top of my desk and looked over the pile of papers I had left there in the morning. I called George Walsh and was told that he had left for the day.

I pulled out the list of names and numbers that Andrea had given me. There were nine names altogether. Eight of them were labeled as relatives, and one was an old high school friend of Raymond's. A note at the bottom of the page from Mrs. Fidel said that these were the only names they could come up with other than people at Fenner, Covington & Pine, and that she had already spoken to everyone on the list. How could a guy know so few people? And suddenly I laughed out loud and looked back at my reflection. "What would your list look like, wise guy?" I asked Eddie Margolis. Murphy and Kate, your father and his girl friend, Mary Lou. Maybe a woman named Holly, if you could find her. And a handful of drunks and junkies. So Raymond knew more people than you do.

I dropped the list of names on my desk. I was getting nowhere. There had to be a way to figure out what had happened to Raymond Fidel. In two days I had learned a lot, and a lot of things weren't making sense, and if I thought about all of it, there had to be a way to pull it all together.

It would be another half an hour yet before Murphy came in, and I began pacing the floor and thinking about Raymond. One thing slowly become clear. Raymond Fidel was running away from something. The Rolodex, the police and the call to Bill Bryant all supported that conclusion. And if Raymond was running away from something, then there were two questions: What was he running from? And where did he go?

I stood at the window near Murphy's desk and stared out past my reflection at the office building across the street. What was he running from, and where did he go?

I put my hands in my jacket pockets, and suddenly I felt the postcard that I had taken from Raymond's apartment.

I read it again and I rechecked the postmark for a date, but it was useless. There was a little printed commentary in the upper left-hand corner that said something about Fort Lauderdale's marvelous beaches. I read the postcard again and then grabbed the telephone off Murphy's desk and dialed information for south Florida.

Thirty seconds later I was sitting in Murphy's chair, listening to the telephone ring at The Beach House in Fort Lauderdale. A woman answered in a rushed voice, "Beach House."

"Hi, is Scott there?"

"Scott Nelson?" she asked quickly. There was loud rock and roll blasting in the background.

"Yeah."

"He hasn't come in yet. He starts around seven."

"You got a home phone number for him?"

"What?"

"Do you have a home phone number for him?" I asked more loudly. The music sounded like an old song from The Doors.

"Who is this?" the woman asked, her voice wary.

And then, just for the hell of it, I said, "It's Raymond Fidel."

"Ray, it's me," her voice relaxed and she seemed less distracted. "What's the matter?"

"I just need to talk to Scott," I managed to say.

"Who *is* this?" she asked again, now furious.

"Actually, I'm a friend of Ray's, and I—" but she hung up on me before I could finish.

I was sitting at Murphy's desk with my feet up on the antique wood when I heard the key in the outer door. It occurred to me that I was not in an appropriate position to greet my boss, but it also occurred to me that I did not give a damn. I waited while he hung up his coat in the closet and puttered around in the reception area, and at last Charles Murphy appeared in the doorway to the inner office.

He had a khaki green overnight bag slung over his left shoulder and he held a briefcase in one hand and wad of message slips in the other. There was nothing sloppy about him anymore. He had lost a lot of weight and he looked good in his suit. His tie was loosened around his neck and gave him a casual appearance. His face was thinner and he looked younger and less tired. The only thing that was exactly the same was the penetrating smirk, that half smile with the right side of his mouth that always made me feel like I was lying.

He dropped his bag and briefcase to the floor and leaned against the doorway. "Margolis, what are you doing?"

I shrugged but didn't move my feet.

"Are you trying to impress your new boss with your nonchalance?"

"Boss? I don't have a boss. There is some guy that calls me every once and a while just to see what I'm doing, but I don't think I'd call him a boss. A phantom maybe, or . . ."

"Margolis, what's the matter with you? Get your feet off my desk."

"Oh, is this your desk?" I swung my feet down and sat up and looked at the desk, as if noticing it for the first time. "Gosh, I'm sorry." I used my hand to dust off the place where my feet had been. "You know, I've been here for two days and haven't seen anyone using it, so I figured it was up for grabs."

"Okay, okay," he said, walking into the room. "I get the idea. Let's pick on Charlie for being a delinquent boss. You ought to have some sympathy for delinquents, Margolis, being one yourself." He sat in one of the seats across the desk from me and put on the full smirk. "Don't forget it was me who pulled you out of the gutter."

"At least in the gutter I knew what I was doing."

We both laughed and then I proceeded to tell him everything. I retraced all my steps for the last two days, beginning with my interview with George Walsh and going right through to my last telephone call to The Beach House in Fort Lauderdale. When I finished, I watched him stare up at the ceiling and tap his fingers lightly on his knees.

"You did all right, Margolis," he said, dropping his eyes from the ceiling. "I gotta say. You did all right. Let's walk through this, now, okay? There's a couple of things here that I would call sixth-sense items. Don't look at me like that. Listen to me. Never mind any of this metaphysical stuff you might have heard about the sixth sense, just listen to what I'm saying. Your senses take in a lot more information than your brain can possibly process. It sits up there and it brews and if you let it, it can give you a lot of information. Part of being a good detective is paying attention to this stuff. You're still looking at me funny. Okay, forget the sixth sense. Call it a hunch. It's the same thing."

"Good, I was beginning to feel like I was in the twilight zone."

"You got no respect, Margolis. Okay, let me tell you

exactly what I'm talking about. Let's take Norens and Pulaski. From everything you tell me, there is nothing unusual or suspicious about them, except for the fact that Norens called Pulaski after you got out of the helicopter." He frowned and shrugged. "Could have been for lots of reasons. Could have had something to do with Fidel, I guess. But, I think there is something else that you saw or heard from one of them that makes you suspect them. Don't try to figure out what it is, because you won't be able to. But your sixth sense tells—"

"You mean my hunch?"

". . . whatever you want to call it, tells you that they have something to do with Fidel. Am I right?"

"Are you ever wrong?"

"Hold the sarcasm, Margolis. Don't think about it, because you'll drive yourself nuts. Just go with your feeling. Maybe Pulaski and Norens do have something to do with it. Keep the door open. Now, what about this sister?"

"My sixth sense tells me that she doesn't really know where Raymond is."

"Margolis, sometimes you're too smart for your own fucking good, you know that? But, I'm willing to go with that. If we had an endless number of operatives we could put a tail on her just to make sure, but we don't. I say ignore her."

"It would be a pleasure."

"Now, what about this call to Bill Bryant?"

"It's a hunch."

"Oh, Jesus, I've created a Frankenstein monster. Let's move on. What's left? The Rolodex and the cops. And Fort Lauderdale. Here's what we do. You get on the phone right now and book yourself on the first available flight to Fort Lauderdale. I'm going to make some calls around downtown and see what I can find about this search-warrant business, but I got a hunch of my own about that."

"What's that?"

"Well, if the cops were looking for Fidel, they would have been to Fenner, Covington and Pine. That's definite. If they went to Fenner, Covington, chances are they would have talked to more than one person. I can't get myself to believe that Fenner, Covington would have lied to us."

"What are you saying?"

"I'm saying that whoever is looking for Raymond Fidel is sophisticated enough to break into his office and steal his Rolodex. That's quite enough sophistication, as far as I'm concerned, to fake being a cop with a warrant to get into Fidel's apartment. But let me make a few calls. I'll find out if the cops were there or not. You get yourself a flight."

"For tonight?"

"Why not?"

"My sixth sense tells me that might be difficult."

"Don't you have any respect at all, Margolis?"

CHAPTER

—12—

In high school I drove an old El Camino that my friends affectionately named Rusty. I lived in Homestead, Florida, a town whose biggest redeeming feature was its proximity to points of interest, and on weekends we used to pile into Rusty and take off for the Keys, or the Everglades, or Fort Lauderdale.

It had been over six years since my last visit to Fort Lauderdale, and as I approached the strip in my rented Toyota, I began to feel sadly old and nostalgic. My plane had gotten in at midnight, and I had picked up the car and checked into the airport Hilton. I had gone up to the room long enough to unpack and change. The room had a queen-size bed and a color television and a clean shower. It was a far cry from the days when we used to sleep in the back of Rusty with blankets over our heads.

The Fort Lauderdale strip, more formally known as Route A1A, ran along the ocean, with the beach on one side and the hotels and bars on the other. November was a quiet time of year for Fort Lauderdale, but on the strip there was still plenty of action. The traffic slowed down to a crawl as motorists and pedestrians watched each other. Boys watched girls, girls watched boys, and boys watched boys. It was Fort Lauderdale's favorite pastime. I drove inland a few blocks and found a place to park and then I walked through the warm night back toward the beach and the strip.

From the looks of things, The Beach House was still a major gathering spot. A couple of giant bouncers sat in the doorway checking IDs and collecting money, and there were a lot of people just sort of hanging out in the front, gathering the courage, or the money, to go in. The inside of The Beach House was a tremendous room that seemed to unfold as I walked through it. There were about five different bars plus an outdoor area in the back with a swimming pool. I looked out at the pool and felt vaguely out of place. Everyone was so young, so tan and so healthy. The boys all had blond hair and big chests. So did the girls.

I chose a small circular bar toward the back of the room and managed to find a stool and a piece of bar to lean on. There was only one bartender and I watched her as she took care of some customers on the other side of the circle. There was something compelling about her. She had a broad forehead and big cheekbones and there was a small gap between her two front teeth. Her hair was chopped short and dyed red and blonde in blotches; she wore red high-top sneakers and a pair of blue jeans, and her black T-shirt was too small. She had all the accoutrements of someone who was young and thin, but she was neither, and yet she was ultimately sexy. I caught her attention and ordered a ginger ale, and as she leaned down to scoop ice into my glass, I got the feeling that she was an ex-topless dancer who now led a domestic home life with a steady boyfriend. Something about her made me think that she was finally pulling her life together, and I guess in that way she reminded me of myself.

I held out the money for my ginger ale and asked my question, "Scott around?"

She didn't stop, but grabbed the money and rang it up on the cash register. "Yeah, he's around," she said, banging the change down on the bar.

"Where is he?" I asked.

She emptied out a couple of ashtrays and wiped them with her cloth while she spoke. "You the guy who called before?"

Maybe it had been my sixth sense that had led me to this particular bartender, or maybe it was a coincidence, but whatever it was, it was unlucky. I managed to put on a confused look and shake my head.

"What do you want with Scott?" she asked.

"I'm a friend."

She stopped all her activity and looked at me carefully. "You a cop?"

"Nope. Are you?"

Her mouth closed and the corners of her lips went back. It might have been a smile, but I doubted it. "You from the tank?"

I nodded noncommittally and didn't say anything.

"Yeah," she said, nodding slowly herself. "He's around somewhere," and she left to take care of another customer. It was an easy trick. She would leave me alone and see if I picked Scott out from the crowd. If I was a friend of Scott's, then I would know who he was and I would not be offended. If I was a fake, I would be in trouble.

But I had a few tricks to play myself. I caught her attention and she came over again. She was trying real hard to look annoyed.

"Scott's girl friend around?" I asked.

It was not the question she had expected, but she composed herself quickly. "You mean Cindi?"

"I don't know who I mean. He told me he had a new girl friend."

"Yeah, he's got a new girl friend."

"Wouldn't be you by any chance, would it?"

"Nope. Her," and she nodded her head toward the service area of the bar. A waitress was standing there unloading a tray full of empty glasses. She was beautiful. She had a dark and intense small face, with perfect features and a head full of dark wavy hair that she held back behind her ear with a flower. She looked herself a little like a flower. She wore one of the black T-shirts that said, "The Beach House, Staff," and she had cut off the collar in the front so that the tops of her breasts showed.

"That's his new girl friend, huh?"

But the bartender was already taking someone else's order. Cindi loaded her tray up with drinks, and I watched her wiggle as she walked across the floor. Between her cleavage and her walk, I guessed that she cleaned up in tips. When she came back toward the bar a few minutes later, she walked right by me, and I reached out and touched her arm. "Hi, Cindi."

"Hi," she said, without stopping.

I jumped off my stool and grabbed her arm. "Wait a second."

The muscles in her arm tensed up as she spun around, and suddenly there was nothing beautiful about her. She looked nasty. "You're Scott's new girl friend, right?"

"Yeah?"

"I'm a friend of Scott's. I just wanted to say hi." I let go of her arm and she took a small step back to take a look at me.

"A friend of Scott's?"

"Yup."

"What's your name?"

"Eddie."

"Eddie what?"

"Eddie Margolis."

She shook her head slowly. "He never said nothing about no Eddie Margolis."

"That's all right. He never said anything to me about a girl friend. How is Scott?"

"Why don't you ask him yourself?"

"I will, as soon as I find him."

"He's down in the cooler. He'll be up. Don't grab me no more. I hate that shit." And she walked off. If she was a flower, it was one with thorns.

I finished my ginger ale and walked back toward the pool. I needed to get some distance from Cindi and the bartender. Chances were they would tell Scott Nelson I was asking for him, and if I was in the right place to watch, I could figure out who he was before Scott Nelson figured out that he didn't know who I was.

I leaned against the wall, just inside from the pool. Rock and roll was blasting from giant speakers all over the room. As I looked around it seemed as if I could see the same faces that had been there six years ago. The real genius behind singles bars is that they don't really work. If young people could actually meet each other at singles bars, then they would go once and never have to go back. But places like The Beach House never really cured anyone's loneliness. It gave the illusion of having the answer to your problems, but in truth, all you got was drunk. And waitresses like Cindi took home a couple hundred dollars every night from drunk, horny college kids, who somehow thought that giving the waitress a ten-dollar tip was going to get them laid. "Everybody's always looking for something," my friend Jack used to say, and nowhere was that truer than in a Fort Lauderdale pick-up joint.

A man showed up at the circular bar with a handtruck loaded up with cases of beer. His face was hard and strong, and he had a big forehead and intense little eyes. His hair was chopped short and spiked, with a tail in the back that was dyed blond. He needed a shave and he had an earring in his right ear. I knew I was watching Scott Nelson.

It was disconcerting to watch him effortlessly toss the cases of beer up onto the bar. The bartender took them one at a time and stowed them under the bar and they talked to each other while they worked. Cindi joined them at the bar, and after the beer was put away, the three of them huddled. Scott's back straightened as they talked, and he started looking nervously around the room. I was clearly visible where I stood, and so I stayed put, confident that they would find me.

The bartender gave Scott Nelson a shot of Jack Daniel's and he drank it. She poured another and he drank that and she poured a third and he drank that. Then Cindi saw me and I waved and smiled, and she pointed me out to Scott.

We stared at each other across the room. With one finger he pointed toward the men's room, which was along the other wall, and then he downed a fourth shot of Jack Daniel's. He had a big head start on me and the two women watched him as he disappeared behind the privacy wall outside the bathroom. As I crossed the room, it occurred to me that I was about to find Raymond Fidel. It was just a hunch. Maybe Murphy had been right about that stuff. Maybe there was a sixth sense.

I turned the corner into the bathroom and Scott Nelson

stuck his fist into my gut. Sixth sense, my ass. There were about five guys standing around the urinals and the sinks, and I felt an urge to know if they were all going to join in the festivities, and while I thought about it, Scott got me with another punch in the ribs.

The first punch had hurt like hell, and the second took the wind out of me. I was beginning to realize that I was going to have to do something about defending myself, when Scott backed off, into the middle of the bathroom floor. He had his fists up and he was prancing around wildly. It was his showmanship that saved me. If he had worked me immediately after the first two punches, he could have had me down in a matter of seconds. The others in the bathroom backed off against the walls and started hooting and yelling. They weren't going to join in, but they sure as hell wanted to watch.

"Can't a guy take a piss?" I asked.

"I don't care where you came from pal, but you're going back in a box." Scott's voice was low and mean.

I went in and took a couple of punches at him, which he blocked pretty well, and then I blocked a couple of his. He was going to be hard to get to, and I decided I was going to have to be creative. I looked down at his feet and saw his beach sandals. Showing off was his problem, mine was surviving. I took a wild punch to distract him, and then I jumped down on his foot as hard as I could.

As I was looking down he connected squarely with my nose and blood started to flow, but I heard him scream as I landed on his foot. It's funny how it's the little things that hurt. You can punch a guy in the face until he's a puddle of blood, and you can pound a guy in the stomach and chest until he's black and blue, but it's not until you twist a finger or break a toe that he'll yell. I used the opportunity to get a couple of more punches in before he could block them, and he began swearing at me. I was dripping blood all over the place and the cheering had picked up. Somehow the bathroom had become packed. I took a kick at his knee, but he moved out of the way, and then he tried a few kicks himself. Then we were back to punching, and suddenly he connected, and then I connected, and pretty soon we were both punching like mad, without making any attempt to block.

Things got blurry. There was a lot of screaming and yelling as we went down on the floor, and there was the sticky feeling of blood and the smell of Jack Daniel's and piss. I felt the back of my head throbbing, and I heard him grunt once when I got my elbow into his rib. At the rate we were going, we would both be dead pretty soon. Then someone grabbed me from behind, and Scott got a few more punches in before they grabbed him too. Suddenly the bathroom filled with big cops and billy clubs and they were yelling at everyone to get out. They dragged Scott out first, and then they dragged me out. I guess I was walking because they had me by both arms and we were traveling across the floor toward the front door. Somewhere in the crowd I saw the woman bartender smiling at me, and she screamed to me, "You have fun, buddy?" I noticed a crowd of cops up ahead with Scott, and Cindi was buzzing around somewhere looking mad. They frisked me when we got outside, and then they pushed me through the crowd and shoved me into the back of a patrol car. Someone threw a towel in my face and told me not to bleed on the seat.

From behind my towel, I noticed that they had put Scott into the car in front of me and he sat there by himself. A bunch of cops stood around outside talking and laughing. Every once in a while one of them would stick his head in and talk to Scott, but nobody talked to me. I tried to figure out what the cops were talking about, but the blur began to fade, and the pain was taking over. I closed my eyes and bled into my towel. At last, the car doors opened and two cops got into the front seat.

The one in the passenger seat turned around and looked at me, "Yawl alive, son?" He had one of those south Florida accents that sounded like a Texan talking through a swamp.

I waited the appropriate amount of time that it would take for a real Floridian to answer. It seemed to be about ten minutes, and then I slipped into the best Florida accent I could remember. "Yeah, I'm alive."

"Good," and he turned to the front and we took off down the middle of Route A1A. They didn't use the siren, but I could see the reflection of the overhead lights on the traffic, which parted on both sides of us, like the Red Sea.

The same cop did all the talking. "What's your name, son?" he asked without turning around.

I waited again and then said, "Margolis. Eddie Margolis."

"Yawl got some ID?"

"Yeah."

He turned just slightly in his seat and pointed to an opening in the metal screen between the front and the back seat. I pulled my wallet out of my pocket and handed him my driver's license. Then I sat bleeding into my towel while he held it under his flashlight.

"Yawl from Homestead?"

I had left Homestead over five years ago, but I had never bothered to change my driver's license, and I didn't feel a compulsion to give this guy my life history. I waited a few seconds and then said, "Yup."

"Yawl go to Homestead High?"

"Long time ago."

"Yeah? What year you graduate?"

"Seventy-five."

"No shit." He turned in his seat and looked at me. In the orange light from the streetlights I could see that he had a square face with a pug nose, but I couldn't see much else. I guessed that he was about forty years old. "Yawl know Bobby Leonard?" He pronounced it Lennert, but I knew who he was talking about.

"Yeah. I remember Bobby Leonard."

"Yeah? He remember you?"

I shrugged. "I doubt it. Bobby was a football star. I don't think he'd remember me."

"Was he really a football star?"

"Yeah, he quarterbacked junior and varsity teams, if I remember right."

"Shit. He's always tellin' us how he was a football star, but none of us ever believed him. He says he got hurt in his first year college."

"Could be."

"Well, I'll ask him if he remembers you."

We had gotten to the end of the strip and we crossed the canal and started inland. I watched the shopping malls and the stores and thought about how much Fort Lauderdale had changed in six years. I tried to remember what buildings had been there and which were new, and when I couldn't hold out any longer I asked them where we were going.

"Aww, we're just takin' you to the hospital so you could get yeself fixed up. You pickin' on the wrong guy."

"I could have had him."

"Less, of course, you wanting to press charges."

"No."

"Didn't think so. I know Scott ain't gonna press no charges."

Nobody said anything for a little while. This was the way things went in Florida. In New York, time was such a valuable commodity that people felt compelled to fill every second with information. Silence was a waste of time. But in

Florida, silence was a time for thought and introspection. Anybody who talked all the time wasn't thinking about what they were saying. Southerners knew that New Yorkers thought they were stupid, but they also knew that New Yorkers were superficial.

"Yeah, that Scott. He's dangerous, that one," the cop said finally.

"I would of licked him," I said.

He turned around and stared at me for a minute. "Well, you're a damn fool." It wasn't the type of comment that you were supposed to respond to, so I just sat still and bled into my towel. "You on vacation?"

"Yeah."

"How long you here for?"

"I don't know. Couple of days."

He stared at me some and then said. "You are a damn fool." And then he turned front again and said something to the driver that I couldn't hear.

"What were you two fightin' 'bout, anyway?" he asked without turning around.

I hadn't really lied too much yet, but I knew I didn't want to start talking about Raymond Fidel. I quickly convinced myself that Scott had socked me because of the way I had grabbed Cindi. "A girl," I said.

"Shit. You even a bigger fool than I thought."

We pulled into the driveway of the hospital and they stopped the car outside the door to the emergency room. The driver stayed in the car, but the one who had been talking got out with me. We stood just outside the hospital door, and now in the light I realized that he was a lot younger than I had thought. It must have been the way he called me son that had made me feel like he was older, or maybe it was the quickly fading conviction I had that cops were always older than me.

"Let me tell you something about Scott Nelson," he said. Now in the light I could also see his badge pinned neatly over his shirt pocket. His name was Deputy Colifax. "You ever meet him before?"

"Nope."

"Yeah, well, let me tell you a thing or two about that boy. He just got hisself outta prison. Five years for assault with a deadly weapon. Boy ran into some liquor store wavin' a piece around. Never did understand the technicality they used to get him off armed robbery. Anyhow, he served his full five years, on account that there was no good behavior, if you get my meaning." He looked off at an ambulance that came racing up the driveway, and we moved just slightly to make room. "Yeah, that boy's just no good. The arresting officer, deputy by the name of Lake, was kilt just a couple of weeks 'fore Scott went to trial. Never could pin that on him, but the talk down at the station was that he had something to do with it. That boy ain't liked much around this town, and ain't nobody gonna complain that you gave him a bloody nose."

The ambulance doors opened and two medics poured out with an old man on a stretcher. He had bottles attached to his arms and an oxygen mask over his face. His skin looked pure white. Deputy Colifax watched them wheel him in and then turned back to me. "I'm gonna give you a bit of advice now, son. They took Scott over to Broward County, on account of not wanting you two to be at the same hospital. But I know that boy, and he's gonna be wanting to finish what you two started. I suggest that after you get fixed up here, you go on back to Homestead. You got a car?"

"I left it down near The Beach House."

"All right. We'll get somebody to drive you over there. You don't have to be no macho man about this. That boy Scott ain't never played a fair game in his life. You wouldn't be no prissy for leavin' this town. Just smart and alive. And any more trouble between you two ain't gonna be handled quite so nicely, if you get my meaning. You hear what I'm saying?"

"Yeah, I hear you."

"Good. Now, they'll fix you up in there. Tell 'em that Deputy Colifax . . . oh, hell, let me go in there with you and we'll get you through quick as we can. The bleeding stop?"

CHAPTER
—13—

I was choking on the dryness in the back of my throat, my head felt as if I had been hit with a brick, and the telephone was ringing. It was one hell of a way to wake up. I managed to crawl across the bed to the telephone without upsetting my broken ribs, but when I swung my feet over the edge a shot of pain went through me like a dagger and reminded me, in the most unpleasant way, of Scott Nelson's fist. It was Bill Bryant on the telephone. Murphy had told him that I was in Florida, and he was calling to see if I'd had any luck finding Raymond Fidel. I mumbled something about possibilities and then we hung up. I sat perfectly still, breathing carefully and waiting for the pain to subside. It was nine o'clock. I took a couple of the codeine pills they had given me in the hospital and then I got up and drank three glasses of water. I looked in the mirror and adjusted the bandage they had put around my head. Then I got back into bed and fell asleep.

The second time I woke up I was still dying of thirst and the telephone was still ringing. This time I wasn't so graceful getting across the bed, and I lay in throbbing pain as Murphy told me that there had been no warrants issued for Raymond Fidel's apartment. He asked me how things were going and I told him that I didn't feel like talking about it. He told me to call him later when I did. I got up and drank three more glasses of water. It was noon.

I took a long hot bath and ordered some lunch from room service. I looked up Scott Nelson's address and then, after two more glasses of water, I headed out into the blinding Florida sun. It was two o'clock and hot, even by Florida standards, and I worked up a good sweat just crossing the hotel parking lot to my car.

Getting into the car was a slow and painful process. I backed into the driver's seat and left my two feet outside on the pavement. Swinging my right foot in was pretty simple, but there was no way I could lift my leg. After several painful attempts I picked up my leg with both of my hands and dragged it into the car. The next problem was closing the door. It was my left ribs that were broken and I couldn't pull with my left arm. I managed to get the door closed enough so that I could reach it with my right arm, and then I took a deep breath and pulled it shut. I put the air-conditioning on full blast. I was hurting and sweating and I felt like crying, but I just sat and let myself fry until the air-conditioning got going.

I drove north on U.S. 1 and stopped off at a liquor store for a quart of Jack Daniel's, and a Coke for myself. It was a little bit easier getting out of the car than it was getting in, but it was no picnic. I got back onto U.S. 1 and continued north until I was past the strip. Then I turned right on Oakland Park Boulevard and headed toward the beach.

Scott Nelson's address turned out to be a cheap motel called The Casa Loca, the crazy house. The sign advertised weekly rates and efficiencies. I pulled off the highway and parked my Toyota next to an old pickup truck that reminded me of Rusty. The dust from the graveled parking lot mingled with the heat, and I sucked on my Coke as if it were oxygen. Old, sickly palms bordered the edge of the lot, and a few decaying coconuts lay rotting in the dirt and gravel. There were about twenty rooms, and an assortment of lawn chairs, barbecues and bicycles were scattered around outside the doors, but there was no sign of human life. The crazy house. Just what I needed.

A gold Plymouth pulled in off the highway and stopped suddenly at the entrance to the driveway. There was too much glare for me to see the driver, and it backed out of the driveway as fast as it had come in. A car on the highway blasted its horn and had to jam on its brakes to avoid the Plymouth. Then both cars took off and disappeared behind the motel.

When I turned back toward the rooms, Scott Nelson stood leaning against a doorway, about twenty yards from me. He was wearing a pair of beach shorts and he held a bandaged foot up in the air behind him.

"What the fuck is wrong with you?" he called out to me. His voice was deep and it sounded as if he had just consumed half of the gravel from the parking lot.

I held up the bottle of Jack Daniel's. "I brought you a present. A peace offering." I started to walk toward him.

"Fuck you, man. Go away."

"C'mon, Scott. Have a drink." I kept walking.

He turned and disappeared into the room, but he left the door open, so I followed him in. The only light in the room came from the open door. The curtains were drawn, and a television played without sound in the corner. I found Scott sitting on the bed with a large automatic pistol in his hand. "Go the fuck away," he said softly.

"You want a drink, or no?"

"You know, you must have your fucking head up your ass. You see what I'm holding here? You see this? This is a fucking Colt forty-five, okay? I pull this little fucking trigger here and your fucking guts are all over the place. Now go the fuck away, 'cause I been dying to use this thing."

I began to question the wisdom of my direct approach. I remembered Deputy Colifax saying, "Scott ain't never played a fair game in his life." I could have turned and walked away, but Scott could also put a bullet into my back. I had gotten myself this far, I was going to have to take it the rest of the way. I stepped further into the room and closed the door behind me.

A little bit of light came in from the edges of the curtains, and in the light from the television, I could see Scott's outline, still sitting on the bed. The room smelled stale and clammy. A small fan in the corner blew the hot air around, but it didn't really help. I stayed perfectly still. "You got a good jab there, Scott. Broke a couple of my ribs."

"You broke my fucking foot," he said from the bed.

"Drink?"

"I broke your fucking ribs, huh?"

"Yup." I lifted my shirt and pointed to the two broken ribs. Even if it had been light enough to see, there wasn't anything to look at.

"What happened to your head?" he asked.

"I don't know. Banged it on something on the way down. Had to get a couple of stitches."

I heard him laughing softly to himself.

"What'd you sock me for?"

"I don't like strangers who think they know me. Give me that bottle."

He kept the gun pointed at me while he took the bottle and put it between his legs. With his free hand he twisted the top off the bottle and raised it to his lips. My eyes had begun to adjust to the darkness, and I was beginning to see the mess. The unmade bed was the main piece of furniture, and it was covered with clothes and magazines. There was a table near the television and it was covered with beer cans and ashtrays. There was also a bag of pot and a bong, and an old bag of cheese doodles. A small kitchen area in the back looked as if it would burst if you put one more dirty dish in the sink.

"Can't go nowhere," he said, bringing the bottle down. "Might as well get drunk."

I walked further into the room and sat in a chair by the table. It was too hot to stand up.

"Have some?" he held the bottle out toward me.

"No, thanks."

"Go ahead, man. Have some."

"I don't drink."

"You don't drink? Have some pot, then. It's good."

"No, thanks."

"You don't smoke pot either, right?"

"Right."

"Don't drink, don't get high. You must be hell at a party."

"Why are you protecting Raymond?"

"Fuck you." He took another hit off the bottle. Then he waved his gun around. "You know, I ought to blow your fucking brains out. I don't know why I don't."

"It'd be a little hard to explain to the cops what my guts were doing splattered against your wall."

He let out a low grunt that might have been a laugh. "Fucking forty-five would do that too. This one's my baby here. Brand-new. Used to use a three seventy-five Magnum, but in this town I had to have something bigger than the pigs. Cost me five bills this thing. Man, would I love to . . ." He jerked the gun up and down like he was shooting it. Then he took another long hit off the bottle. "There's something called self-defense, you know. Man's got a right to protect his home. Could say I blew your brains out to save my own tail."

I laughed and shook my head. "I don't know, Scott. From what I hear, your word doesn't mean much around this town."

"Shit. They got it in for me, man. I don't even know what I'm doin' here. And now I'm stuck in this goddamned shit hole for two weeks because you broke my fucking foot. Man, you piss me off!" He moved back on the bed and leaned against the wall with his broken foot stretched out in front of him. He had his gun in one hand and the bottle in the other. "I gotta get the fuck outta this place, man. If I'm stuck in here for two weeks, Cindi's gonna drive me nuts." He took another hit off the bottle. "You know, I would've whipped your ass last night if those cops hadn't come. Piece of fucking cake."

"Maybe, but I'm the one walking around today."

"Fuck you, man."

"So how is Raymond Fidel these days, anyway?"

"Double fuck you. You're a pain in the ass, you know that? You think you're slick or something?"

I shook my head. "No, I'm not slick. I'm just looking for Raymond."

"Well, you ain't gonna find him here. You can look around if you want," and he laughed to himself. "Who knows, maybe he's under the bed or something." And he laughed some more and then drank some more.

"No, I don't think he's here, Scott. But I think you know where he is."

"Well, I don't care what you think. Who are you, anyway? You some kind of cop or something?"

"I think you know where he is, and I think that bartender last night knows where he is too. What's her name again?"

"Karen don't know where he is, man. Why don't you just go away."

It was an old cop trick I had learned from my father. If you assume something harmless enough, long enough, it becomes admitted. Scott didn't know it, but he was already beyond trying to deny that he knew Raymond Fidel. The fact that he knew Raymond Fidel, and wasn't claiming that he hadn't seen him in years, was enough for me. The rest would fall into place in time. "And I'll bet Cindi knows where he is too," I said.

"You get on my nerves. I think you better chill out. Here, take a drink of this." He put the top back on the bottle and tossed it at me. I caught it and put it down on the table. "No thanks," I said.

"Drink it!"

"No, thanks."

"If you don't take a hit from that fucking bottle right this fucking minute, I'm just gonna blow your fucking brains out." He held the gun out toward me. "Now drink it, scum bag!"

In some ways it was a fantasy come true. There was no better justification for taking a drink, than having some raving maniac who was going to blow my brains out if I didn't. He was going to make me have a drink, against my will. Clearly it was more important to stay alive than to stay sober, but for some reason I didn't pick up the bottle. Sometimes I was too smart for my own good. I could make myself believe that if I didn't take a drink, I would die, but I would be fooling myself. If Scott Nelson was going to shoot me, he would have done it already. "Forget it, Scott," I said. "I'm not drinking. Blow my brains out if you want," and I threw the bottle back to him.

He laughed and dropped the gun down on the bed and caught the bottle with both hands. I cursed myself for being so smart.

"I might be starting to like you, man," he said. "What'd you say your name was again?"

"Eddie."

He took a long drink and stared up at the ceiling. "Whose friend were you supposed to be, now, I forget. Mine, or Raymond's?"

"Raymond's."

"And I'm supposed to believe that shit?"

"Why not?"

"C'mon, I wasn't born yesterday, you know."

"Did he come down here to see you, or to see Karen?"

He laughed and took a drink. "Karen, man. That girl could fuck you right in half." And he laughed some more and drank some more.

I smiled at him. "Speaking from experience?"

"Bet your ass I am," and he drank more.

"Cindi doesn't look like a bad girl to have around."

"Oh man, let me tell you something about Cindi. That girl may look real hot, but she fucks like a wet rag," and he drank. "But that Karen Fletcher. Man, she could fuck you in half."

"Raymond's probably getting it right now, huh?"

He sat up quickly. "Fuck you, man. You don't know what you're talking about."

"Educate me."

"She used to hang with Ray back in the old days. She was working The Cat Club out on the highway, and Ray and I were working at The Seaside. Man, those were the days. Work till ten, party till four, sleep till noon. Walk on the beach and then go to work. It was the best life, man. Piece of cake."

"Seems like you still got it pretty good."

"No man," his speech was slowing down. "It ain't the same no more, man. Everything's different. Ray's a lawyer. Karen's old and fat. Everyone else is married and shit. Cindi's just a dumb little cunt. No, it ain't the same no more, man. Shit." And he drank.

"The Cat Club. Topless place, wasn't it?"

"Yeah."

I gave myself a mental pat on the back. "So now you all work at The Beach House?"

But he didn't hear me. "Yeah, man. Ray and I used to get off around ten and go over and see her. Man, that girl could move. And after Ray left, I was hanging with her for a while, until I got my ass thrown in the can. I don't care about her now. I love Ray like a brother, even if he is a lawyer now. And Karen, she ain't the same girl she used to be. She got fat now. Pretty soon she'll be having babies and rolling them around in a carriage in the park. Shit, that ain't for me, man. No fucking way."

Scott turned and stared at the television. I watched the fan in the corner of the room, going around and around: Scott, Cindi, Karen and Raymond. Four people going around and around, trapped in their own little lives. The only thing that didn't make sense was Raymond. Why would a lawyer from New York come back to this? When I looked back at Scott, his eyes were closed. The half-empty bottle was leaning against his hip, and his hand had fallen off it. The gun was about two feet from his hand. I watched him for a few minutes. Then I stood up and walked to the foot of the bed. "Scott," I said. He didn't move. "Scott," I said louder, but he still didn't move.

The telephone was on a little table near the head of the

bed, and there were some telephone numbers written on the wall. There was a number for Karen, but I had already spoken to her on the telephone once, so I pulled out a telephone book and I looked up her address. Then I took one last look at Scott Nelson, with his broken foot sprawled out on the bed, and I stepped out into the steaming afternoon.

I was driving south on A1A, and the gold Plymouth was behind me. I had noticed it in the Denny's parking lot across the street from The Casa Loca. It was late afternoon, and the traffic was already starting on the strip, so I turned inland on Sunrise Boulevard, and the Plymouth followed me.

When we got to Route 1, I turned north, and then took a quick turn off the highway onto a small residential street. I pulled into a driveway about halfway down the block and waited. The Plymouth came cruising down the block a few seconds later, and I watched it go by in my rearview mirror. It took a turn at the end of the block and then reappeared facing back toward the highway. Someone wasn't being very subtle.

I pulled out of the driveway and headed back to Route 1, but I stopped at the corner, with the nose of my Toyota practically sticking out onto the highway. I put the emergency brake on and left the motor running and I eased myself out of the car. The Plymouth was sitting about halfway down the block, and I walked down the middle of the street, trying to be as obvious as possible. The Plymouth began to back up as I approached it, and it kept going until it was at the end of the block. I kept walking. As I approached for the second time, the Plymouth backed up again, this time going through the intersection and about halfway down the next block. Someone wasn't being very friendly.

I turned and walked back to my car. The hell with it, I thought. It was someone who wasn't subtle, wasn't friendly, and as far as I could tell, wasn't particularly dangerous. Just another wacko playing with my mind.

By the time I had dragged my feet in and closed the door, the Plymouth was behind me again. I pulled out onto Route 1 and watched in my mirror as it followed me back out onto the highway. Someone was getting on my nerves.

I knew I didn't have a prayer trying to outrun a Plymouth in my little Toyota, so I drove slowly, trying to decide if I should go back to my hotel. And then I saw the police car, sitting on the median strip, about half a mile down the highway. I thanked Fenner, Covington & Pine in advance for covering my expenses, and I **push**ed the pedal to the floor. I quickly got up to fifty miles per hour, and I kept the pedal down. There were a few cars on the road, and I had to weave in and out of them to keep my speed up, and by the time I was even with the cop, I was doing seventy-five. I checked my rearview mirror. The cop had pulled out after me, and the Plymouth was lagging way behind.

I pulled over as soon as the cop put his lights on, and I slowly worked my way out of the car, vowing that the next time I broke my ribs I would travel by train. I stood up outside the car and watched the Plymouth go by. I didn't get a good look at the driver, but I waved anyway.

The cop had pulled over behind me and he was walking toward me. We recognized each other at the same time.

"Goddamn," he said. "I heard you was in town, Eddie."

"Hiya, Bobby."

"Yes, sir, Colifax told me you was in town." He came up and stood in front of me. Bobby Leonard had always been a good-looking boy. He had looked good in his football uniform, and now he looked good in his police uniform.

He'd probably look good in his coffin. "How the hell you been, Eddie?"

"Good, Bobby. How you been?"

"Pretty damn good. Shit, look what old Scotty boy's done to you. Hurt your head, did he?"

I leaned against the car and put my hands in my pockets. "Just a couple of stitches."

"Shit. You're lucky, you got off easy."

"Couple of broken ribs too."

"Yeah, he's a motherfucker, Eddie. Anybody could of told you that. What'cha got there, Eddie?" he made like he was trying to look around me at the car. "One of them imports, ain't it?"

"Toyota."

"Rented too, ain't it?"

"You think I'd buy one of these?"

He laughed. "Goddamn, Eddie. Let's see. You used to drive an El Camino, wasn't it? Let's see. Sixty-seven, I think, right?"

"Pretty good, Bobby. You had a Thunderbird. Brand-new. Seventy-three?"

"Four. Yes, sir. Seventy-four Thunderbird. Colifax asked me if I remembered you, and I said sure as hell. Where you keeping yourself these days? I heard your old man moved outta Homestead."

"Yeah, he moved to the Keys."

"Which one would that be, Eddie?"

"Big Pine."

"No shit. He was a customs agent, wasn't he?"

"Yup."

"Hey, whatever happened to that guy you used to hang with, what was his name? The big ugly fella."

"Spike?"

"Yeah. Whatever happened to Spike?"

I shook my head. "He's dead. Took my car out for a ride one night, and neither of them made it back."

"Oh, I'm sorry to hear that, Eddie. I always liked Spike, even though people used to make fun of him. Wrecked your El Camino?"

"Yeah."

He let out a laugh. "Guess that's why you're driving a rental, huh? What'ya doing with yourself these days, anyway?"

"A little of this, a little of that. How's your family, Bobby?"

"My old man passed away a couple of years ago. My mom's still in Homestead, though. I see her every once in a while. You know, Eddie, you musta been going close to seventy, and this is zoned forty-five. You sort of putting me in a bad position, here."

"Yeah, I fucked up, Bobby."

"Listen, Eddie. I ain't gonna write you a ticket or nothing. But you gotta be careful, 'cause the whole station's already talking about how you took on Scotty boy last night. And some of them guys was putting money on whether you'd be dead today. This is serious business, Eddie. That boy just ain't no fun. Now, between you and me, Eddie, he got his time way before I was on the force, so I don't see what the big to-do is all about, but man, they don't like that boy. Now, don't expect that to help you none, though. I'm telling you, Eddie. You better watch yourself."

"I will, Bobby."

"Well, I gotta get back to things. You know how it is. It was real nice seeing you again, Eddie."

"Yeah, Bobby, likewise."

He started walking back to his car, but then he turned again. "Hey. You drive slow now, Eddie."

"Yeah, okay, Bobby. Take care of yourself."

He turned and waved over his shoulder. After he pulled

away, I stood there for a few minutes watching the cars go by. A salty, late-afternoon wind blew across the highway, and a couple of palm trees on the median swayed in time. The cries of seagulls were occasionally drowned out by a passing truck or bus. Once again, I eased myself into my Toyota. I made a U-turn at the first light and there was no sign of the Plymouth, so I headed back toward the strip, toward Karen Fletcher's.

CHAPTER
—14—

It was an enigmatic little street, just off the strip. I drove down to the end of the block and parked the car in front of an old and tired-looking drugstore. The sun had already set, but the heat clung to the street with a sickening determination, and I stopped into a tiny gift shop and bought myself a Coke. Then I stood outside and looked out across the parked cars and the wandering tourists at the old wooden house.

It was set back from the street, wedged between a sporting goods store and the neon cactus of a Mexican restaurant. Paint peeled from the outside walls, and the big porch in the front looked like it had barely survived the years' hurricanes. It was the kind of house that people walked by and never saw. I crossed the street and followed the cracked pavement up the front steps. Garbage was strewn across the front yard, and the dried remains of a garden lay crumpled around the edge of the house. I took my time climbing the steps, afraid they might collapse beneath my weight, and then I gingerly crossed the porch and rang the bell.

An old man in pajamas answered the door. After complaining about the heat and his flu, he told me that Karen Fletcher lived in an apartment in the rear. I told him that winter would take care of the heat soon enough, but that he was on his own with the flu. I thanked him and followed the dirt driveway back between the house and the Mexican restaurant. The smell of burned tacos and stale beer permeated the hot air. I peeked into an open door in the back of the restaurant and saw a couple of chefs smoking cigarettes and banging pots on the stove.

A small apartment stuck haphazardly off the back of the house. It had its own door and a little staircase that led out into the driveway. There were windows along the side and back walls of the apartment, but they were too high to see into from the ground, so I borrowed a metal garbage can from the restaurant and quietly placed it under one of the windows. It took me a while, with my broken ribs, but I managed to get my feet up onto the top of the can, and then I grabbed a piece of windowsill and hoisted myself up.

Raymond Fidel was alone, lying on a couch with his eyes closed. He wore blue jeans and sneakers, but had no shirt, and there was a beer in his hand, which he appeared to have forgotten. He had his mother's deep-set eyes and his sister's cheekbones, and he already had a good tan. I watched him breathing slowly on the couch and I laughed to myself. It had taken me only two days to find him.

I was so preoccupied with congratulating myself that I didn't hear them coming, and suddenly everything turned upside down. As I fell, I caught a glimpse of a white chef's hat, and then I hit the top of the overturned garbage can, ribs first. The world exploded from inside me and I felt as if my ribs were spewed out onto the dirt. I bounced and rolled and landed on my back, and I heard a low groan. My whole body shivered in pain as the two chefs watched me. One of them left and one of them stood leaning over me. I was totally overwhelmed by the mathematics of it all. Two chefs. Minus one, equals one chef. I realized that the groans were coming from me.

Karen Fletcher suddenly appeared, wearing a pair of shorts and a T-shirt. Scott Nelson had said that she was getting old and fat. I couldn't help thinking that she must have started pretty young, and pretty thin. Even in my pain, I wondered what she must have looked like at The Cat Club. She squatted next to me. "You're getting to be a regular pain in the ass, you know that?"

I studied the gap between her two front teeth and tried to figure out if she was smiling. I was having a hard time breathing, and I considered asking her to get me a doctor, but then I noticed the gun in her hand, and I realized that my well-being was not high on her priority list. "And you're a barrel of laughs," I managed to say.

"What are you doing, looking in my windows?"

Somewhere I found some air. "I'm with *People* magazine. We're doing an article on female bartenders, and I . . ." One of the men in white kicked me, but it wasn't on the side with my broken ribs. After enough abuse, you become thankful for small things.

"I'm not a patient person," Karen Fletcher said. "Now tell me who you are and what you want, or else I'm just going to blow you away."

It all sounded very matter-of-fact, and I was beginning to feel like I had a better chance of being blown away by Karen Fletcher than I had by Scott Nelson. I was going to have to say something, and I lay still and concentrated on my breathing.

"You heard the lady," one of the chefs said. "Start talking!"

I looked at Karen. "Raymond's in your apartment," I said. "I was hired to find him, and I have to talk to him. You think I'm a pain in the ass. The way I see it, either you bring me inside and let me talk to him or I just keep going on being a pain in the ass."

One of the chefs laughed. "Or maybe Karen here'll blow your brains out," he said.

That made the other chef laugh.

"Listen," I said, starting to breathe better. "I think I smell some enchiladas burning. Why don't you guys go check on it?" That got me another kick and started the shivering all over again.

"I *could* blow your brains out," Karen said, considering it as an alternative.

"I guess so, but maybe you ought to check with Raymond first."

"Get up."

"I can't."

"The lady said get up."

"All right, all right. Give me a minute."

They all backed away from me and watched me maneuver. First I took the long and slow roll over onto my stomach, and I realized that I had been lying in the scattered leftover meals from the garbage can I had been standing on. I noticed some tortilla chips and some green globs of guacamole, and I noticed my can of Coke, spilled in the dirt. I carefully lifted myself into a kneeling position, and I stayed there and caught my breath. Then, using my arms as a brace around my ribs, I pushed down on my legs until I was standing. I stood clutching myself as if I were trying to hold myself together. Maybe I was.

"Who hired you?" Karen asked, still pointing the gun at me.

"That's not a three seventy-five Magnum, by any chance, is it?"

"That's right. Now who hired you?"

"Did Scott Nelson give you that?"

"Listen. I'm not interested in answering your questions right now."

"Well, I'm not interested in answering yours. Take me inside away from these goons and let me talk to Raymond."

One of them came at me, but Karen held up her hand and stopped him. She was studying me carefully. She handed the gun to one of the chefs. "Keep him here a sec, Ron. I'll be right back." She ran up into her apartment, no doubt to check with Raymond. I smiled at Ron, but he didn't smile back.

I poked at my ribs. "Couple of broken ones right here," I said. "Got them in a fight last night. You guys know Scott Nelson?"

They didn't say anything. Talkative guys.

We were all relieved when Karen came back out and she took the gun back from Ron and sent them back to their tacos and burritos. Then, with the gun pointed at the bandage around my head, she led me into her apartment. The apartment itself was small, but cute, and I guessed that she had spent a lot of time fixing it up. The cabinets were freshly painted and the curtains looked homemade. Karen pushed a chair out into the middle of the kitchen and made me sit. I could smell her sweat and her perfume, and it made me feel better to realize that she was nervous.

Raymond was sitting up on the couch, with a beer in his hand. His naked chest looked smooth and muscular and he seemed older than I had imagined. His personnel file from Fenner, Covington & Pine had said that he was thirty-five.

He lived in an apartment in the Village and smoked pot and I knew he had at one time run ski lifts and been a bartender. It all added up to someone who didn't fit in too well at Fenner, Covington & Pine, and for that person I had expected a guy who was a little bit lost in the world. And yet, now in front of me, Raymond's posture exuded confidence. He was a man fully capable of taking care of himself and fully in control of his own life. "Who are you?" he asked.

"My name's Eddie Margolis. I'm with the Charles Murphy Detective Agency. We've been hired by Fenner, Covington and Pine to find you."

"You're a detective?" he asked, his voice ringing with incredulousness.

I felt embarrassed, as if I were part of a paranoid conspiracy to check up on Raymond Fidel. "That's right."

"Who hired you, exactly?"

"Fenner, Covington and Pine."

"Yeah, but who at Fenner, Covington and Pine?"

"Well, I don't know really. George Walsh was the person I spoke to originally. But I think somebody named Cadell had a lot to do with it. And maybe Bill Bryant."

"I don't believe you."

"Neither do I," Karen Fletcher added.

Kate had ordered business cards for me, but I didn't have them yet. I had nothing on me that could prove that I was a detective. It was a silly problem and I decided to ignore it. "What are you running from, Raymond?"

"How'd you find me?"

"There was a postcard in your bathroom from Scott."

"Jesus," and he threw himself back into the couch.

"I was lucky," I admitted. "You didn't leave much of a trail."

"I still don't believe you."

"Look, Raymond. You left work at four o'clock last

Wednesday afternoon. For a couple of days people worried and exchanged telephone calls. Your mother wanted to go to the police, but they had a big meeting at the firm and they talked her into going with a private investigation. I met your mother and I met your sister. I've been through your office, and I've been through your apartment. I know a lot about you. The firm is worried that your disappearance might give them some bad publicity if it's related to your work. That's why I'm here. If you don't believe me, call your firm, or your family, or my office. Now can you get that gun off me, 'cause it's making me nervous?"

Raymond waved his hand at Karen and took a long drink from his beer. Karen lowered the gun and walked over to the couch to sit next to Raymond.

"So what do you want from me?" he asked finally.

"I need to know what you're running from."

"Who says I'm running from anything?"

"It's written all over your face."

"I don't have to talk to you," he said, blushing with anger.

"You're right. But I might be able to help you."

"And I'm telling you I don't need any help."

"And I'm telling you you do."

"Look," Karen said, breaking in. "You were hired to find Raymond, right? You found him. Now he doesn't want to go back and that's all there is to it. You can't force him to go back."

"And I don't intend to try."

"Great," she said, waving the gun. "There's the door."

I didn't move. "I wish it were that easy," I said. "Raymond, if you want to stay here, that's your business. But you've got to give me something to go back with."

Raymond nodded his head and moved forward on the couch. "It's no big deal. I just got tired of it all. I got tired of the day-in-and-day-out drudgery of it. So I ran away. Maybe

I'm irresponsible and maybe I'm crazy. I know it's not the right way to do it. The right way to do it is to quit your job and give up your apartment and say good-bye to your family, but who wants to go through all of that? I can take you to the place I was sitting when I decided to go to law school. If I can decide to be a lawyer, than I can decide to quit. The whole law trip was a mistake, and so I'm back where I belong. I'm just pissed that it took me so long to figure it out. Now you can go back and tell them that you saw me, tell them that it had nothing to do with anything, and tell my family I'll send them a postcard. It's as simple as that. I'm not going back."

I knew there was more to it. "No one can force you to go back, Raymond."

"Damn straight. Those fucking clowns could all walk up to me and kiss my fucking ass and I wouldn't go back."

Karen laughed and then saw the anger in his eyes, and she moved closer and put her arm around him.

"You don't know the kind of shit that goes down in a place like that. I mean, I'm telling you, those people are fucking evil. We used to sit around and play this game called 'Can You Bill It?' A guy would make one telephone call that lasted thirty seconds and he'd bill his client for a full fifteen minutes. Guys'd take a shit and bill it to the client."

Karen laughed again.

"I'm serious. Lance used to call his time sheets the Great American Novel. I mean he'd add up his time and it would come to sixty hours, and he'd feel like he worked harder than that, so he'd boost it up to seventy. I mean, what kind of shit is that? And the client doesn't even care. The client is some goddamned bank or insurance company. Nobody really cares. And that's what really started getting me sick. All this money being wasted, and nobody really cares. It's just a big game."

Karen pulled his head toward her and he rested it on her shoulder. They looked good together, I had to admit. And Fenner, Covington & Pine was no place for an honest lefty like Raymond Fidel. His anger was genuine, I had no doubt about that, and I knew that he meant every word he said. And yet, it still didn't add up to a disappearing act. There was still the missing Rolodex and the fake cops and the Plymouth. There was still the urgent telephone call to Bill Bryant.

"I think there's more to it, Raymond."

"Think what you want," he said, keeping his head on Karen's shoulder.

"I mean, for starters there's the fact that there's someone else looking for you."

He picked up his head. "Who?"

"I don't know. I thought maybe you could tell me."

"You trying to scare me?"

"I'm doing a good job of it, if I am. You still have that key to your office door?"

"Yeah, I got it somewhere. Why?"

I pulled out my copy of the key. "Here's the other one. There's only two, and we've got them both. I locked the door to your office on Monday afternoon. On Monday night someone broke in and stole your Rolodex."

"So what? Let 'em have it." And he finished off his beer in defiance.

"Fine with me. Was Karen's number on it?"

"What if it was? What's the big deal? Hey, babe, let me have another beer."

Karen went to the kitchen and brought back a beer for Raymond. She didn't ask me if I wanted one, which was just as well. I'd already turned down booze once today. Raymond opened his beer and took a sip. "Look. I appreciate what you're trying to do here," he said, back in control of himself. "But the truth is, I'm not running from anybody."

I ignored him and pushed on. "Then there's the fake cops at your apartment."

"What fake cops?"

"I don't know. Probably nothing to worry about. A couple of guys with a phony search warrant tricked your super into letting them into your apartment."

"Jesus. How do you know they were fake?"

"Would it make you feel any better if they were real?"

"Did they—"

"No, I got the postcard, and I don't think they saw it. But you never know."

Raymond took another sip of beer and let out a big sigh.

"I also had someone tailing me this afternoon. You know anyone who drives a gold Plymouth?"

That was the one that did it. Raymond jumped off the couch and began pacing wildly around the room. *"Tailing you? Here? In Fort Lauderdale?"*

"Yup."

"Jesus. Did they follow you here?"

"Nope. I lost them."

"Are you sure?"

I tried to act casual. "I think so."

"Jesus."

Karen had been quiet, watching Raymond pace back and forth, but she couldn't hold it in any longer. "Ray, what's going on?"

"Jesus. I don't believe this!"

"Ray?"

Raymond stopped and stood behind the couch, resting his hands on Karen's shoulders. "Honey, we gotta go."

"Go where?"

"Go. Leave. Like we said. Leave tonight."

"Tonight?"

"Yeah, like right now," and he started pacing again.

She looked at me and then back at Raymond. "Ray, I don't have any money. I've got to get to the bank. Besides, I get paid Friday. Let's at least wait until—"

"No! Let's go! We got to get out of here!"

"Raymond," I said. "If you let me, I can help you."

"How can you help me?"

"I can help you, but first, I got to know who you're running from."

"I told you," he stopped behind the couch again. "I'm not running from anyone."

"Oh, come on, Raymond. Tell me about Alfred Norens."

"Norens? What's he got to do with it?"

"You tell me."

"Look, I don't want to play games. I told you what I'm doing. You tell me someone else is following me and that scares me. How would you like it if someone was following you?"

"Someone *was* following me."

He ignored me. "All I'm telling you is that I'm sick of Fenner, Covington and Pine, and I'm leaving. Okay? I'm gone. I'm out of there for good. You go back and you tell those jerks I left because I was sick of them. Nothing more than that. Karen, we gotta get out of here."

"One more question," I said, stopping him. "How come you called Bill Bryant before you left?"

He seemed to think about that one, but then he waved me off. "Look, no offense. Okay? I don't want to talk to you. That's all there is to it. I said what I have to say, and that's it. You're welcome to hang around and drink some beer, but I'm not talking anymore. Karen, let's go. You don't have to go to the bank or get your paycheck. I got bucks. I want to get out of here, tonight."

It took them about twenty minutes to pack. I helped

myself to a glass of water from the kitchen and sat on the couch and watched them. Raymond was running from something, but I knew he would never tell me what it was. I guessed that he hadn't even told Karen. Raymond Fidel was every bit his own man, and there was no way I could force him to talk to me if he didn't want to. There was no way I could stop him from running. I had been hired to find him, and now there was nothing else to do. I sat on the couch and drank my water.

Raymond wouldn't tell me where they were going, of course. He told Karen to call someone named Susan, who I gathered had a car, and they made arrangements to meet her at the beach in an hour. Raymond didn't want to wait around the apartment, so when they were finished packing, I helped them with their stuff, and we left the apartment and headed for the beach. It had gotten dark, and once we crossed Route A1A, the beach was empty and the ocean stretched out in a wall of blackness. I felt a strange sense of desperation as we walked toward the water. I had Raymond Fidel in the palm of my hands, and now I was going to let him go.

We dropped their luggage in a big pile and made ourselves comfortable in the sand. A breeze came up off the water and it reminded me, once again, that I was back in Florida. I listened to the wind and the surf and after a while I asked Raymond about his sister.

"I don't know," he said in the darkness. "For a while we thought there was something wrong with her, you know. My mother kept sending her to all kinds of doctors and shrinks. There's nothing wrong with her, though. She's just a little slow and a little different. My mother was always sort of overly protective." His voice trailed off, but I knew there would be more. "Tell her I'll be back to see her soon. Could you?"

"Can I tell her when?" I asked.

"I don't know," he said, his voice sad and quiet. He got up and walked down to the water.

Raymond had been sitting between me and Karen, and now I looked over at her and watched her outline against the hotels on the strip. I could see her playing with a small pile of sand between her legs. "You believe what Raymond says? About why he left?" I asked.

"I believe what I want to," she said, without looking up. "I think he's running from something, but I don't know what the hell it is, and frankly I don't care. Whatever it is, it brought him back to me, and I'm happy for that."

"Don't you think he might be in trouble?"

She didn't answer right away, and I looked back out toward the water and watched Raymond's figure by the surf. "I don't know," she said finally. "I take it one day at a time. I'm better off that way."

"I could help him."

She laughed, but didn't say anything.

I nodded my head in the darkness. There was nothing else for me to do. It wasn't my job to follow Raymond all over the world. I couldn't handcuff him and bring him back to New York. Nor could I lock him in Karen's apartment. Raymond Fidel was a free man.

I waited with them until their ride came and I helped them load their luggage into the trunk of an old Buick. Raymond grabbed my hand and held it tightly. Just before he let go he said, "Don't trust those guys, Eddie. Don't trust anybody," and then he ducked into the front seat of the car. I saw Karen's hand go around his shoulder. The car made a U-turn at the first light and I watched it pass me and head south toward the strip.

CHAPTER

—15—

They were waiting for me in my hotel room. Bobby Leonard was stretched out on the bed in his perfectly pressed uniform, with his big police boots dangling over the edge. He looked bigger indoors than he had out on the highway that afternoon, and he seemed less like the quarterback I remembered and more like a cop. I had never known him very well, and yet there he was, sprawled across my bed as if we were old lovers. He propped himself up on his elbows and watched me as I came in the door. His sandy-blond hair was sticking up in the back and his eyes were bleary with sleep. The room was filled with smoke, and there was another cop, younger and smaller than Bobby, sitting in the chair by the television, smoking a cigarette.

"Have a seat, boys," I said, closing the door behind me. "I'm sorry I'm late."

Bobby Leonard sat up and rubbed his eyes. "I knew you'd be back here, Eddie."

The cop in the corner stuffed his cigarette out into an ashtray and leaned over to turn the television off. I was pretty sure I had never seen him before, and that made me nervous. If Bobby Leonard had merely wanted to pay a social call to an old high school classmate, he wouldn't have come with a stranger.

"What's the matter, Bobby? Did you think I'd skip out on my bill?"

Bobby moved up to the foot of the bed. "Colifax, that dumb ass, is waiting with a bunch of men down at the rental car place, but that just didn't make no sense to me. I mean, if a guy's gonna run, why would he bother returning his rental car?"

I looked at Bobby and then at the one in the corner. They were both southerners and they were both cops, and so they were going to take their sweet time getting around to business, but trouble hung like cigarette smoke in the air. I decided to play their game. "Mind if I wash up?"

I left the bathroom door open and slowly peeled my shirt off over my broken ribs. In the mirror over the sink I could see the reflection of Bobby Leonard, sitting on the edge of the bed, not quite facing me. "You know, Eddie," he was saying. "I'm not sayin' it's your fault or nothing, 'cause it was my decision not to give you a ticket this afternoon, but I'm really in a bad position now, seeing as I never even asked to see your license or registration or nothing. Lucky enough I saw that rental sticker and remembered it was one of those Toyotas. Otherwise the Sheriff'd have my tail. No hard feelings, Eddie, but I hadda tell him about stopping you."

"No hard feelings," I said, and then I leaned over carefully and cupped my hands under the running tap. I imagined that with the first splash of cold water, I would wake up from this dream and I would be back in New York or down in the Keys or anywhere but in a hotel room with a couple of Fort Lauderdale cops. The first splash didn't work. Neither did the second. Or the third.

"I mean, I wouldn'ta said nothing if it had just been the speeding you understand, Eddie."

I turned off the water and came out of the bathroom patting my face with a towel. He was warming up to it now.

"I mean speeding is one thing, Eddie, but when someone fires a gun in this town, everyone can hear the shot. You know what I'm saying?"

He had swung around to the corner of the bed now so that he could face me, but he was staring down at the floor between us, as if he was shy or apologetic. And suddenly it struck me that he was acting as if he was intimidated. That was bad news. I had to have done something pretty horrible to intimidate Bobby Leonard. "Who's the unlucky soul?" I asked.

"I mean, believe me, Eddie. I stuck up on your behalf. It wouldn't be like the old classmate of mine, son of a customs agent and all, to go around blowing holes in people. But Sheriff Grant was asking a whole lot of questions that nobody seemed too good at answering. I mean, you gotta admit, Eddie, you being down here from New York with a rented car and all, it just don't look too good."

"A man's gotta right to take a vacation."

Bobby's face flushed red with anger. "Eddie, ain't nobody's gonna buy that vacation crap no more." He got up and crossed the floor, planting his big self in front of me. "Now, I don't rightly know why, Eddie, but I believe in you, but you best be giving up with that vacation crap, because it ain't gonna do you no good down at the station. Yawl gonna have to come clean with Grant, now, or else he's gonna have your tail, Eddie. It ain't no fooling around, no more."

I could smell stale coffee on his heated breath, and I wanted to back away from him, but there was no place to go. We stared at each other, two old high school classmates peeling away those layers of loyalty and innocence and realizing that people grow up, and grow up in different ways. It had been over ten years since we'd seen each other, and neither of us had any reason to trust the other.

"Who got shot, Bobby?"

"Scott Nelson, Eddie. Scott fucking Nelson."

"Dead?"

"As dead as they come," and he moved past me into the bathroom to urinate.

It all came together in my mind. The fight. The lecture from Deputy Colifax. Being caught speeding by Bobby. Nothing in the way of alibis. I didn't like the way things were sizing up at all. "I need to talk to a lawyer," I said.

Bobby flushed the toilet and then checked his hair in the mirror. "Yeah, I reckon that's the smartest move you could make right now, Eddie. Yawl got a specific attorney you want to use? They could assign one for you if you want, Eddie."

"No, I'll get my own."

"That's good, Eddie. Between you and me, I wouldn't trust none of that sleaze that the court gives you."

They put me in a holding cell down at the station with two other guys: a muscular beach bum, who sat in the corner and smoked one Marlboro after the other, and a skinny Hispanic man, who paced back and forth in front of his bed like a tiger I had seen once at the Bronx Zoo. Neither of them seemed inclined to talk, and that was just fine with me, so I stretched out on the empty bed and stared up at the cement ceiling.

It had been pure luck that I had caught Murphy when I

called him from Sheriff Grant's office. I told him where I was and that I thought I might need a lawyer. Murphy promised to get me the best criminal lawyer that money could buy, but he spent most of the time lecturing me, making sure that I wouldn't answer any questions until I had spoken with a lawyer. It was an odd lecture coming from him. I don't think he doubted my innocence, but that didn't mean I hadn't messed up in a very big way. You have to do something very, very wrong to get yourself pinned to a murder.

Sheriff Grant had tried to question me, and in the old days I would have given him all the answers he wanted to hear. Perhaps I would have been let go. But, now, I was being responsible, and being responsible meant spending the night in jail until Murphy could arrange for a lawyer to come and see me. It just wasn't happening the way it was supposed to.

They served us some dried-out meat loaf and soggy vegetables for dinner. It was pretty disgusting, but I ate it anyway, and at ten o'clock they turned the lights out. I knew I was never going to fall asleep, and I couldn't even move around much because of my ribs, so I laid on my back and stared at the orange ash of the beach bum's cigarette, glowing in the dark.

I don't know how I got to thinking about Alice Pinder. Somewhere in the darkness, I saw her sitting in the back of the taxi cab outside Grand Central Station. She was leaning forward just a bit, and she said, "I'll bet we could get past all this." She couldn't look at me when she said it, and her voice sounded almost as if she were speaking to herself. "I'll bet we could get past all this."

"Now, where exactly is it that you live, Mr. Margolis?"

Sheriff Grant had only a hint of a southern accent. He was a big, good-looking man, with a short, stubby mustache that he pulled at constantly, as if he were trying to make it grow, and he had intelligent blue eyes. He wasn't the kind of sheriff to beat confessions out of people, but his voice filled the room and it didn't leave any space for anything else. It felt like I was being suffocated. He leaned back in his seat with his hands behind his head, and he kept his eyes focused on a spot of air over the top of his desk.

To my right sat a man introduced to me as Ken Aldrich from the district attorney's office. To his right was Bobby Leonard and a stenographer who recorded the meeting. My lawyer, Tony Merlino, was stuffed into a chair on my left. He was a fat man and he introduced himself as a friend of a friend of a friend of Murphy's. We had met for five minutes in my cell, and then on the way up to Grant's office he had given me instructions. I was to answer all of the questions as honestly as possible, but I did not have to answer any questions relating to the case I had been working on, and he would interrupt if there were any questions I should not answer. I looked at him now, and he gave me a shrug.

"I live in New York," I said.

"New York City?" the Sheriff asked, now focusing his eyes directly on me.

"That's right."

He slipped on a pair of glasses and looked down at the open file on his desk. "One nine five Christie Street," he read. "Is that right?"

"That's right."

He looked at me over the top of his glasses. "That's your official place of abode, son?"

"It's my home, if that's what you mean."

He pulled his glasses off and fell back into his seat. "But, according to your driver's license here, you live in Homestead, Florida."

"I'm from Homestead originally."

"Originally?"

"I was born and raised there."

"But now you live in New York City?"

"That's right."

"Well, then, how come you still have a Florida driver's license?"

"I never got around to changing it."

"Hmmm. And why is it that you told my Officer Colifax that you were from Homestead?"

"I *am* from Homestead. Originally."

He suddenly sat up and put his big hands on his desk. "Son, I don't appreciate you playing games of semantics with me now. I want to know why you lied to Officer Colifax."

Merlino grunted and shifted his weight around in his chair. "Come on, Dick," he said, seeming annoyed. "It's not semantics. He lives in New York, but he grew up in Homestead." His voice had a nasal quality, and it changed in pitch on almost every other word. Listening to him talk was like riding the roller coaster at Coney Island. "So he didn't get his license changed. You're trying to make something here out of nothing."

The Sheriff shook his head. "Now, Tony, I beg to differ with you. Mr. Margolis here showed my officer his driver's license with a Homestead address on it and told my officer that he was from Homestead, Florida. Now, if you want to argue semantics and say that what he meant to say was that he grew up in Homestead, you just go right ahead, but in my book, Tony, and this goes for you too, Mr. Margolis, it looks to me like an out-and-out lie. And I'm gonna make a note here for the record that Mr. Margolis falsely tried to pass himself off as a resident of Homestead, Florida, when in fact he resides at . . . ," and he slipped his glasses back on and read, "one nine five Christie Street, in the city and state of New York."

Merlino grunted some more. "You can make any note you want, Dick," he said. "We'll maintain it was an innocent misunderstanding."

The Sheriff proceeded. "Now, Mr. Margolis. Seeing as you have admitted that you are a resident of the State of New York, would you mind telling me exactly what your business is here in Broward County?"

I looked over at Bobby Leonard, but he was staring at the stenographer's legs. I looked at her legs and made a note for my own record that they were worth staring at. Then I looked at Merlino and he made some noise and nodded his head, so I answered. "I'm here on business."

"Okay," the Sheriff said. "That's just fine. Now we're getting someplace. Would you care to tell me just what type of business you're in?"

"I'm a private detective."

"Uh, huh. A private detective," he faced the stenographer and continued, for her benefit. "Originally from Homestead, moved to New York, and now conducting his business in the city of Fort Lauderdale."

"He's not conducting his business in Fort Lauderdale," Merlino interjected with obvious annoyance. "He conducts his business in New York. He happens to be in Fort Lauderdale."

The Sheriff ignored him. "I don't recall the boys telling me that they found any kind of private investigator's license in your wallet. Perhaps you don't like to carry that with you. Where would that be?"

"I don't have a license."

"You don't have a license?"

"No, sir."

"You practice as a private investigator in the state of New York, and you don't have a license?"

"He's employed by a licensed private investigator," Merlino said. "He doesn't need a license."

Grant pulled on his mustache slowly. "Could be. Could be. In New York, I suppose, it could be. But then again, he ain't in New York. He's in Fort Lauderdale. And I haven't looked at the books for a while, but I believe you need a license to act as a private—"

"Come on, Dick. We got reciprocity and—"

"—investigator in this state. Now, son, it seems like on every issue we deal with, you got a problem, and we ain't even started the serious stuff yet."

"Okay, okay," I said. "So I lied to a cop and I acted as a private investigator in the state of Florida without a license. . . ." Out of the corner of my eye I saw Merlino sit up and hold his hand up, but I couldn't stop myself. "I might have jaywalked crossing the strip last night, too. You have a death penalty in this state?"

The Sheriff smiled. "Son, what is it exactly that you're investigating?"

Merlino answered for me. "A missing person."

"And who would that be?"

"Come on, Dick. You know I'm not going to let him answer that."

"Now, Tony. We've got a murder on our hands."

"Still, Dick, unless you can prove that his investigation is directly tied—"

"Now just hold on a minute, Tony. I refuse to be the receptacle here for a lot of your bullshit. Now, none of us here are going to miss Scott Nelson very much, but just the same, we've got a job to do. Now, Mr. Margolis, you've had a chance to talk to your attorney, and now I'm asking you who it is you were hired to find."

I shook my head. "If my attorney says I don't have to answer, then I'm not going to answer."

"And I suppose you don't want to tell me who your client is, either."

"Right."

"And I suppose you don't want to tell me what Scott Nelson's unfortunate entanglement with your missing person might be."

"Right."

"And I suppose you believe you're being very self-righteous in protecting your client by holding back the truth."

"Until my lawyer tells me otherwise."

"Well, why don't you suppose again, son! Last night you got in a fight with Scott Nelson and you broke his foot. He busted a couple of your ribs and took off a piece of your head. Today his girl friend found him hung up in his shower with half of his goddamned fingers broken and shot full of holes. It wasn't a pretty sight. Now we have information that places you at Scott Nelson's apartment between two and three this afternoon. The coroner says that Scott Nelson died sometime this afternoon. Now, Mr. Margolis. Unless you can fill in some of the missing information here, I'm inclined to believe that you came down to Fort Lauderdale from New York City for the specific reason of rubbing out one of our fine citizens."

"Fine citizen?"

"Son, don't interrupt me. I'm doing you the favor of letting you know just how deep the shit is that you're standing in. Now, I understand that Officer Colifax told you to clear out of town last night. But you didn't. Now, would you mind telling me why you took it upon yourself to visit Scott Nelson this afternoon?"

"I brought him a bottle of booze."

"You *what?*"

"I brought him a bottle of booze."

"What the hell you do that for?"

"It was a peace offering."

"Oh, bullshit." He threw his glasses down on his desk. "He dented in your head and busted a couple of ribs, and I'm supposed to believe that you go ahead and bring him a bottle of booze as a peace offering?"

"I was never much on holding grudges."

He banged his big hand down on his desk. "Tony, you get him to start giving me some straight answers here, or else we're really gonna have us some trouble!"

"He's giving you straight answers, Dick. I can't help it if you don't like them."

"Shit. Mr. Margolis, what time did you arrive at Scott Nelson's apartment this afternoon?"

"About two."

"And what condition was he in when you arrived?"

"He was sober, if that's what you mean?"

"Now, was it a bottle of . . . ," and he slipped his glasses on and looked again at the file, "Jack Daniel's. Was it a bottle of Jack Daniel's that you brought to Scott Nelson's apartment?"

"Yup."

"And you gave this bottle to Scott Nelson upon your arrival?"

"Yup."

"And he accepted it?"

"Yup."

"And then what happened?"

"Well, he waved his gun around at me and—"

"He waved his gun at you?"

"Yeah."

"Did you happen to notice what kind of gun it was?"

"He told me it was a Colt forty-five."

Merlino grunted. "Did you see the gun, Eddie?"

"Yes."

"Did you see for yourself that it was a Colt forty-five?"

"No, it was too dark. I didn't see what kind of gun it was."

The Sheriff continued. "Okay, what happened after he waved his gun at you?"

"I sat down and he drank and we talked."

"He drank? What about? You musta had a hit or two off that bottle."

"No, sir."

"What'd you talk about?"

"Nothing in particular."

"Mr. Margolis, I'm afraid you're going to have to do better than that."

"We talked about the person I was looking for."

"And did Mr. Nelson know where this person was?"

Merlino shook his head.

"Oh, Christ, Tony. Okay, Mr. Margolis, how long did you stay there at Scott Nelson's apartment?"

"About half an hour, maybe an hour."

"Maybe an hour?"

"Maybe. Probably less."

"And what was Scott Nelson's condition when you left?"

"He was drunk."

"How drunk?"

"Very drunk."

"Drunk enough so that you could move him around and he wouldn't be able to resist?"

"Probably."

"Drunk enough so that you could haul him into the bathroom and tie his hands to the shower sprocket with a piece of heavy rope?"

"Dick, come on," Merlino said.

"Drunk enough so you could break his fingers one by one, and then turn on the shower and stuff his own gun into a pillow and blow him full of holes?"

"Dick!"

"Drunk enough so that you could leave him there in the shower with the scalding-hot water burning his skin and ransack the place?"

"Dick! Enough!"

"I'm just asking Mr. Margolis here a question. How drunk was Scott Nelson when you left?"

"He was sleeping on his bed," I said.

The Sheriff leaned forward over his desk and spoke softly. "That's some bullshit, Mr. Margolis, and you and I both know it." He let that sit for a few seconds and then turned back into his chair. "Now, Bobby, what time did you stop Mr. Margolis?"

Bobby turned away from the stenographer's legs and looked at me sheepishly. "It musta been about three-thirty."

"Yeah, about three-thirty. Now the coroner placed the death somewhere between three and five o'clock. In my professional opinion, I'd say that three o'clock'd be just about right. What do you say, Bobby?"

"I don't know, sir."

The Sheriff sat up in his seat now and looked closer at me. "Yeah, I say about three o'clock. That'd give you about fifteen minutes to ransack the place and about fifteen minutes to get out to U.S. One, where Bobby picked you up, trying to hightail it outta here. Where were you headed, Mr. Margolis?"

I had not mentioned the gold Plymouth to my lawyer. I knew the Plymouth could not have been with Sheriff Grant's office, because it had disappeared as soon as I got stopped by Bobby Leonard. In fact, I guessed that the Plymouth had gone back to Scott Nelson's apartment after it left me out on U.S. 1. There was no specific reason for keeping the gold Plymouth to myself, but somehow I felt that it might come in handy later on. "I was going back to my hotel," I said.

"To your hotel?"

"Yup."

"But your hotel is south of the point where Bobby stopped you, and you were heading north on U.S. One. Would you like to explain that?"

"I was taking the long way around."

"You're gonna be taking the long way around our state penitentiary system, son, unless you can come up with a better answer than that."

"I was lost."

"You're feeding me a whole lot of bullshit here, son. Bobby, what time did you get to his hotel room? About seven, right?"

"Right."

"And what time did Mr. Margolis show up?"

"About eight."

"Okay. So we lost him between three-thirty and eight o'clock. Where'd he go?" Then he looked at me. "Mr. Margolis?"

"I can't answer that."

"Well, lookey, here. Here's an idea. I say maybe you did go to your room. Who knows where you went. But you started getting nervous that someone was going to get you. So you went back to Scott Nelson's to get the body. But by then you saw it was too late because there were officers all over the place."

"So I went back to my room?"

"To pack up your stuff and catch the next plane to New York."

"Are we talking about me or an idiot?"

I heard Bobby laugh.

"Son, don't sit there and poke holes in a theory that you can't talk your way out of. Now, you ask Ken over here if what we've got is sufficient to charge you with murder. Ken, don't answer that just yet. I have a few more questions for Mr. Margolis. Why were you at The Beach House last night?"

I looked at Merlino and he shook his head.

"Oh, come on, Tony. Why can't he answer that?"

"No way, Dick. That's privileged."

"What was the fight about?"

"He doesn't have to answer that either."

Grant pounded his fist down on the desk and stood up. "Well, goddamn it, then, I'm gonna throw the goddamned book at him. Son, I hate to do this to you, but your attorney is forcing my hand here. Now we've got you for making untrue statements to an officer of the law, for practicing as a private investigator in the state without a license, and for murder. Now, I understand that you claim you are innocent, but you understand me that I don't have to take your word for that. We're gonna nail your ass, son!"

"Wait a second, wait a second," Merlino moved around in his seat. "I've had quite enough of this, Dick. My client has been trying very hard to cooperate as much as possible without compromising the interests of his client. Now, Dick, you know as well as I do that you've got nothing but very circumstantial evidence, at best. Now, if you want to book Margolis here for some petty-ass little bullshit, then just go ahead, and we'll pay our bail and get out of here. But let's not fool ourselves about booking him for murder."

"I don't believe what I hear! Ken, say something for Christ's sake!"

Ken Aldrich shook his head slowly. "Well, Sheriff, I suppose I could get him for obstruction of justice for refusing to cooperate with—"

"Obstruction my white hairy ass!" Grant screamed, and he jumped out of his seat. "I don't want no goddamned obstruction charge. I'm talking murder here! What the hell is the matter with you?"

"Dick," Merlino said calmly. "Can we go off the record, please?"

"No! We're not going off the record and we're not releasing this ... this boy, until I'm convinced that he is fully cooperating with us. Now, Ken, I need you to reconsider. After all—"

"Dick," Tony said with forced patience. "We need to go off the record."

"Just a goddamned minute!" Grant was up and pacing around behind his desk. "Ken, now I'm asking you and I need an answer. We have motive, we have him placed at the scene of the crime at the time of the crime, and we have him trying to make his getaway—"

"And you have him showing up in his hotel room to be arrested," Aldrich added.

"I didn't say he was smart. I said he was a murderer."

"Dick?"

Aldrich continued. "Sheriff, you got nothing to tie him to the murder weapon. You have no witnesses, and you have him giving a perfectly reasonable explanation for his visit."

"Christ! I honestly don't believe this!"

"Dick."

"Okay! Okay! Off the record. Now, what the hell do you want, Tony?"

"Well, I think we could work out a deal that might be mutually beneficial."

"I just don't believe this! Bobby, can you believe this shit?"

I looked over at Bobby Leonard and he winked at me.

"You ready to listen to me, Dick?" Merlino asked.

"Okay, okay. What?"

"Look. You're not going to get my client on a murder charge. Ken's told you that, and you can rant and rave, but it just isn't gonna happen. Okay? Now you've got a few minor things on him, but between you and me, even if you sock him with the full regalia, he's gonna be walking by this afternoon. Now, that doesn't mean that my client doesn't want to cooperate with the enforcement of justice. In fact, my client would like to do everything possible to help you, provided it doesn't compromise the rights of his client privilege. Now, from the way my client tells me, his case is getting ready to wind down. I suggest that my client makes a good full-faith effort to get his client to agree to a full-scale cooperation with your department here, and so perhaps we can clean this mess up. For the record, Dick, let me just add that my client has no idea who killed Scott Nelson, or why Scott Nelson was killed. As far as my client knows, Scott Nelson's death is totally unconnected to his case. And that's important, Dick, because what I'm saying is that my client is not willfully withholding important information from your department. So, why don't we just drop everything here, and maybe we'll have some more information for you. On my word, Dick, we are not trying to hide anything from you, and as soon as my client can cooperate, he will. What do you say?"

Sheriff Grant was standing behind his seat, with his big hands resting on the back of his chair. I could practically see the smoke coming out of his ears. He fixed me in a stare, and then I knew I had him. The old cop-staring contest I'd learned from my father. I stared back. Not smiling, blinking, or looking away. We stared and stared and, at last, he began to nod.

I heard Bobby Leonard giggling behind me as we walked out of Grant's office, "Man, Eddie," he said, under his breath, "you really got his goat, man. I ain't never seen that bastard so mad before."

"Hope I didn't get you in any trouble, Bobby."

"No man. It ain't nothing I can't handle. Yawl going back to New York now, Eddie?"

"First plane I can catch."

"Yeah, I knew you wasn't stupid, Eddie. It's good to see you and all, Eddie. If this all clears up, yawl stop down sometime and meet my wife. I got me a cigarette you wouldn't believe. We'll cruise down to the Keys or something. What do you say?"

I nodded at him. "Sounds great." But I hoped that I would not be back in Fort Lauderdale for a long time.

CHAPTER
—16—

Bill Bryant was a handsome and solid man, full of energy. His tanned skin wrinkled around his narrow eyes. His lips were thin and elegant, and his small mustache was a perfect shade of aristocratic gray. He wore a light blue shirt and a deep blue tie and no jacket. There was something confident and clean about him. He sat behind his desk in a large leather chair, a king upon a throne, his elbows resting gracefully on the arms of his seat, his big hands wrapped around a mug of coffee. There was no doubt he was the kind of a man who was always in control, a man who could make things happen.

"We have reviewed your report," he said, his low voice rumbling across the desk at Murphy and myself. "My partners and I have discussed it at some length. It's an interesting report. Although, I might add, it is not the one that we had expected."

"It usually isn't," Murphy said. He slouched down in his seat, and he looked at me and winked. He had totally rewritten my first draft of the report, and when I read his revisions, I had to look hard for any of my original words. It wasn't easy being edited into oblivion, but I was happy that it was not *my* report on Bill Bryant's desk.

"I find it hard to believe," Bryant continued, "that Raymond Fidel dropped everything and ran off with an old girl friend simply because he had 'grown tired' of being a lawyer."

Murphy was wearing his smirk now, not the least bit intimidated by Bryant's imposing manner. "I can see how you would," he said.

"Well, Mr. Murphy, would you care to offer a more reasonable explanation?"

Murphy frowned and put his hands out with his palms to the ceiling, a dramatic gesture of being empty-handed. "I would if I could," he said.

"So you buy this explanation?"

"I don't buy anything. I investigate and report. You hired us to find Raymond Fidel, and we found him."

"You found Raymond Fidel, yes. But you also lost him. We still don't know where he is or what he's doing."

Murphy sat up and raised his voice. "Well, then, perhaps you should have hired a baby-sitting service, Mr. Bryant."

"It's not baby-sitting I want, Mr. Murphy," Bryant came back quickly. "It's explanations."

"I can understand that," Murphy said, smirking again. "Raymond Fidel's explanation for his disappearance is hardly believable. There are a lot of unanswered questions, as you can see from our report. I don't buy Fidel's explanation any more than you do, Mr. Bryant, and we'd be happy to investigate the matter further, but let's not forget that we were hired to find Raymond Fidel, and we did that."

Bill Bryant sipped quietly from his coffee, his silence even more intimidating than his voice. At last he let out a low sigh. "Mr. Murphy, we are all very happy here that Raymond is alive and well. As human beings, we were concerned for him. It is not, however, a part of our firm policy to spend our resources checking up on the well-being of our associates. Strictly from a business point of view, Mr. Murphy, we are less concerned with Raymond's health than we are with the possibility that his disappearance was connected to firm business. As far as I am concerned, we still have no assurances on that."

"I take it, then, that you would like us to continue our investigations."

"That remains to be seen. The committee has asked me to make the final decision." Bryant sipped again from his coffee and then turned his attention to me. "Mr. Margolis, as the primary investigator on this case, do you have any idea where Raymond might have gone after leaving you in Fort Lauderdale?"

"No."

"Do you think that the murder in Fort Lauderdale had anything to do with Raymond's disappearance?"

"I don't know. There could be a connection. It's possible that, if there is someone else looking for Raymond, they might have tried to get information from Scott Nelson in a more forceful way than I did."

"Do you think Raymond knows about the murder?"

"I was with Raymond when Scott Nelson was killed, and I stayed with him until he got into a car to leave Fort Lauderdale. Chances are he never found about it, but then again, we don't know where he went or whether he kept in touch with people in Fort Lauderdale."

"Mr. Margolis, was there anything at all in your investigation that concretely ties Raymond's disappearance to his work here at the firm?"

Murphy answered for me. "If you read the report, the summation lists some of the loose ends, any one of which could lead to involvements with your firm. It seems likely that someone, besides my agency, is looking for Raymond Fidel, and the murder in Fort Lauderdale may or may not have been connected with our investigations. There's nothing to indicate that his disappearance was related to his work, but then again, there's nothing that indicates it wasn't."

Bill Bryant nodded slowly. "If we asked you to find Raymond Fidel again, could you do it?"

"It would be a lot harder now. He's been scared away twice. My hunch right now, Mr. Bryant, is that he'll be very hard to find. If he's running, which he appears to be doing, then tracing him down will take a lot of man power. It's the kind of thing that the police would be better at doing than a private firm. However, I doubt the police would be interested since Raymond is known to be alive, and, as far as we know, he's not a criminal. They'd have no reason to look for him."

"Well, then, Mr. Murphy. What would you recommend, if you were to continue on the case?"

"We'd continue our investigations of his files."

"In search of?"

"Anything unusual. We wouldn't know what it is until we found it."

"Mr. Margolis, I understand that you met with Alfred Norens and Sam Pulaski. Were you satisfied with your meetings?"

"Not really."

"Why not?"

"I didn't like Sam Pulaski."

For the first time Bryant smiled. "Nobody does, Mr. Margolis. Unfortunately, you take your clients where you can get them. We're in business, and Sam is an important client."

"What is the connection between Norens and Pulaski?"

"Connection? They are both clients of mine. They've done business together in the past. They were both involved in the development of the Interchange Building a few years back. They are not particularly fond of each other, but with Sam Pulaski in the picture that is not unusual. It's a small industry, Mr. Margolis. Everyone knows everyone else."

"Mr. Bryant," Murphy interrupted. "Can you think of any reason that any of your clients might be looking for Raymond Fidel on their own?"

Bill Bryant frowned and shook his head. "Raymond left in the middle of some important deals. His files, I understand, were a mess, and we've been having some trouble picking up where he left off. Understandably, this has aggravated our clients, but in answer to your question, no. Particularly, since the clients are all aware that we have instigated our own investigation."

"Well, Mr. Bryant. We would be happy to continue our investigation, but I can't promise any concrete results."

Bill Bryant placed his coffee cup on the desk and rested his chin in his hands. Even Murphy seemed to squirm in his seat as we waited for an answer. Bryant's office was on the northeast corner of the fifty-eighth floor of the Pan Am Building, and from where I sat, I could see La Guardia Airport and half of Queens. I watched three planes take off before Bryant broke his silence.

"Well, gentlemen. I don't believe that further investigation would be advisable at this time. It is unfortunate that we have lost an important associate, and I feel a little disconcerted by the loose ends, but I *am* glad that Raymond is alive and healthy, and we will simply have to terminate his position here. We will be meeting with Raymond's mother this afternoon and will inform her of your findings. She will be free to pursue the matter on her own, and we would, of course, be happy to cooperate in any way we can. There is one small item that remains to be discussed. In your report you indicated that you might be compelled to report back to the Fort Lauderdale police about the nature of this investigation. It would be quite awkward for us if our name, or Raymond Fidel's, was in any way connected with the murder. I'm afraid it would not be good publicity for the firm. I'm sure you can understand."

Murphy stood up and stretched his arms. "We'll keep you out of it as long as we legally can," he said, suppressing a yawn.

Bill Bryant stayed anchored in his chair. "I would hope that you could do better than that, Mr. Murphy."

Murphy let out a short laugh. "I'm sure you're not asking us to do anything contrary to the law."

"Of course not, Mr. Murphy. I'm asking you merely to help us to preserve the good reputation of our firm."

The sun was shining on Forty-fifth Street, and the sidewalks were crowded. Murphy plowed through the hoards of people and the street vendors toward our office, oblivious of the rest of the world. I had a hard time keeping up with him, but he didn't seem to care. "Fucking bastard," he said at last, not slowing down. "You did a first-rate job this week, Margolis, and it isn't your fault if those assholes don't appreciate it."

"I did a first-rate job?" I asked, practically jogging alongside him.

"You're damn right you did. Let me buy you lunch."

My boss was telling me that I had just done a first-rate job. That was supposed to make me feel good about myself and make me feel worth something, but for some reason all I felt was angry. "No thanks."

As we passed Orvis, I looked in the store windows at the fishing gear and the outdoor clothing and wondered what was wrong with me. I missed fishing. I missed the Keys. I wanted to be out on a boat, in the water and the sun. I wondered if I would ever adjust to being back in New York.

"Margolis, what's the matter with you?"

"I did a first-rate job?"

"Yes! You did a first-rate job! And I'll take you out to lunch if you want, but I'm not gonna beg you. You want to go back to work, we'll go back to work."

When we got to the corner of Madison Avenue, we had to wait for the light to change, and I could feel Murphy's eyes on me. I tried not to look at him.

"Margolis, what the hell is wrong with you?" he asked.

"Nothing," I said, watching the light change and waiting for the last few taxis to zip through before the crowd closed in upon the street.

Murphy followed me into the street. "Margolis, I don't understand you."

"I spent a night in jail and almost got hung for murder, but I did a first-rate job."

"What do you want from me?"

"Nothing. I'd just rather not spend any more time in jail."

When we got to the corner, Murphy grabbed both of my arms and forced me to face him. "Okay. I'm stupid. I admit it. I don't know what the hell you're talking about."

"I'm stupid too," I said. "You send me down to Fort Lauderdale. I have no idea what I'm doing. I get my ass thrown in the can for fucking murder, and you tell me I did a first-rate job."

"Okay, okay." He kept holding me. "I'm stupid, I'm stupid, I'm stupid. It takes me a long time to get things. You're mad at me for sending you to Fort Lauderdale, right?"

"Right."

"You're mad at me because you're inexperienced and you feel like I'm throwing you into things headfirst, right?"

"Right!"

"Okay, now we're getting someplace. Let's go out to lunch and we'll talk," and he let go of me and started to walk.

I was about to tell him that I didn't want to go out to lunch, and then I saw Alice Pinder coming toward me. Murphy was already walking away, and I stood still and waited for Alice.

She stopped when she saw me. "Hi Eddie." She was wearing a gray plaid business suit and carried a giant briefcase. The pearls hung loosely around her neck, but were partly covered by her blouse and her jacket. There was nothing sexy about her, but I found it hard to breathe.

"Hi," I said.

"I heard you saw Raymond."

"Yeah."

"Is he all right?"

"I guess so."

"You're off the case?"

"Yeah."

"Well, I got to run to a closing. It's been nice working with you," and she headed off down Madison Avenue.

"Hey, Alice!" I called after her.

She turned quickly, the briefcase banging against her thigh, her hair caught in her face.

"I may call you," I said.

"What for?" she asked, and suddenly I wanted to be back out in the middle of Madison Avenue so a cab could hit me. I smiled and shook my head and she disappeared into the crowd.

"Who the hell was that?" Murphy asked, coming back to where I was standing.

"Alice Pinder."

"You sure go for those blondes, don't you?"

"She works at Fenner, Covington and Pine."

"I know. You told me about her. You gonna call her?"

"What for?"

He shrugged and smiled. "Call it client development. Take her out and bill it to the firm. C'mon. Let's have lunch."

CHAPTER
—17—

Someone once told me that coldness was merely the absence of heat. Nowhere was it more true than in my loft. I awoke on Saturday morning to the bitter realization that I was doomed to another winter of electric blankets and telephone calls to the landlord. Why had I ever come back to New York City? As I waited for the coffee water to boil, I stared out at the dismal gray streets of the Lower East Side. There was only one thing to do on a day like this, and that was to be in Florida. I took my coffee to the bed and sat with my back against the wall, staring out at the emptiness around me.

Loneliness wears many disguises. Sometimes it was the reflex action of reaching for the telephone when the stillness got too loud. Other times it was the lingering scent of perfume that women left behind when they went to work in the morning. For a long time, loneliness was the magnetic pull that sucked me into my neighborhood bar, The Pit, every night and made me drink Scotch until I couldn't see. Loneliness, in its many disguises, had always been there for me; this morning I sat on my bed drinking coffee and feeling paralyzed by its presence.

In the afternoon I took the slow, cold ferry ride to the Statue of Liberty. I stood by myself in the back of the boat and watched the sea gulls dance in the windy grayness. The Hudson Harbor Office Complex fit in perfectly among the downtown office towers, with its stately granite and glass rising up into a light cloud of wispy fog. The Manhattan skyline slowly receded, an island of steel towering over the Hudson Bay. I turned and watched the Statue of Liberty grow larger against the dull sky. Her copper robes hung motionless in the wind and her right arm shot up like an arrow into the mist.

There were some families on the boat, mostly Hispanic and Oriental, and the children laughed as they chased each other around the decks. I tried to think about America, about immigrants, about freedom and peace, but all of that was too lofty for me. I couldn't even think about Raymond Fidel. When it came right down to it, the only thing I could think about was me, and New York City. When we got to the island, I didn't even bother to get off the boat, but simply rode it back with the returning group. The rest of the weekend was downhill from there.

By late Sunday afternoon I was back on my bed, staring up at the ceiling, too tired to go out, but not tired enough to go to sleep. I knew that if I lay still long enough, either I would think of something to do, or I would die, but an hour had gone by and neither had occurred. When the telephone rang, I grabbed it like a man overboard reaching for a lifeline. "Hello."

"Margolis, get up here!" It was Murphy, of course.

"I'm fine. How are you?"

"Quit the small talk and get your ass up here!"

I felt relief spreading through my body. "Where are you?"

"In the office. Where do you think I am?"

"What's going on?" I couldn't help but notice the excitement in my voice. I *wanted* to go to work.

"We're back on the job. I'll tell you about it when you get up here. Grab a cab."

I was out the door in less than a minute, and I walked quickly through the early-evening cold to the Bowery, where I hailed a cab. For some reason the word *workaholic* hung in my mind as I rode uptown. Well, it was better to work than drink, I told myself, but somewhere in the back of my mind a voice told me that sooner or later I was going to have to get my life together.

Murphy sat behind his big oak desk wearing a blue shirt and a pink tie. His travel bag sat in the middle of the floor between us, and his suit jacket was draped carefully over one of the chairs. He was wearing his infamous smirk.

I stepped further into the room. "Glasses?"

He pulled them off his head and looked at them as if he had never seen them before. "For reading. You'll be wearing them yourself one day. And if you're as lucky as me, you'll hold on to your hair."

"Are we really back on the case?"

"Like they say, it ain't over till the fat lady sings."

Mrs. Fidel put us back on the case. After Fenner, Covington & Pine had informed her of their decision not to pursue the matter, she had gone to the police. Apparently the police had not been very helpful, so she had called over the weekend and left a message that she wanted to hire us to find her son again. Murphy had called her and explained to her how difficult it might be at this point to find Raymond, and after some discussion it was agreed that we would focus our attention on finding out why Raymond had left.

"So what do you want me to do?" I asked Murphy.

"Oh, I don't know. I thought maybe I'd let you handle this on your own. . . ."

"Shit! Here we go again!"

"I'm just kidding! Jesus, Margolis, you're a hyper kid. I'm kidding, okay? I'm going to tell you exactly what I want you to do."

I took a deep breath and tried to quell the anger inside me. I knew one thing for sure: I was not going to go to jail again.

"You still have all that stuff you took from Fidel's office, right?" Murphy asked.

I nodded.

"Good. I want you to go through it, just like you were doing, and just make a note of anything that doesn't make sense to you."

"None of it makes sense to me."

"Good, then make a note of all of it. Here," he reached over the desk and handed me a blue and white message slip from Alice Pinder. "She called Friday night and left a message on the machine. Call her up, take her out to lunch and pump her. I'll bet she knows more than she's letting on." He looked at his watch. "Shit, I gotta go."

"Poughkeepsie?"

"Where else? Look, Margolis, I'll be back tomorrow night. I promise. We'll sit down and do this together. Okay?"

I didn't say anything.

Murphy laughed and put on his coat. "You know, you're going to overwhelm me with your enthusiasm if you're not careful. Go home, and I'll see you tomorrow night."

I wandered back over to my desk and looked at the pile of papers from Raymond's office. I had been planning to return everything on Monday, but now it sat there, as if it had know all along that I would come back to it. I could have gone home, but I knew what waited for me there, so I sat down at my desk and started to work.

I read through all of the things that had constituted the top layer of paper on Raymond Fidel's desk. Most of it seemed to relate to Sam Pulaski and the new loan on the Travis Building. There were a few things about the Norco Construction Company and a few other things that I could not identify. I listened to the tape Fidel had left in his Dictaphone and found an unfinished letter addressed to a lawyer named Barry Fried. I pulled the tape out and put it in the pile of unidentified documents.

By ten o'clock there was still another four inches of papers and documents to go through. I leaned back in my seat and decided to leave the rest for tomorrow. Then I spotted the manila envelope that Raymond's secretary had given me. It contained copies of all the telephone messages that Raymond had received in the two weeks before he left. I opened the envelope and poured the message slips onto my desk, about a hundred of them. In the morning I would go through them one at a time and make a list of all the people whose names I didn't recognize, but right now it was time to go home. I started to scoop the little pink pieces of paper back into the manila envelope, and then one of **them** caught my eye. It was a message from Michael Dorfman.

I had to think about the name for a moment before I realized why I knew it. Michael Dorfman had been murdered just a few weeks ago, thrown through the window of his thirty-second-floor office. I sat with the little pink piece of paper in my hand and looked at my reflection in the windows. George Walsh had mentioned the Dorfman murder when they had first hired us to find Raymond Fidel, but if I had been told the date of the murder, I could not remember it now. All I knew was that at 5:15 P.M. on October 18, Michael Dorfman had called Raymond Fidel. Sometime after that, Michael Dorfman had been murdered. And sometime after that, Raymond Fidel had disappeared.

CHAPTER
—18—

The Picasso seemed out of place. It came from a world outside the law, away from the daily routine of Fenner, Covington & Pine, away from mortgages and conference calls and billable hours. The framed poster supplied the only color in the office, its blues and reds standing out in sharp contrast to the otherwise drab decor. The central figure stood tall and thin, her arms outstretched above her, her left leg bent at the knee and crossed behind her. I could not take my eyes off her. Like a prisoner calling out for freedom, she demanded my attention. I stared at her obediently, as if merely by watching her, I could set her free.

"We have to call Barry Fried," Alice Pinder said.

Alice was sitting comfortably behind her big desk with her arms resting gently on the arms of her chair. Her steel-blue eyes were pointed in my direction, but they seemed blank and unfocused. The collar of her dark blue blouse was turned up, hiding all of her honey-colored neck except for a few inches in the front. She looked down at Raymond Fidel's Dictaphone in her left hand, and a shrill sound filled the office as she rewound the tape. Then she played back the slow, monotonous drone of Raymond's dictation. ". . . your client to complete the repairs as quickly as possible. It is my understanding that your client has spent approximately. . . ."

The dictation stopped and Alice turned the tape off, set the Dictaphone on her desk, and crossed her arms over her chest. "He stopped in the middle of a sentence," she said. "It's hard to know what he was going to say, but it could have been a specific dollar amount that had been spent on repairs. Maybe he stopped because he didn't know what the amount was."

"And you think he would have called the guy he was writing to?"

She shrugged, disinterestedly. "It's worth a shot."

Alice Pinder had told me in the morning that she was too busy to have lunch, but she said she would be willing to help me if I came to her office later in the afternoon. When I arrived, she told me that she had called on Friday night to apologize for her behavior that day on the street. The apology seemed to leap from her mouth too quickly to be sincere, like a child saying "thank you" after being told to do so. It left me wondering if there hadn't been another reason for her call on Friday.

Now she picked up her telephone and I heard her give instructions to her secretary. "Kim, get the number of a lawyer named Barry Fried, at Lockhart and Adams on Third Avenue. See if you can get him on the phone."

A few awkward minutes passed as we sat across the desk from each other and waited for the call to be put through.

Since that first night, when she held my arm as we walked through the dark midtown streets, Alice Pinder had intrigued me, there was no denying that. After years of hanging out with prostitutes and waitresses and rock and rollers, I felt intimidated by Alice's successful career. But there was more to it than that. Alice Pinder had a rock-steady exterior, perfectly tailored for the business world. She showed no signs of weakness or frailty, but something made me think there was another person in there, crying to get out. We sat in her office, a lawyer and a private investigator, doing their jobs, but I wasn't thinking about Raymond Fidel. I was thinking about me and Alice Pinder. And I was wondering if it was all in my head.

At last her telephone rang, and Alice leaned across her desk and hit the button on her speaker phone. "Mr. Fried? This is Alice Pinder at Fenner, Covington and Pine," she said, leaning back into her seat. "I'm here with Eddie Margolis, a private investigator. Do you have a minute?"

There was a brief pause. "Sure. What's this about?" Barry Fried's voice sounded hard and dry, and also slightly metallic through the speaker phone.

Alice raised her right hand and gestured to me. "Mr. Fried," I said, "my firm has been hired to find Raymond Fidel, and I understand that you've had some dealings with him recently. I'd like to ask you a few questions."

"What happened to him?"

"Well, that's what we're trying to find out, Mr. Fried. When was the last time you spoke to him?"

Again there was a brief pause. "Well, let's see. It couldn't have been too long ago. There's still an open matter on a deal we closed about two years ago, and Fenner, Covington and Pine is still holding some money in escrow. It's not a lot of money, but Raymond's been wanting to close it out. Seems to me I was supposed to be getting a letter of agreement from him. He called me, I guess it was about two weeks ago."

"Do you remember what day it was?"

"I probably took some notes, let me look at my file. Hold on a second." Alice Pinder had turned around in her seat and was staring out the window at the office buildings uptown. From where I sat I could only see the very top of her head sticking up over the back of her seat, her blond hair against the black leather upholstery. "Okay, here it is," Fried's voice came back. "I remember now. He called to get some figures from me for the letter agreement. I guess it was Wednesday afternoon, that's two weeks ago."

"Can you tell me what you talked about?"

"Like I said, he needed some figures for the agreement, but you know, Raymond and I were always on pretty good terms. We always talked a little business. Hey, is there somebody there handling this now?"

"I will be," Alice said, turning just slightly in her seat. "Would it be all right if I called you about it later on in the week?"

"Fine with me. It was your client who seemed to be in a hurry."

"Mr. Fried," I persisted. "Do you remember anything more specific about your conversation with Raymond? Anything at all?"

"Yeah, I seem to remember telling Raymond about a deal I had been working on with Michael Dorfman. You know who Dorfman was?"

I sat up in my seat. "Yes."

"Yeah, well, I was working on a deal with him when he got murdered. I got questioned by the cops and everything. It was pretty crazy, really. Ray was real interested in what I was working on. Seemed particularly interested in the fact that

Dorfman was representing Sam Pulaski. Now, there's a character for you. You know who Pulaski is?"

Alice swung around, her eyes now clearly focused. "I know who Pulaski is," I said, watching Alice. "What was Dorfman doing for him?"

"I'm afraid I'm not really at liberty to talk about it. Raymond seemed real interested in it, too, and asked me a whole lot of questions, but I'll tell you what I told him. My client has given me strict instructions to keep this under the hat. I can tell you it's a refinancing, but I can't tell you what property it is."

"Can you tell us who your client is?" Alice asked.

"Sure, it's Metro City Bank. Look, I don't mean to be telling you your job or anything, but there's really no big mystery here. It's just a simple refinancing. Honestly, I can't see how it has anything to do with Dorfman's murder or, for that matter, with whatever happened to Raymond. I'm not trying to be a wise guy here. I'm just trying to save us all a lot of time."

"Can you remember exactly when you spoke to Raymond?"

"No, not offhand. Sometime in the afternoon, I think, but hell, I can't remember two weeks ago, the shit that happens around here. Look, I'll do what I can to help you find Raymond, but, frankly, I don't think I can be of much help. You think he's all right?"

"I don't know."

"Well, like I said, I'll be happy to help, but I'm at a loss for what I can do."

"Well, thank you for your time, Mr. Fried."

"No problem."

"I'll call you later in the week," Alice said, and she leaned forward and turned off the speaker phone. "Wow!" She was grinning with excitement, and she held on to the arms of her chair as if riding a roller coaster. "What do you think that was all about?"

I reached into my pocket and pulled out the message slip I had been fingering all afternoon. I had not shown it to her yet because I wanted her to concentrate on a few other things first, but there was no longer any holding out. I reached across the desk and handed it to her, and I watched the look on Alice Pinder's face turn from excitement to fear. "Eddie, what's going on?" her voice cracked as she spoke.

"Do you remember what day Michael Dorfman was killed?"

She nodded, but couldn't seem to get the words out. She held the slip in her hand and wiggled it up and down, as if she were trying to shake it loose. Finally she spoke. "About three hours after this message."

I stood up and took the message slip from her, and then I walked back and closed her office door. When I turned around again, she looked like a different person. Her arms were resting on her desk with her hands clasped together, and her eyes were suddenly soft and real. "How is it that Michael Dorfman represented Sam Pulaski?" I asked. "I thought you guys represented him."

She shook her head, dismissing the issue. "It's not unusual for these guys to have more than one lawyer. Pulaski's got a lot of property around, so I guess he's refinancing some other building he's got."

"Okay, so both Raymond and Michael Dorfman represent Sam Pulaski. Would they be in competition?"

Alice laughed. "In competition? Yeah, competing to get rid of him, maybe. Pulaski is Bill Bryant's client, and Raymond never really liked working for him. Neither do I, for that matter. From where Raymond and I sit, nothing could be better than to *lose* Pulaski as a client."

"What about the fact that Pulaski wants the other deal kept quiet?"

"That's pretty common. He's doing that with the Travis Building too. The whole industry is like that. Nobody ever wants to let anyone else know what they're doing."

"Okay," I said, now standing behind the chair I had been sitting in. "Let's just walk through this a second. Michael Dorfman calls Raymond Fidel and leaves a message. Three hours later he gets killed. Nobody knows what it's about. Two weeks later Raymond talks to Barry Fried and finds out that Michael Dorfman represented Sam Pulaski in another refinancing deal. A few hours after that, Raymond disappears from the office and runs away to Fort Lauderdale, claiming he's fed up with being a lawyer."

Alice Pinder shook her head. "Something's not right, Eddie. You think Raymond knows something about Michael Dorfman?"

"It could be, but I think I've got to find out more about him myself."

"Eddie, I think I should call Bill Bryant." She turned on the speaker phone and dialed. "Bill, it's Alice," she said when he came on the line.

"Yes, Alice," his voice boomed through the speakers and filled her office.

"Eddie Margolis is in the office with me. We just talked to an attorney named Barry Fried."

"Lockhart and Adams, isn't it?"

"Yes. He told us that Michael Dorfman was representing Sam Pulaski on another refinancing project. Apparently, Fried talked to Raymond about it the day Raymond disappeared. We also found a message slip to Raymond from Dorfman from three hours before Dorfman was murdered."

There was a long silence on the other end of the telephone. Even over the phone, Bill Bryant's silences were powerful. "What else did Fried tell you?" he asked, at last.

"Nothing. He wouldn't tell us what property they were working on, just that the client was Metro City Bank."

"Mr. Margolis, what do you make of all this?"

"I don't think we can ignore the possibility of a connection between Dorfman's murder and Raymond disappearing. And I think we have to look carefully at the possibility that Pulaski is somehow involved."

"Well, I see what you mean, but I wouldn't get too crazy about it. Pulaski owns close to fifty properties throughout the city, and he must use about ten different law firms. Frankly, I don't see what his involvement could be, but I'll call him and ask him about it. In the meantime, let me know if you find anything else. Alice, who are you billing your time to."

"Um, the Employment Committee, I guess."

I had been staring at the Picasso again, but the sudden strain in Alice's voice made me turn back to her. Her face had turned brilliant red. I watched her as she turned off the telephone and sank back into her seat.

"He never asks me how I'm billing my time," she said. "He doesn't want me working on this, Eddie. That's what he meant with that question."

"Well, that's okay," I said, not quite getting it. "You've been a big help, Alice. I can probably handle the rest myself."

She was shaking her head. "No, Eddie. I mean, I don't think he wanted me working on this at all."

I stood in front of her desk, suddenly feeling very dumb. What was she trying to tell me? There was something I was missing, but before I could even formulate a question, the red had drained from her face, and she was smiling. "Oh, I don't know, Eddie. I just got scared. The whole thing has just sort of thrown me for a loop."

"Yeah, it threw me too," I said. "Look, I can take care of this now. There's no reason for you to get involved. Thanks a lot for your help." I headed toward the door, but she stopped me.

"Eddie?" She looked better. Her skin was back to its normal color and she was still smiling. "Eddie, you can call me if you want."

I smiled back at her and then took one last look at the Picasso. It hung boldly among the files and documents, like a vestige of a life forsaken.

CHAPTER
——19——

I stood a few feet from the tracks on the subway platform underneath Grand Central Station. There must have been a thousand of us waiting for the downtown Lexington Avenue train. We were packed solid. It was a typical rush-hour mix of faces and newspapers, and I could feel them rubbing up against me, as close as lovers. I stared up at an advertisement for blue jeans on the station clock and tried to ignore the smell and the chaos.

Murphy, of course, had not made it back from Poughkeepsie, but I had spoken to him from the office. I told him about my meeting with Alice Pinder and about all the leads pointing to Michael Dorfman. Murphy promised to arrange for me to talk to someone from the police department about the Dorfman murder investigation. I was feeling pretty good. My meeting with Alice Pinder had made me feel stronger and more competent, and it felt good to have a concrete lead. I felt almost like a private detective.

I leaned over and looked down the tracks into the dark and endless tunnel. There was a white light of a distant train barreling toward us, but it was too soon to tell if it was an express or a local. I watched until I was sure that it was not going to veer off onto the express track, and then I stepped back to wait. I stared ahead at the dirty tiled walls and listened to the roar of the Number 6 train as it came into the station. I was one foot from the tracks.

I remembered Alice Pinder's face when she got off the telephone with Bill Bryant and then suddenly I felt something hard slam into my back. It felt like someone had just taken a swing at me with a baseball bat. For some magical reason, my feet stayed in place, and as my midsection flew forward, my knees buckled. I fell backward into the crowd and my arms got tangled in a mess of pocketbooks and shopping bags. I fell through the bodies and smashed into the ground, my legs bent backward and my arms somewhere underneath me. I probably looked like a figure in a Picasso painting.

I saw a pair of blue jeans and dirty sneakers moving through the crowd, and I saw a pretty set of legs with black nylon stockings and red shoes. My face was pressed against a newspaper, opened and wrinkled, with footprints all over it. There was a man leaning over me, wearing a khaki beige coat.

My ribs throbbed once again in pain, making it impossible to breathe. I swallowed hard and tried to pull my legs and arms up from under me, every move sending a wave of pounding agony through my side. Somehow I managed to get into a sitting position with my knees up and my hands in my lap. The train came to a stop and the doors opened, regurgitating more commuters onto the crowded platform.

They rushed past me, their legs dragging over me and around me, their briefcases and book bags bouncing off my head and my shoulders. A woman got her foot caught in the tails of my coat and she cursed at me as she pulled it loose. Then the flow of the crowd changed directions. I was not ready to stand up, so I sat dumbly while they pushed past me to get onto the train. The platform seemed to clear quickly, and suddenly I was sitting alone.

The man in the beige khaki coat was holding the door open for me. "Are you okay?" he asked. Showing concern for others was not typical for a New York commuter, and I wondered if perhaps there was something wrong with him.

"I'm fine," I said. "What happened?"

"Some kid. He's gone now. You sure you're all right?"

I nodded, and he let the door close.

I stood up slowly, now feeling a new pain across my back where I had been hit. It couldn't have been a baseball bat. There had not been enough room. More likely it had been someone's forearm shoved squarely against me. As the Number 6 pulled out of the station, I tried dusting off my coat and my pants, but it hurt too much to move my arms. Besides, there was no dusting off subway grime. An express train pulled into the station, and suddenly the platform was packed again. I followed the crowd up the stairs to Grand Central Station. My ribs ached with each step. Once upstairs, I went out onto Forty-second Street, and only then did the fear rise up inside me with a throbbing intensity. Someone had tried to kill me.

CHAPTER
—20—

"I told Charlie we're not talking small potatoes," Detective Jack Branby said, standing behind his big wooden desk.

Branby was a thin man with olive-green skin. His face looked sallow and tired, and when I looked into his pale brown eyes I thought that perhaps he had a hangover or the flu. His office was fairly neat, at least by a policeman's standards. It had that old New York look, with big bulky furniture and a worn tiled floor. Papers were stacked neatly on his desk and he had one of those gizmos that pulled the smoke in from cigarettes. From where I sat I could see the back of a framed photograph on his desk and a potted plant on top of one of his file cabinets. It was obvious that Branby was an organized man and that he took some pride in the appearance of things. But the office still had a stale smell of cigarettes and after-shave lotion. There was an old wooden coat stand in the corner and next to it a framed mirror that he probably spent a lot of time looking at, not that it helped his appearance.

"I'm not sure what we've got here," Branby said, peeling off his corduroy jacket, "but whatever it is, it's pretty fucking big. You know what a MAC is?" he asked.

"It's a computer," I answered.

Branby laughed and hung up his jacket. "Yeah. It's a computer, but I'm not talking about computers," he said. "I'm talking about a MAC: a Mutual Assistance Committee. It's a real simple gig, and it goes like this. I help you guys. You guys help me. Everyone keeps their mouths shut. There's only one rule," he said, holding up a finger to make his point. "Mum."

"Mum?"

"That's right. You see the papers? You see the articles on Dorfman? You see anything in there about the investigation? No. I'm telling you right now, if you or Charlie have any inclination toward the press, and I know Charlie sure as hell don't, one word to the press, and I'm gonna find out about it. Okay?"

He didn't wait for an answer. "And I'll tell you something else. You guys are conducting an investigation, and I know what you guys do. You go around and talk to everyone in the world. I know because I do it myself, but let me tell you something. You guys are gonna do what you have to do, but if you say one word about anything that goes on in this office . . ." again he held up his finger for emphasis, "One word. When I say mum, I mean mum. Got it?"

"Mum," I said, settling back into my seat. From the way things were going, it didn't look like I'd get a chance to do much else.

"Okay, let's talk about Dorfman." Beneath the corduroy jacket Branby was wearing a white short-sleeved shirt and a shoulder holster, and he pulled the holster off and played with the adjustment straps while he talked. "Michael Dorfman, aged forty-two, wife, four-year-old kid, and a house in Greenwich, Connecticut. Graduated New York Law School in 1974, and he's worked at Torens and Clarke ever since. No record, no nothing." Branby hung the holster up next to his jacket and then began pacing behind his desk. "Belonged to the debate club in high school. Remember those guys? He was one of them. I mean, we're talking clean. Guy didn't even cheat on his taxes. Got the picture?"

I nodded, but Branby wasn't looking at me. He had pulled the chair out from under his desk and was looking into it, as if trying to figure out what it was for. Then he picked up a pack of Pall Malls from his desk and lit one with a fancy gold lighter.

"His wife works at a real estate office in Greenwich. She had an affair about five years ago with a guy in her office by the name of Webster. Ken Webster." Branby paced behind his desk and talked through a cloud of smoke. "No big deal. It lasted a few months and was over. The guy got transferred up to Hartford. She hasn't seen the guy since. So, it could be a lot of things. Could be the guy came back and knocked Dorfman off to get him out of the way, or could be the wife got pissed and wanted her freedom, or maybe Dorfman had his heart broke and did himself in. Lots of possibilities, but we're not looking at them." Branby moved around to the front of his chair and did a crash landing.

"Because you got something more," I said.

"Right." Branby dropped his cigarette into an ashtray and picked up a big green folder from his desk. He flipped through it and I watched the smoke from his cigarette get sucked up into the filter gizmo.

"Okay," Branby said, resting the folder in his lap and reaching for his cigarette. "Let's go to the night of the murder. Dorfman's sitting in his office, eight o'clock at night, in the Baker-Stone Building on Third Avenue. They got what they call security downstairs. A guy sits by the elevators and makes you sign in. Not hard to get past if you want to, especially if you're experienced at these kinds of things. Okay, so our man sneaks past the guard and rides the elevator up to the thirty-second floor. The doors from the elevator bank are locked, but it's an idiot lock. My senile aunt could pick it. Our man picks the lock and walks in. There's no receptionist on duty, but Torens and Clarke at eight o'clock at night is still like Grand Central. There's attorneys all over the place. And there's a couple of cleaning ladies. The guy walks right through the halls to Dorfman's office and closes the door. This guy's got balls.

"We got a cleaning lady probably looked right at him, but she's Oriental and all whites look alike to her. Anyway, we know our man is white and was wearing a suit. Big help. So now he's in Dorfman's office, and the door's closed. Nobody sees or hears a thing. How could that be? The goddamned cleaning lady is running a vacuum cleaner down the hall. They say they can't hear themselves think. Anyway, our man's in Dorfman's office and now he's breaking fingers—"

I tried to stop him.

"I know, I know. Same thing as your friend in Florida. Charlie told me. Four fingers, two on each hand. Oh, let's back up a second. Dorfman was a big guy, six-one, but light as a rail. So maybe our guy was bigger than that. Or maybe he had a gun. In any case he must have had his hand over Dorfman's mouth when he snapped the fingers, else the whole world would've heard. So our man breaks a bunch of fingers and then he picks Dorfman up and throws him out the window. Right through the glass. Ouch."

I had the same feeling in the pit in my stomach that I had that first time I had heard about Michael Dorfman from

George Walsh, and I thought about the way my knees went weak that day up on the sixtieth floor of the Hudson Harbor Office Complex.

Branby was still talking. "Got a lot of this from the autopsy report. Four broken fingers, lots of cuts from the window, and then smash. Our man, having done his job, walks right out through the halls, takes the elevator downstairs, and walks out into the night, like it's just another day at the office."

"How do you know it's not the boyfriend?"

"The fingers. People have their fingers broken for two reasons. Loan sharks do it, you know, one finger for every day you don't pay. But you don't do that if you're gonna send the guy out the window. Doesn't make any sense. Besides, Dorfman wasn't the type. Second reason is it makes people talk. You're probably too young to remember the Local Four-twenty-eight trials out in Jersey about fifteen years ago. Witnesses kept disappearing, and when they showed up, they'd be dead and their fingers'd be broken. Company had a couple of informers in the union, but it's hard to keep a secret when someone's cracking your thumbs. Does that mean we got a union problem on our hands? I doubt it. Torens and Clarke does some labor law, but Dorfman never went near it. I think we're talking about the same guy, but a different cause. You know what I mean? Someone who hires himself out for this kind of thing."

"Like a hit man?"

"Yeah, like a hit man. Can't be sure about that, but I'll tell you one thing. We ain't talking about a lovers' quarrel." He smashed out his cigarette and then picked the file up off his lap and set it on the desk. "We got no suspects. We got a million and one leads. And we got a great big headache because we know we're onto something big." He leaned forward across the desk and tapped his finger on the file.

"This is hot stuff. This is the kind of stuff that disappears overnight if anyone knows you've got it. Real hot." He reached for his cigarettes. "Now tell me about Fort Lauderdale."

"I was down there looking for someone."

He stopped me with a wave of his hand while he lit his cigarette. "Guy named Raymond Fidel. Spare me the background, I already spoke to Charlie. You went down to see this guy Nelson, the one who bought the farm. You got in a powwow with him in the bathroom of a club, and the next day you went to visit him. Before we know it, Nelson's dead and you're in the can. I spoke to that Sheriff Grant too. He's a real friend of yours, let me tell you. Now, I really only got one question, Did you notice anyone following you when you were down there?"

The surprise must have shown on my face.

"It's the only way it works," Branby said. "Your buddy Fidel knows something about all of this, and somebody knows you're looking for him. Did you see who it was? The guy who was following you?"

"No. It was a gold Plymouth with Florida tags, but I didn't get the license."

"Did you see the driver?"

"No. Just a shadow."

"Who knew you were down there?"

"Just Murphy, and our secretary. And our client."

"Fenner, Covington and Pine." His voice suddenly seemed softer. "Who'd you talk to about Fidel before you went down there?"

"A lot of people. People at the firm . . ."

"Besides the firm."

"Let's see. Fidel's mother and sister. Some old man at Fidel's apartment building and some of Fidel's clients. A guy named Alfred Norens."

"You mean the guy from Norco Construction Company?"

"Yeah."

"What's that guy like?" Branby's voice had gotten still softer, and his questions were asked gently now, as if curiosity were the only motive.

"He's eccentric. He's short and he loves to talk. He took me for a helicopter ride out to New Jersey. I think he's a little crazy."

"He's rich enough to get away with it. Who else?"

"Sam Pulaski."

Branby grunted. "Your friend and mine. Guy's got a lot of lawyers, but only one reputation. I wish I could show you the report on *him*. What a piece of work. Who else?"

"This guy Barry Fried, the lawyer who worked on the case with Dorfman."

"Anyone else?"

"Bunch of people in Florida."

"Who knows you guys are back on the case?"

"I don't know. Fenner, Covington and Pine. Maybe some of their clients."

Branby inhaled from his cigarette and leaned back into his seat. "You know, you're lucky nobody's tried to kill you."

"What makes you think that?"

Branby sat up fast. "Are you serious?"

"Someone tried to push me in front of a train on the way home from work yesterday."

"You sure they were trying to kill you?"

"No. I fell down and never saw a thing, but it didn't feel like an accident."

He puffed some more on his cigarette, and for the first time since I had entered his office, there was silence in the room. I suddenly became aware of the sounds of telephones and typewriters from the other offices.

"I'm gonna tell you something right now," Branby said at

last. "You guys got your hook into something so big it's gonna pull you right out of the fucking boat. I'm not saying that there's necessarily any connection between your gig and mine. I'm just saying that for your sake I hope you know what you're doing. What's Charlie doing in Poughkeepsie, anyway? Chasing Vassar girls?"

"I feel like you know something that I don't," I said.

Branby laughed. "I know a lot of things that you don't, but I don't know anything about this case that's gonna help you. I never really got along with Charlie. Did he tell you that?"

"No," I answered honestly.

"Charlie and I used to work a squad car together in Hell's Kitchen, back in the seventies. Just a couple of months really, and then I got transferred to Homicide, and a few months later he got Narcotics. Oh, he's all right, Charlie. I mean they gave him the screws on that Santucci thing and I don't like to see that happen to anybody. I guess he's better off now anyway, to hear him tell it. I never had anything against him. Charlie's honest, and that means a lot more to me now than it used to."

Branby held his cigarette in front of his face and stared at me across his desk. I got the feeling that he wanted to tell me something more, and that if I just sat still long enough he would. At last he put out the cigarette and leaned forward. "Close the door a minute, would you?"

His voice was rock steady and quiet and I got up and closed the door, suddenly feeling nervous.

"You been at this long?" he asked before I could sit down.

"This case?"

He shook his head. "No, this private-dick stuff."

"No."

"Neither has Charlie. You know, he's got a lot of experience at being a cop, but he don't know beans about being a private dick." He held up the file. "I'm not sure there's anything in this file that could help you, but it doesn't really matter because I can't let you see it anyway. If it ever got out that I leaked this stuff, my goose would be cooked. You know what I mean? Now, I gotta go talk to someone for a few minutes, but why don't you wait here for me. Maybe you'll think of some more questions." He held the file up in his hand a minute longer than he had to and then dropped it square in the middle of the desk. "I'll see you're not disturbed."

"Thanks."

Branby left the office and I heard the door shut behind me. I thought of waiting a few minutes, but there wasn't really any reason to. I reached across the desk and picked up the big green file, my hands shaking slightly as I felt its weight. I rested it in my lap and began shuffling through the notes and papers. On the inside left flap there was a list of names under the heading "Preliminaries." I read down the list quickly. Jennifer Dorfman must have been the wife. Ken Webster was the boyfriend. There were a lot of lawyers under the subheading of Torens & Clarke, and there were a lot of names I didn't know, probably neighbors and friends. I found Sam Pulaski's name among the list of clients and then I flipped through the file and found the report on the preliminary interview with Pulaski. The report was authored by a detective named Jack Older.

I almost laughed out loud at the opening description:

This guy is one of the most unpleasant human beings I have encountered in my twenty-one years on the force, or for that matter during my forty years on this planet. He is rude, obnoxious, unhelpful, demeaning, and in fact, quite suspicious. Recommend a follow-up interview just to find out if it was me, or if I caught him on a bad day.

The rest of the report was about how Pulaski had met Michael Dorfman, how he had come to use Dorfman as his lawyer, and how well he knew Dorfman, which was not very well at all. I caught my breath, when I got to the third page, where there was a description of the work Dorfman was doing for Pulaski:

> *Dorfman was representing Pulaski, in Pulaski's capacity as president of Travis Realty Corp., which is the managing general partner of Travis Realty Limited Partnership. The Partnership owns an office building on Madison Avenue, known as the Travis Building, which is currently mortgaged to a Panamanian corporation, Ocron S.A. Pulaski's partnership is taking out a twenty-million-dollar loan from Metro City Bank to pay off the Panamanian loan. There were no problems or unusual circumstances surrounding the loan. Metro City Bank is represented by Barry Fried, Esq. Suggest preliminary.*

I read the paragraph three times. Then I looked up the preliminary interview with Barry Fried. The interview was short and confirmed that Metro City Bank was lending Travis Realty Limited Partnership twenty million dollars in order to pay off its loan to Ocron S.A.

I looked up and stared out over Branby's desk. Raymond Fidel had been representing Pulaski on a loan from the National Bank of New York, which he was going to use to pay off the Ocron S.A. loan. Sam Pulaski had told me that himself. But Pulaski was now borrowing money from Metro City Bank for the same reason. Why would he do that? Why would he borrow money from two banks to pay off the same loan? What was he up to?

CHAPTER
—21—

At four-thirty in the afternoon, the air was already buzzing with pre-rush-hour jitters, and a blast of wind swept out through the doors of Grand Central Station, as if to make room for the impending masses. I pushed against the warm rushing air and managed to work my way through the crowds to a public telephone. It was warmer inside, but I felt a continued tension in my shoulders as I dialed the number of my office.

The line rang once and Kate answered, "Charles Murphy Detective Agency."

"Hi, Kate, it's me."

"Jesus, Eddie! I thought you'd never call! I've been waiting for you for three hours. You already missed the guy, but he called again and gave another time. You know, it gets pretty boring around here with you two guys gone all the time."

"Kate, what are you talking about?"

"He said you should be at the telephone on the southwest corner of Twenty-third Street and Sixth Avenue at four o'clock—"

"Whoa! Just slow down a second," I said, switching the receiver to the left side of my head as if things might make more sense through the other ear. "Kate, start from the beginning. Who are you talking about?"

"I don't know who he was. He wouldn't leave his name. He just said he was your friend from Florida. Look, I don't know what kind of Dick Tracy games you guys are playing. He just said I should tell you to be on the corner of Twenty-third and Sixth at four o'clock."

"My friend from Florida?"

"That's all he said. I thought you'd know who he was. So just listen a minute, would you? He told me you should be there at four. And he told me you had to go by yourself. Must have said it five times." Then her voice dropped into a deep mimicry, " 'Tell him he betta be alone.' Just like that. Well, I didn't hear from you, so I couldn't tell you about it, and so of course you didn't make it. The guy called back just a few minutes ago and told me to tell you to be at the same place at ten o'clock tonight."

"And you don't know who it was?"

"Would you listen? No I don't know who it was. The nerve of this guy. He told me to make sure you get the message, and I told him that I couldn't give you the message unless you called in. I told him that if he'd like to leave a number, like any normal person, I'd make sure you called him back as soon as you could. Then I told him that if you didn't call in by five, it would have to wait until tomorrow because I was going home. The guy told me not to leave until you got the message! Well, I told him I'd go home whenever I goddamned pleased."

"So I'm supposed to be at the telephone on the corner of Twenty-third and Sixth at ten o'clock tonight?"

" 'And you betta be alone,' " she mimicked again.

"Is Murphy back yet?"

"Oh, he's another one. The two of you, I'm telling you. One day you're both gonna come back to the office and the whole building will have been burned to the ground with little old me in it, and there won't be anyone here to give you your messages. No, Murphy's not back, and he never calls."

"Well, when is he supposed to be back?"

"He was supposed to be back last night. C'mon, Eddie, you talked to him. You know he doesn't know when he's coming back. He'll be back when he gets back. Probably tomorrow sometime. Listen, I'm getting ready to go here. Let me give you the rest of your messages. Bill Bryant called at noon and left a number. Mrs. Fidel called at two-thirty and left a number. Andrea Fidel called at four o'clock and didn't leave a number. Now, I gotta get going. I need to pick some things up on the way home, and I don't want to miss *Cagney and Lacey*."

"Of course not. Just do me a favor and call Murphy at his hotel and leave a message that I'm in over my head, that someone's trying to kill me, and that I need him to get his ass down here."

"Should I quote verbatim?"

"No, spice it up a little. Twenty-third and Sixth?"

"Eddie, you're not really going to go down there, are you? Oh, hell, suit yourself. You going to be in the office tomorrow?"

"I don't know."

"You and Charles. What the hell am I going to do with you two? Bye." And she hung up.

I leaned against the telephone and stared out at the rush of people, the world slowly slipping out of focus. I couldn't seem to hold on to any single thought or feeling. Everything was just zipping through me, random and confused, like the growing hordes in Grand Central. My friend from Florida. Was it the driver of the gold Plymouth? Was it the one who had killed Scott Nelson? Was it the man who broke people's fingers for a living?

"You using the phone?"

My eyes snapped in focus and a man's face loomed in front of me. I shook my head and slowly moved away from the telephone. "No, go ahead," I said.

The big *Newsweek* clock said it was twenty minutes to five as I pushed my way toward the north end of the station. There were three escalators pouring people onto the main floor, as if emptying the entire Upper East Side, and there was one escalator, almost empty, going up. As I left the main floor and rode up into the Pan Am Building, I looked down at my fingers, and it occurred to me that I liked them just the way they were.

CHAPTER
—22—

I stood perfectly still as the elevator raced through the up-
per floors of the Pan Am Building to Fenner, Covington &
Pine. Everything was suddenly coming together and I felt
my muscles tense with excitement. The elevator doors
opened into the massive lobby on the fifty-eighth floor, and
I approached the reception desk and looked Mrs. Fenner,
Covington & Pine dead in the eye. "I'm here to see Alice
Pinder," I said.

She nodded her matronly head and told me to have a seat,
and as I walked away from the desk, I heard her instruct
one of the other receptionists, "Tell her Mr. Margolis is
here."

After I was told that I could go in to see her, I followed
the already familiar hallways, past the nameplates and the
historic portraits, to Alice's office. I knocked lightly on the

open door, suddenly feeling happy to have a reason to be there.

Alice pushed her chair back away from the desk, literally distancing herself from her work, and looked up at me with a light and airy smile. She was wearing a soft blue dress that matched her eyes. "I'm not supposed to talk to you anymore, you know," she said, her smile widening. There was something different about her. As my eyes drifted toward the Picasso, I noticed that it didn't seem quite so out of place anymore.

"Why not?" I asked.

"I don't know. Bill told me that that if you have any more questions about Raymond Fidel or Sam Pulaski, I should tell you to talk to him." Her lips pulled together into a puckered grin, as if daring me to get around this apparent barrier to our conversation.

"It's not about either of them," I said, stepping into the office and closing the door.

"Oh, good," she said, her voice bubbling in delight. "Then come on in and let's talk. I'm in a great mood, Eddie. The Travis deal closes tomorrow, and I'm all ready to go. I got one more document to get back from word processing and then I'm out of here. I feel great."

I settled into the chair across the desk from her, feeling strangely comfortable. "You *look* great," I said.

Her smile stayed in place. "Thanks, Eddie. How's my favorite private detective?"

"He's a little confused, to tell you the truth," I said. "Maybe you can give him some legal advice."

"Not if it's about Raymond or Sam Pulaski."

"It's not. It's just sort of a hypothetical problem."

She broke out in a laugh, but played along. "Okay. I'll take a stab at it."

"Well, let's just say I own a building with a mortgage on it, and let's just say I'm taking out another mortgage to pay off the first mortgage."

"That's what we call a refinancing," she said.

"Right. Now, with this refinancing, when the new bank gives me the money—"

"Stop there," she held up a hand to interrupt. "The new bank isn't going to give you the money. They want to make sure that you use the money to pay off the first bank, so they're going to give the money directly to the first bank."

"Why do they care if I pay off the first bank or not?"

"Because they want to have a first mortgage. If you don't pay off the first bank, then they are going to be holding a second mortgage."

"What's the difference?"

Her eyes seemed to soften. "I think maybe we better start from the beginning. May I?"

"Of course."

"Okay. You want to buy a building but you don't have enough money. So you go to the bank, we'll call it Bank One, and you get a mortgage. They lend you the money to buy the building and you sign a note and a mortgage. The note is your promise to pay back the loan, and the mortgage is their security. It means that if you default on your loan, stop paying, or something like that, they can foreclose on the property. Very simply, what usually happens is that they'll sell the property and pay themselves back with the proceeds of the sale. So now Bank One has a first mortgage on your property. With me so far?"

"Yup."

"Okay. Now you decide that you want to make some improvements to your building, but you still don't have enough money. So now you go to Bank Two, and you borrow more money and you give them a mortgage. Bank Two now has a second mortgage. If you go into default and the banks foreclose, Bank One is going to get all of its money out before Bank Two sees a penny. The first mortgage has priority over the second mortgage. Now, foreclosure sales are always way below the market value, because its a forced sale, so Bank Two may never get all of its money. Depending on the sale price and the amount of equity in the building, a second mortgage may not be worth as much as a first."

"How do you know who has a first mortgage and who has a second?"

Alice leaned way back in her seat, with a knowing smile. "Oh, that's an old law school kind of question," she said. "They have all these statutes and rules to figure out which mortgage would come first. Usually it's the first person to record the mortgage at the county clerk's office. In reality, you don't really have to worry about it because you get title insurance. The title insurance company will search the title and tell you who owns the property and what other mortgages or liens there are. They'll tell you if you have a first mortgage or not, and then they'll issue insurance. If they insure that you've got a first mortgage and then it should turn out, for some reason, that you don't, then you can collect any money you lose from the title insurance company."

"Okay, so back to my problem. Bank Two is going to pay the money directly to Bank One, so that Bank Two is sure that they have first mortgage."

"Right."

"And then I owe the money to Bank Two instead of Bank One."

"Right."

"Okay, now what happens if Bank Three comes along and lends me money?"

"Well, it's the same thing. Either they make you pay off

your loan from Bank Two or else they'll hold a second mortgage."

"Hmmmmm." We stared at each other across the desk. The sky outside her window had grown darker, and the office seemed quiet. Everything she had said made sense, and yet I still couldn't understand why Sam Pulaski would be borrowing money from two different banks. I was going to have to take a more direct approach. "Okay, let me go on. Let's just say now that I hired you to represent me in the refinancing. And now let's say that somehow you found out that I was borrowing money from another bank to pay off the first loan. What would you do?"

"Oh, God, Eddie, I can see you're not going to give up. We're still not talking about Sam Pulaski, right?"

I couldn't quite keep myself from smiling. "Right."

"Okay, you mean, you hire me to represent you in a loan from Bank Two to pay off the loan to Bank One, and then I find out that you're also borrowing money from Bank Three to pay off the loan to Bank One? Is that what you mean?"

"Exactly."

"Well. . . ." she stared up at the ceiling, lost in thought, and continued without lowering her head. "Let's assume that the deal I was working on was going smoothly, and let's just say it's going to close tomorrow. There are no contingencies, everyone's ready. You can never be a hundred percent sure, but we've got a commitment letter from the bank, so they can't really back out and you've already paid a mess of points so you wouldn't back out." She brought her head down and looked at me. "I'd have to say I don't see any reason that you would go to another bank."

"There's got to be a reason. Think about it. Think dirty."

Suddenly her face got bright red, and she started to laugh. "Eddie, I don't think you want me to do that!"

I felt myself blush, and suddenly I understood how things were different. Ever since I had met her, Alice Pinder had been a lawyer who just happened to be a woman, but today, from the instant I had walked into her office, she had been a woman who just happened to be a lawyer. I couldn't be sure if she was any different, or if it was just the way I saw her, but I knew I didn't really have the time to figure it out. We were very close to solving the puzzle.

Alice suddenly began talking nervously. "Okay. So, let's say that right after our closing you go down to Bank Three and borrow more money. Right?"

I nodded.

"Now, Bank Three would see the mortgage to Bank One on their title report."

"I thought Bank Two already paid off Bank One at the first closing."

"They did, but Bank Three wouldn't know this."

"Why not?"

"You see the title insurance company does a title report that tells you about all the mortgages that are recorded on the property. That's how you know if you've got a first mortgage or not. In most states the title company will actually send someone down to the clerk's office from the closing to record the mortgage before they will issue their insurance. Makes sense, right? In New York, of course, they have to do it differently. In a New York Style Closing, on the day of the closing the title company will do what they call a continuation, which simply means they go down to the clerk's office and check to see that nothing else has been recorded. If it looks okay, the title company will issue a commitment to insure before they've actually recorded the mortgage. Once the bank has this commitment from the title company, it lends the money. The title company is actually at risk until they get down there and record the mortgage. If you go to another closing on the same day, Bank Three isn't going to see the mortgage from Bank Two, because it won't have been recorded yet. They're only going to see the mortgage from Bank One."

"So Bank Three would pay the money over to Bank One?"

"Theoretically. It's a small world and chances are Bank Three would find out about the loan from Bank Two some other way, unless there were a lot of people trying to keep it a secret."

"And if they pulled it off, Ocron would get paid twice?"

"We're not talking about Sam Pulaski."

"Of course not. Bank One gets paid twice?"

She shrugged. "Yeah, I guess. And you're in a whole lot of trouble because you've got two banks who each think they have a first mortgage."

"What can they do to me?"

"They can sue you. And you won't have the money because it all went to Bank One."

"So why would he do it?"

Alice laughed. "I don't know, Eddie. It's your hypothetical."

"No it's not," I said. "In fact, it's not a hypothetical at all."

Alice bolted upright in her seat. "Come on, Eddie! You can't be *serious*!"

"Completely."

"But Eddie, it doesn't make any sense."

"It's got to make sense, because Pulaski's doing it. Now you can sit there and tell me that it doesn't make sense or you can help me figure out what he's up to."

"Eddie, how do you know he's doing this?"

"I can't tell you that. You just have to believe me."

"Oh, come on, Eddie! I know Pulaski's an ass, but I can't just go accusing him of stuff like this unless I know what I'm talking about."

I felt myself starting to get mad. "Alice, I need you to help me."

"I can't help you, Eddie. My job is to protect the interests of my client. That means that I'm not *allowed* to do anything that will compromise his interests."

"Even if he's breaking the law!"

"Now wait a minute. Nobody said anything about breaking the law. Even if what you say is right, then all I can see is that he's taking advantage of a loophole in the closing procedures to borrow more money than a bank would otherwise lend him. I'm not even sure if there's a law against what he's doing. In addition to which, Eddie, even if it was illegal, I can't turn him in just because you say he's doing it. I have to know, beyond a reasonable doubt, that my client is committing a crime before I can turn him in. *That*'s the law, Eddie!"

I was out of my seat, standing over her desk. "Don't you remember Michael Dorfman? Can't you see what's going on here, Alice? Dorfman figured this thing out and Pulaski had him killed. And then Fidel figured it out and had to skip town. Pulaski had him followed down to Fort Lauderdale and killed Scott Nelson. We've got two murders on our hands. Is that enough 'against the law' for you?"

Alice was sitting stiffly in her seat. "Eddie. I don't think it's a good idea for you to be telling me how to do my job. If you want to keep talking about this, then I suggest you talk to Bill Bryant." She reached for her telephone, but I leaned over the desk and held it down.

"You're scaring me, Eddie."

"Alice, you said that if someone was trying to pull this off, there would have to be a lot of people in on it. Well, between you and me, I don't feel like guessing who's in on it and who's not. Now, someone's already tried to kill me and I don't plan on letting it happen again."

"Eddie, what are you suggesting?" she said, leaning back into her seat, her voice suddenly rock solid. "This is my job here. You can walk out of here tomorrow and be put on a new case. But this is it for me. I work here. Sam Pulaski is my client and Bill Bryant is my boss." She was staring steadily into my eyes. "You come in here accusing my client and my boss of being crooked, and you still haven't given me any proof. And now you expect me to *help* you? Come on, wake up!"

"Alice, I've got nobody else to turn to."

"I'm sorry, Eddie. I already feel like I know more about this than I want to, and I'm scared. Now, this deal closes tomorrow, and all I want to do is walk in there and just do it the way I know how. I'm a good lawyer. You show me some other third-year associate who can handle a twenty-million-dollar loan on their own. Most people would be scrambling around the night before a closing trying to get ready. I'm good, and I don't want to get screwed up now. Can you understand that? Goddamn it! This isn't just my job we're talking about here. This is my life!"

I slowly retreated to my seat. It's funny the way things go. The words and the anger did not keep us apart, and in fact, I sat there, feeling like I was finally beginning to know who she was. I couldn't believe what I heard myself say. "Can I take you out for dinner?"

She was smiling again. "I'd like that, but it's laundry night tonight. How'd you like to come over for some Chinese takeout?"

CHAPTER
—23—

I remember my old bedroom window, which looked out the back of the trailer and across the field of vegetables into the eastern Florida sky. My father had installed a special shade, which blocked out the early-morning sun, and each day before I opened the shade, I would lie in bed and try to imagine the weather. For years I believed that if I concentrated hard enough, I could make the sun shine, or I could make it rain when I wanted a ride to school. Then I would get up and open the shade, and if the weather was not what I had wished for, I would blame myself for not concentrating hard enough. I remember the way it suddenly hit me one day, like a spiritual realization, that I could not control the weather. All I could ever do was find out what it was.

I got the same kind of feeling climbing into a taxi cab with Alice Pinder. I felt it in the way she slammed the door and moved closer to me, and the way she leaned forward across my lap and gave our destination to the driver. As we took off up Park Avenue, her head fell back against the seat, resting comfortably beside me, and she let out a long and mournful sigh. "Boy, sometimes I forget there's a world out here," she said, staring up at the ceiling of the cab.

Neither of us said anything after that, but I could feel her next to me, thinking and breathing. I was grateful for the silence as we weaved in and out of the traffic going uptown. She had intrigued me from the beginning. But I was going home with her *now* because *she* wanted to. This was all her game, and it made me nervous not to be in control.

We stopped in front of a stately brick building on Sixty-fifth Street just off Third Avenue, and I held the door of the cab while Alice paid the driver. Then she held out her hand, and I automatically reached for it and pulled her gently to the curb. Alice took my arm and led me toward the building, where a doorman held the outer doors open for us.

He smiled at Alice as we approached. "Hello, Ms. Pinder. Haven't seen you around much. I guess they're working you pretty hard, huh?"

"You wouldn't believe it if I told you, Danny."

He laughed and followed us in. "Well, you tell them to be good to you, young lady. Tell them Danny Levelli is looking out for you."

I followed Alice across the big, quiet lobby and I held her briefcase while she got her mail. I watched with a strange sense of jealousy as she pulled a handful of magazines and letters from her box, more mail than I got in a month.

In the elevator our eyes met briefly, and for an awkward second I thought she was going to say something that would break the spell. Instead, she smiled at me and I felt a sudden rush of nervous energy. Not only was Eddie Margolis not driving this train, but he had no idea where it was going. It was time to talk to the conductor. I looked back into her eyes, their blueness now soft, warm and enticing, and I forced myself to speak. "Alice," I said.

"What, Eddie?"

But before I could say anything else, the elevator stopped and the door opened. Without waiting, Alice stepped out into the hallway and led me to her door. I held her briefcase again as she fiddled with her keys, and then suddenly we were in her apartment.

The first room was a large, empty foyer, with a polished wood floor, but no furniture and nothing on the walls. We walked through it into the living room, where there were scattered pieces of furniture—a couch and a television—and against the far wall there was a huge stack of moving boxes, still unpacked. She took the briefcase from me and put it down on the coffee table with the mail.

"Alice," I said, not able to say much else.

"What, Eddie?" she asked again, now smiling and stepping closer.

One last step broke all the boundaries. Suddenly I felt the warmth of her body and the heat of her wet mouth. We stood, kissing, and I could taste her breath. This was not the Alice Pinder I had thought about, and yet she felt so delicious in my arms that I couldn't let go. We began peeling off each other's clothes, slowly, piece by piece, step by step. We continued, until we were naked and standing next to the only piece of furniture in the bedroom.

Suddenly I felt as though all life was being choked out of me, leaving me with nothing but my own aching desire. I pulled away and tried to stop, but she stepped forward and grabbed me gently. She pulled me down onto the bed, and all of the nervousness and confusion disappeared. My ribs made it difficult to move freely, so we rocked slowly, saying nothing, and gently falling into a peaceful and loving rhythm.

Afterward, we lay quietly, our sweaty bodies sticking together, my head resting gently on a soft pillow. I felt her breathing beneath me, each breath lifting and carrying me like a wave and gently bringing me back to the softness of her body and the bed. With my eyes closed, I rode the waves and slowly floated away into a peaceful memory.

I was with my teenage buddies, Jimmy and Spike. We lay on our backs in a big Florida field and watched a thunderstorm forming to the southeast. Usually we spent our time running around and looking for trouble, but for some reason, that afternoon, we just lay quietly, with our heads close together and our feet pointing away and watched the sky. The big gray clouds billowed and fell into themselves as they gathered up strength, and the whole sky turned silver and yellow. We didn't talk for a long time, and I remember feeling stuck to the ground, as if gravity had made it too hard to stand up. Finally the rain began in big drops that splattered as they hit. We all stood up to try to beat it home, but Spike grabbed us by our arms and held us to our places. His eyes were heavy and he looked like he was about to tell us something, but he didn't speak. Then Jimmy made a joke and Spike laughed, and we all ran home, laughing in the rain.

I lifted myself gently off Alice and rolled onto my back, suddenly feeling alone. Spike was killed about a year later when he drove my car off a bridge. A lot of people never understood him, because all they saw was his bigness and his ugliness. But I would always remember the way he looked, running across that muddy field and laughing, his eyes wet, though whether from rain or tears I'll never know.

Alice rolled on top of me and held me gently in her arms, and slowly I felt myself start to get hard again. We made love once more, this time with her on top, and as I watched the soft curves of her breasts and shoulders in the warm shadows of her bedroom, I felt a deep longing swell up inside me. And when at last I came, I held my head between her breasts and felt the wetness from my tears on her skin.

CHAPTER
—24—

It was precisely 10:00 P.M. when I climbed out of a taxicab on the corner of Twenty-third Street and Sixth Avenue. The night had turned cold and brittle, and I made my way to the telephone on the southwest corner, praying that my friend from Florida would not make me wait too long. With each step, I felt a screaming fear rise up within me. What would happen when I got to the telephone? Why was I doing this? Where was Murphy when I needed him? I casually surveyed the intersection, feeling slightly reassured by the fairly heavy traffic still moving up Sixth Avenue and the numerous pedestrians scurrying about in the cold.

As I stood by the telephone, waiting for something to happen, my fear ebbed slowly, and I thought about Alice. We had ordered Chinese food and we had sat naked in bed, eating with chopsticks out of the white cardboard containers, her skin glistening with sweat long after we had finished making love. We didn't talk very much, but there was nothing awkward about it. It felt very right to be with her.

The sharp ring of the pay telephone jarred me back into the present, and I grabbed the receiver, feeling its stinging coldness in my hand. "Hello."

"I can see you," a woman's voice taunted.

I instinctively looked around, as if I might be able to find her.

"Hold up some fingers on your left hand," she said.

It was a familiar voice but I couldn't quite place it. I held up the middle finger of my left hand.

"That's not very nice, Eddie."

Then I recognized the voice. "I'm not a nice guy, Karen. Where's Raymond?"

"Chill out, and listen. When I tell you, you're going to hang up the phone and walk west on Twenty-third Street to the Chelsea Hotel. You know where it is?"

"Of course.

"Good. Go to the front desk and ask for Scott Nelson."

"Scott's dead."

"Do what I tell you, Eddie, or you'll be dead too."

"Oh, you're not going to pull a gun on me again, are you?"

"Time to go," she said, and she hung up.

It only has to happen once. Someone tries to kill you, and suddenly the whole world is your enemy. I didn't feel good walking down Twenty-third Street toward the Chelsea Hotel. My spine tingled the whole way, and I could practically see myself through the scope of a sniper's rifle. Every person I saw carried a gun, every truck and cab on the street was trying to run me down. My skin crawled as I crossed Seventh Avenue. There was no reason to look around. If Karen Fletcher wanted me dead, she would have me.

As I passed beneath the red neon sign of the hotel, I thought of some of its more famous inhabitants: Dylan Thomas, Bob Dylan, Sid Vicious. I climbed the steps and pushed my way through the doors into the main lobby, hoping that I was not about to become another name in the hotel's long and sordid list of obituaries. I went to the desk and asked for Scott Nelson. The desk clerk was an older man with greasy hair and big rings on his fat, stubby fingers, and he barely looked at me as he picked up the phone and announced my arrival. I was instructed to go to Room 706. I rode the elevator up to the seventh floor, wondering which room Sid Vicious had been in when he stabbed his girl friend.

On the seventh floor I knocked at the door of Room 706, and a muffled voice came back from within, "Who is it?"

"Who the hell do you think it is?"

The door cracked open a few inches and I peered into the darkness. From the dim light of the hallway, I could see a gun leveled at my stomach. I had seen the same gun a week ago in Fort Lauderdale, but that already seemed light-years away. The door opened more, and I could make out Raymond's shape, standing in the shadows of the room.

"Welcome back, Raymond," I said. "Why the gun?"

"Shut up," he said softly. "Get in here."

I stepped into the darkness, and Raymond turned on a light and locked the door. He was wearing the same sneakers and blue jeans he had been wearing the first time I saw him, but now he was wearing a heavy red flannel shirt that made him seem older and more masculine. There was something solid about him. His skin had a healthy deep brown tan, and his eyes were steady. Still, his voice wavered as he spoke, "You're a fucking slime ball, Eddie."

"So I've been told."

"How come you didn't kill me when you had the chance?"

"Why should I have?"

"For the same reason you killed Dorfman."

I heard myself laugh.

"It's not funny. Look, Eddie, I don't care what you told the cops. I know that you killed Scott Nelson. And I know you killed Michael Dorfman. So let's cut the crap."

I suddenly felt myself shaking with anger and I forced myself to sit on the bed and stay calm. "Raymond, I don't appreciate being held at gunpoint and being accused of all kinds of shit, when the truth is only a phone call away."

"I'll tell you what's a phone call away, Eddie. The goddamned police are a phone call away!"

The sudden flood of relief must have shown on my face.

"What's that matter, you got them paid off too? Listen you goddamned little fucker. Scott Nelson might have been an asshole, but he was my friend." Raymond moved closer to me, the gun waving about my head. "Now, I don't know just who you think you are, but I ought to blow your brains out right now. You're *lucky* I'm going to call the police. You know what I mean?" He jammed the gun into my forehead.

I felt like grabbing the gun and strangling him, but I took a deep breath and closed my eyes. "Look, Raymond, call the police, shoot me, I don't really care what you do," and now I was losing it, "but get that goddamned gun away from my head because I've had enough of this shit!"

I opened my eyes and he had backed away a few feet, and I took the opportunity to stand up. "Let me tell you something, Raymond," I continued, almost forgetting about the gun. "Scott Nelson was alive when I left his room. I got back to my room after seeing you and Karen off and the police were there waiting for me. Scott was killed while you were handing me that line about being tired of your job. Now, if you really cared about Scott Nelson, you would be here trying to help me rather than flashing your gun around.

And if you really want proof that I'm not who you think I am, why don't you answer your own goddamned question, because I could have killed you, Raymond. You know that. In fact, I'm beginning to wish I had."

Raymond retreated to the other bed, where he sat with the gun in his lap. I decided to keep working him as long as I was on a roll, and I continued in a calmer voice. "Your little story about being tired of your job didn't go over so big up here. Now I'm finding out what this is really all about, and the only thing I've got to thank you for is throwing me off track. You want to do something now? You want to get involved? Fine. Stay away from me. You're in or you're out, but don't come to town waving a gun at me unless you know what you're talking about."

Raymond sat quietly, biting his lip, the gun now on the bed beside him. "I guess I didn't think this through very carefully," he said at last.

I had to laugh. "I'm sure everything would be easier to understand if I was the bad guy, but you know I'm not. Now, just listen to me for a few minutes while I run through this, because right now you're the only person who can help me."

Raymond's eyes seemed to grow deeper and slowly he began to nod his head, and I took that as my cue.

"Okay. Sam Pulaski's got some plan to put two mortgages on the Travis Building. Both banks think they're going to have a first mortgage. Michael Dorfman was representing Pulaski on a loan from Metro City Bank, and somehow or other he found out about the loan you were working on from National Bank and he mouthed off to Pulaski before he understood what was going on. That got him killed. On the day he was killed he tried to call you, but I guess he was out the window before you had a chance to get back to him. The day you walked out of Fenner, Covington and Pine you had a telephone conversation with Barry Fried, and he told you about how he was representing Metro City Bank on a loan to Pulaski. Right?"

Raymond jumped right in. "I mean, what the hell was I supposed to think? I've been in the business long enough to know that you keep your mouth shut unless you know what you're talking about. So I didn't say anything to Barry about our loan. I just got off the phone and I thought about it. And then I called Sam Pulaski, and he told me he'd come up to the office later that night to talk to me about it, and then I called Bill Bryant, but he wasn't there. I was sitting there at my desk, and suddenly I remembered how Dorfman had called me the day he was killed, and I thought about how he was representing Pulaski on the other loan, and suddenly I just got real scared."

"So you left the office."

"Jesus, what was I supposed to do? I mean I just had to get out of there so I could think. Part of me thought I was in deep shit, and the other part of me was laughing, because I was being so paranoid. I'm walking the goddamned streets in the middle of the afternoon, and I'm just getting myself all worked up. I can't even think of who I can talk to. Finally, I'm standing there on Madison Avenue, looking right up at the Travis Building, and I realize that I have no way of knowing whether I'm being careful or paranoid. All I could think was that this was my big excuse to get the hell out of New York City, so I grabbed a taxi and went out to the airport and grabbed the first flight down to Fort Lauderdale."

"How come you didn't call your family?"

"I was scared. I didn't know what I was doing. I was afraid that if I told them where I was, someone would find me. I just needed to be left alone. So, I'm down there a couple of days, still brewing with this thing inside my head. I mean, fuck these people. I'm supposed to put my goddamned life on the line for them? After a while I couldn't keep it to myself anymore, so I told Scott all about it, and he wanted us to come up here and try to get a piece of the action, you know, bribe Pulaski or something. But I didn't want any of Pulaski's dirty money. I'll tell you the truth, there was a part of me that still believed I had made up the whole thing just so I would have an excuse to leave. I didn't want to believe that Dorfman had been killed for knowing what I knew."

"So Scott was protecting you?"

"He thought he was. He shouldn't have gone at you like that in The Beach House, but he was always crazy. And then when you told me you were being followed, I knew it was all for real."

"So why didn't you tell me about it? Why did you lie to me?"

"It wasn't a lie. I had already decided that I wasn't going back. You could say this was just the last straw, the kick in the pants."

"So what changed your mind? Why'd you come back?"

Raymond fell backward onto the bed and talked to the ceiling. "Cindi told me that you killed Scott. She said the cops grabbed you and then you got off on some kind of technicality. It didn't make any real sense to me, but I felt like shit because I knew that whoever killed Scott was looking for me. It was my fault, so I knew I had to come up here and do something about it. You were the easiest suspect."

I sat down on the bed across from Raymond. First, I had been hired to find him, and I had found him. Then I had been hired to find out why he had left, and now I had done that too. Officially, my job was over. But there was still a murderer running around out there.

"Raymond, are you going to help me?"

He sat up and looked at me. "Yeah, I'm gonna help you."

"Okay, look. The way I figured it, with these two loans, Ocron is going to get paid off twice. Right?"

"Right."

"Well, what's in it for Pulaski?"

Raymond shook his head. "I don't know. I've tried to figure it all out, and the only way it makes sense is if Pulaski's got a big piece of Ocron."

"Can't we find out?"

"No, that's the problem. Ocron is a Panamanian company, and Panama's got some wicked secrecy laws. The way the law works down there, if the actual owners of a company want to remain anonymous, it's impossible to find out who they are. We don't know anything about Ocron. We deal with some lawyer down there who acts as their representative, but he's not going to help us. He's getting paid to keep his mouth shut. Besides, even he probably doesn't know who owns the company."

"So Pulaski could own Ocron. Then he'd be taking the money from banks and putting in into his own pocket."

"Exactly. But there's more to it than that. First of all, you gotta understand that Pulaski only has a five-percent interest in the Travis Building. Not only is he ripping off the banks but he's ripping off the limited partners, the investors. If he's going to pull this thing off, he's not gonna be sticking around when the shit hits the fan. You know what I mean? There's no reason for him to stop at two mortgages. Why not go for three, or four, or ten? Why not sell the goddamned building a couple of times while he's at it. The guy could be going for broke."

"What can we do?"

Raymond nodded slowly, giving me a long look in the eyes. "I think I might know a way we can pop his big balloon without exposing ourselves."

There was a soft knock at the door and Raymond's hand

instinctively went for the gun, but he let it rest on the bed at the sound of the key in the lock. Karen Fletcher stepped into the room wearing a long black raincoat and jeans with cowboy boots. Despite all her toughness and strength, there was something ultimately warm about her. She looked at me and then at the gun on the bed, and then at Raymond. "What happened?" she asked.

Raymond smiled at me. "Eddie's with us now, Karr."

CHAPTER
—25—

I met Raymond on the front steps of the surrogate court building on Chambers Street. It was sunny and cold, and Raymond had a gray wool scarf wrapped around his neck and his shoulders were hunched up inside his coat. As I reached out and shook his hand, I suddenly realized how much I liked him. We climbed the steps together to the main entrance, where a small crowd had gathered, waiting for the doors to open.

"I called my family," Raymond said, squinting into the sun. His face and ears were bright red from the cold, and it made me think of the photograph of him and his sister at the beach. "My mother told me to say thank you, and said she would call your boss and thank him too." Raymond looked down at his feet. "Andrea said she liked you."

I caught myself starting to laugh. "She's got a strange way of showing it," I said.

"She's a strange girl."

"Are you going to stick around after today?"

"I don't think so. Karen and I haven't decided what we're doing yet, but I'll tell you one thing. I'm not going back to Fenner, Covington and Pine."

"Somehow I could have guessed that," I said, and we both laughed.

I leaned back and stared up at the surrogate court building. I must have passed it many times over the years, but I don't think I had ever noticed it, and now I felt awed by the richness of the solid gray stone, and the preciseness of the ledges and corners. The gargoyles looked down on me, frozen in time.

Raymond nudged me and pulled out a white paper bag from his coat pocket. "Mrs. Field's Chocolate Chip Cookies," he said, holding the bag out for me. "Want one?"

I shook my head. "No, thanks."

"I've learned over the years that anytime you come down to one of these government offices," and he nodded at the court building, "it pays to bring along a little chocolate payola."

"What for?"

Raymond laughed. "For all the bribable bureaucrats."

A guard finally opened the main door, and the crowd shuffled into the warmth of the building. I followed Raymond through the main foyer, feeling slightly overwhelmed by the smooth marble floor and the warm, rich colors. Voices and footsteps echoed in the quiet as we headed up a large set of steps to the second floor, where a marbled hallway circled the atrium.

"Now, there's probably a couple of ways we could go

about this," Raymond said, "but I think our best bet is to start in here."

He stopped in front of a set of double doors with a sign that announced, "Clerk of the Court, Mortgages and Fees." Raymond pushed his way through the doors and I followed him into a large room with long rows of racks and tables. It was set up like a library, except that instead of books, the racks held big canvas-covered registers, each several inches thick and about two feet high. We appeared to be the first ones there.

"I haven't been here in years," Raymond said. "I was a law clerk one summer during law school, and they had me doing title searches." He led me through the rows of registers to the far well. "I know the lot and block numbers of the property, so all we have to do is look up in this grantor index, which lists all the mortgages and deeds by the grantor's name."

The far wall was covered from floor to ceiling with register books, and Raymond searched the stack until he found the one he was looking for. "This ought to be it," he said, pulling out the register and laying it out on the table behind us. "We know the grantor is going to be Travis Realty Limited Partnership, so all we got to do is turn to the right block, let's see . . . ," and he carefully began turning the big square pages of the book.

"Okay, here's our block. Now, just run down to the bottom of the page, since it would be one of the most recent things recorded. . . ." He stopped suddenly. "That's strange."

"What is it?"

"Well, the last thing in here is a mortgage recorded on November eighth."

I looked over Raymond's shoulder at the long list of names and numbers. "Nothing from Travis Realty Limited Partnership," I said.

"No, but the eighth was two weeks ago." He slammed the book shut and looked at me with a funny smile. "I just thought of something. Come on." I followed him back out into the hallway, around the corner and through another set of doors. This was a smaller room, with a short service counter running down the middle. A young woman with dark hair and a tough-looking face sat behind the counter. She had heard us come in, but she didn't look up.

Raymond pulled the bag of cookies from his pocket and winked at me. We approached the counter, and Raymond held the bag out so the woman could see it.

We stood there for a few seconds and finally she looked up at Raymond and his bag of cookies. "What have we here?" she asked. Her deep voice reeked of Brooklyn.

"Mrs. Field's Chocolate Chip Cookies. Want one?" and he let her look into the bag.

She peaked in and twisted her lips into a smile. "I suppose you'll be wanting something that I don't have time to do."

"No. Just wanted to ask you a few questions."

The woman reached in and grabbed a cookie. "I'm listening."

"Is this where you bring a mortgage to be recorded?"

"Right where you're standing," and she took her first bite.

"I'd give it to you?" Raymond asked.

"Yup. Fill out that form right there you're resting your arm on. I'll stamp the mortgage and the form and take it for recording."

"And when would it be on the books, out there?"

"A week to ten days."

Raymond looked at me and then back at the woman. "You mean it takes ten days between when I bring it in here and when it actually gets recorded?"

"No, it's recorded the day you bring it in. It just ain't on the books for a week to ten days, depending on how busy we are. This time of year it starts getting pretty crazy down here. Are you a reporter or something?"

"No, just a guy with a bag full of cookies." Raymond held the bag out for her.

"I'll take this one for my lunch break," she said. "What else you want to know?"

"What if I needed to know if someone had recorded a mortgage on a specific piece of property in the last week or so?"

She pointed with her thumb over her shoulder. "You see those baskets back there?" There were four metal baskets, each piled about a foot high with documents. "It'd be in there, if it's anywhere. Of course, you're not allowed back here to check, which means you'd have to find someone here who'd be willing to check for you."

Raymond held the bag out again. "Grantor would be Travis Realty Limited Partnership."

She took two cookies this time and smiled. "Honey, you ain't doing a thing for my waistline."

It didn't take her long to find the first one, and Raymond waved his magic bag of cookies and asked her to keep looking. She pushed her eyebrows together and looked at him as if he was crazy, but she went through all four baskets and found two more. Raymond exchanged what was left of his cookies for copies of the mortgages and then grabbed my arm and pulled me out into the hallway.

"Three mortgages, Eddie," he said in a loud whisper as he headed for the stairs. "Can you believe this? Twenty million dollars each! He's already sapped sixty million out! God knows how many he's putting on this building!"

I practically had to run to keep up with him as we headed down the stairs. "Raymond, what can we do?"

"Didn't you tell me that Alice was closing that loan from National Bank today?"

"Yeah. The closing starts at two this afternoon."

"Perfect. All we got to do is sneak copies of these up to the title closer during the closing. One look at these and the title company won't issue the insurance. It'll blow the whole thing wide open!"

We reached the main floor and headed out into the cold and the sun. I knew Raymond was right: we were about to blow the whole thing wide open. I was only afraid of where the pieces would land.

CHAPTER
—26—

I called the office and Kate told me that Murphy was on a train coming back from Poughkeepsie. Then I called Jack Branby, but he wasn't in either, and nobody seemed to know where he was. I left a message that I was standing on Park Avenue, across the street from the National Bank Building, and that he should get there as soon as possible. Raymond nervously paced the Park Avenue sidewalk, stopping to take quick sips of his coffee and to check the revolving doors of the National Bank Building. I sat on the cold stone of a plaza wall, my eyes glued to the same revolving doors. On the twenty-eighth floor Alice Pinder was representing Sam Pulaski on the closing of a twenty-million-dollar loan from the National Bank of New York. We had everything we needed to nail Sam Pulaski except for help. After about twenty minutes, Raymond got tired of waiting and he ran up and left our package of mortgages at the reception desk for the representative of the title company.

The wait was longer than we had expected. I called Jack Branby three times and my office twice, and we were on our second cup of coffee when Sam Pulaski came barreling out of the revolving doors. He was accompanied by another man, short and balding.

I jumped off the wall and landed near Raymond on the sidewalk.

"Mathew Fields," Raymond said, before I could ask. "He's the managing agent. I should have known he'd be in on it. He's got all the paperwork on the building. Pulaski couldn't pull it off without him."

We watched as they crossed the plaza in front of the National Bank Building and headed down the steps to the line of cars and cabs parked out in front. "Shit! He's got a car!" Raymond said.

There was no time to wait for help. I tore across Park Avenue to the sounds of screeching brakes and blaring horns, and as I reached the island in the middle, I looked for Raymond and found him running beside me. In my peripheral vision I saw a cab speeding down Park Avenue with its overhead light on. I guess I could have stopped my momentum, but I let my legs carry me out into the middle of the street, and again I heard the screech of brakes. The cab skidded to a stop, the bumper just inches from my knees. Raymond grabbed the back door and yanked it open.

Sam Pulaski and Mathew Fields were getting into a small dark limousine about a half of a block in front of us. I jumped in behind Raymond and slammed the door.

"Get the fuck outta my cab," the driver said without turning around.

"Could you follow that black limo up there?" Raymond

asked, catching his breath. "The one pulling away from the curb."

"I said get outta my cab," the driver said, now turning in his seat. "That's a hell of a way to stop a taxi, buddy. You have any idea how much I dish out in insurance every year? You guys are nuts, man, and I don't drive for nuts. So get out before I call a cop."

I pulled ten dollars from my pocket and held it out for him. "Look, I'm sorry, but I'm in a hurry. Here, take this, and there'll be more. Just follow that car!"

He looked at the money and then at me. "It ain't the money, pal. It's the principle of the thing. What's gonna happen to me when one day I hit some wiseass who jumps in front of my cab? See what I'm saying? It ain't the money."

"Look, take the ten dollars and drive and we'll discuss the principle! Just *go*, goddamn it!"

"Shit," he said, grabbing the money from my hand and turning around in his seat. He put the car into gear and we started down Park Avenue, now about a block behind Pulaski. "Been driving twenty-five years and seen all kinds of shit, and I ain't never seen anyone stop a cab like that. Why do I always get the screwballs? You guys cops or something?"

"He's a private detective," Raymond said.

The driver looked up in his mirror at me and laughed. "Yeah, right, and I'm the mayor!"

We followed Pulaski down Park Avenue and then west on Forty-ninth Street. "He's not going to his office," Raymond said, "because that's east, and Mathew's office is uptown. Maybe they're going to the airport."

"They're going the wrong way to go to the airport," the cabbie said. "Unless they're going to Newark, and I'll tell you right now, fellas, this ten bucks isn't going to get you to New Jersey. You gotta pay twice the meter and all the tolls.

I don't care if you are a private detective. Who the hell are we following, anyway?"

"Bad guys," I said.

The driver laughed. "Why do I always get the screwballs?"

Pulaski continued west on Forty-ninth Street to the river and then headed down the West Side, picking up speed as soon as they were free of the traffic. Our driver was doing a good job of keeping up with them, grunting at the potholes and cursing out the other drivers. We were somewhere between Twenty-third Street and Fourteenth Street when I figured it out. We were going to the Hudson Harbor Office Complex.

I made the driver stop about a half a block away as we watched Pulaski's car turn into the entrance gate. I told Raymond to find a telephone and call Murphy and Branby and get them down there as soon as possible. I prayed that Murphy was back.

Raymond grabbed my arm as I climbed out of the cab. He didn't say anything, but I could see the worry in his face. "It's okay, Raymond," I said. "Just make the calls."

As soon as I got out I knew that something was wrong. The wide muddy parking area outside the project was empty. Nobody was working, and it was only three in the afternoon, too early for it to be so quiet. I walked slowly around the big, brown puddles and the broken cement toward the gate, wondering if I should wait for Branby.

There were two guards inside the gate, hanging around the wooden security booth. They looked at me but didn't move. One of them crossed his arms against his chest, his pistol sticking out from under his jacket. They showed no sign of being friendly, and they certainly weren't about to let me in, so I walked on slowly, studying the fence as I went. It was a standard chicken wire fence, about ten feet high, with a single strand of barbed wire running along the top. Through the fence I picked out the Norco trailer, closed and quiet. I walked about fifty yards, until there were plenty of trailers between me and the guards. Then I stopped and looked up at the fence. It could be a long wait until Branby showed up. Besides, I was pretty good at fences.

I took off my coat and tossed it up gently, getting it caught on the barbed wire and watching it fall back against the outside of the fence. Then I carefully buttoned my suit jacket and began to climb. When I got to the top I pulled the coat up and arranged it carefully over a section of barbed wire. I climbed higher and lifted my right leg over the coat, and got my foot firmly placed on the other side of the fence. Then I leaned forward and held on to the top part of the chicken wire with my hands. I felt the prickly points of the barbed wire poke at me through the coat. I swung my left leg behind me, working it over the top of the fence and then getting it placed into the chicken wire. Then I slowly straightened my body, pulling away from the coat and the barbed wire. I felt a tug at my neck. My tie had fallen out from my suit, and was stuck to a pointed barb sticking out from under the coat. I guess I had never tried to climb a fence with a tie on before. I tried to pull it loose, but it wouldn't budge. I leaned forward, loosened the tie and pulled it off over the top of my head. Then I jumped to the ground and went on my way, leaving the coat and the tie hanging stubbornly from the top of the fence.

There was a strong wind from the river, and I felt cold and vulnerable as I made my way through the trailers toward the building. I moved quickly, using the boards that were laid out across the mud. I peeked in the windows of the Norco trailer and there was no one there. I walked on until I got past the sheds and then stopped and looked up at the towering fortress of silver and green. It rose up from the mud and disappeared into the late-afternoon sky.

I bolted across the open area to the outside elevator on the south side of the building. Pulaski's limo was parked outside the elevator and I pulled the door open, but it was empty. I pushed the button for the elevator and heard the motors start. It had been at the top and now was coming down to get me. I waited anxiously, looking around and feeling the oppressive quiet. At last the elevator arrived, and when I stepped into the hard metal box, I thought that this was either the bravest or the stupidest thing that I had ever done. I threw down the handle, like I had seen Mitch Dougherty do only the week before. There was no sense in praying. They would be up there.

The ride seemed to take forever. I noticed that the doors did not take up the whole front of the elevator, and I played with the idea of hiding along the front wall, but before I could move, the elevator stopped and the doors popped open. I could not be sure if it was the same floor I had been on the previous week, but it looked the same. Straight across the open floor I saw Sam Pulaski, and Mathew Fields standing by the desk. Mitch Dougherty stood behind them, as did a chauffeur in a clean black suit.

Alfred Norens was sitting at the desk with a rifle pointed at my head. Across the windy floor I heard Norens laugh and call my name.

CHAPTER
—27—

I stepped out from the elevator and felt the cold wind sweep across the empty floor. The sun had long since disappeared behind the dark clouds over New Jersey, and yet the day lingered with a gloomy ambivalence. I walked slowly across the cement floor, making my way through the jutting pipes and wires and painfully aware of the not-so-distant edge. I don't know why it came to me just then, but I suddenly realized that Norco spelled backward was Ocron. I pulled up the collar of my suit.

Alfred Norens had laid the gun down on the desk in front of him, and they all watched me as I approached. I had two goals in mind. I wanted them to do the talking. And I wanted to stay away from the edge.

"Well, Eddie," Norens said, as I planted myself in front of his desk. "I had this funny feeling I'd be seeing you again."

He wore an expensive brown overcoat with a white cashmere scarf, and he was shaking his head with mild amusement. "After I met you, I called Sam and told him to look out for you. I just had this *feeling* you were going to be trouble."

"The feeling was mutual," I said.

Pulaski let out a loud grunt, and I just had to look at him and laugh. "What's the matter, Sam? Did you have a bad day?"

"You're a scum bag."

Norens laughed and held his open hand out at Pulaski. "What do I do with him? The man is out of control. We got eighty million dollars in the bag, and all he can see is the twenty million you screwed us out of. The man's out of control." He turned to Pulaski. "What time is your flight?"

"Five-fifteen."

"No problem. We'll have you there in thirty minutes. Stewart," he said, addressing the chauffeur. "Why don't you help Sam and Mathew here with their bags and take them down to the bird. I think Eddie and I need to talk."

There were no farewells. Pulaski and Fields followed the chauffeur back across the floor to the elevators, and we watched them in silence until they disappeared behind the elevator doors. Norens and Dougherty exchanged a look and then Dougherty began walking around the outer perimeter of the floor, like a sailor in the crow's nest looking for enemy ships.

"Have a seat," Norens said to me.

I settled into a chair opposite his desk, feeling strangely calm. I wasn't talking and I was away from the edge.

"Well, what do you have to say for yourself?" Norens asked.

"It's pretty quiet around here."

He laughed. "Yeah, I sent everyone home. It's good for

morale once in a while to surprise them with an afternoon off. It was a clever move today, Eddie, your shenanigans with the title company."

"It was Raymond Fidel's idea."

He raised his eyebrows. "Oh, is he back in the picture?"

I nodded.

"You know, Eddie, You're one of those guys who gets so caught up in figuring out the truth that you forget to keep an eye on where you're going." He leaned back in his seat and the legs of his chair were just inches from the edge. He looked down the side of the building, sending a wave of nausea through my gut. "Let me tell you the story of the Travis Building, Eddie," he said, still looking over the side. Dougherty was out of hearing distance by now.

"Maybe I already know it," I said.

Norens looked back and smiled at me. "Well, then, indulge me. It's not a story I'm otherwise going to get to tell." He moved his chair forward and put his feet up on the desk. "It all starts with Bill Bryant. Bill is a remarkable man. He's talented, he's brilliant, he's . . . well, you've met him. But I think, like me, he's got some kind of deficiency in his soul. Too smart for his own good, maybe. I don't know. I haven't quite figured it out, but I know this much. People do evil things to make up for their own smallness. With me, it was always a physical smallness. With Bill, maybe it was something more interior, but I'm no shrink. Bill's been a kingpin in the legal profession for a long time. He can get laws passed in Albany simply by calling the governor. What more could a guy want? And yet, for him, it wasn't enough. I know that feeling, Eddie. Look at me. I got more money than I know how to spend. And yet, I'm not satisfied just winning the game. I'm only happy if the other guy loses. Are you following me?"

"That depends on where you're going."

"Well, we're getting to the good part now. It was Bill who came up with the whole idea, and it's so simple that it's unbelievable. The New York Style Closing. Of all the states in this country, New York is the one state where the closing procedures depend on trust and goodwill. You figure it out. It's about the goddamned stupidest thing I've ever heard. And yet it works. Why? Because no one's had the guts to cheat it."

"Until now."

"Bingo. The way Bill tells the story to me, he was preparing some proposed legislation to send up to Albany and he was dealing with some of the problems inherent in the New York Style Closing. Well, he started to sketch out a scenario of how someone might be able to take advantage of the present procedures. One thing led to another, and pretty soon he had me out alone on my boat and he was laying it out for me. It was just beautiful."

Norens brought his feet down and leaned across his desk. "I'm sure you've figured this out already, but I couldn't believe it when Bill explained it to me. Banks lend money based on a commitment from the title company that they're insured. Title companies insure based on what other mortgages are recorded. The clerk's office is a week behind getting mortgages onto the books. The whole goddamned thing works on blind faith. It's amazing! We closed two on Friday, one Monday and one yesterday, and not a single title company figured it out!"

He stood up in his excitement and began pacing along the edge of the floor behind his desk. "But, obviously, somebody's going to be left holding the bag. Right? So Bill comes up with the idea of using an offshore company as the first mortgagee and working the deals as refinancings. That's where I come in. He needs me to lay out twenty million for the first mortgage. That Ocron loan is a bona fide mortgage.

But now, instead of signing our names on the mortgages and having everyone on our tail, we get some other sucker to sign, and we let all the banks just cut checks to our offshore company. The money's transferred into Swiss accounts and everyone's chasing Pulaski. We're sitting pretty behind a Panamanian Corporation."

"So what's in it for Pulaski?"

He stopped and looked at me with a devilish grin. "Pulaski? Well, he's our sucker. We needed someone who had some money and credibility in the real estate industry, so no one would question what he was doing. Pulaski was perfect for the job. He's been around. Everyone hates him. He's stupid and greedy. Bill and I spent a year looking for the right guy with the right building. We offered him half the take and a nice big condo down in the Caribbean. After a couple of years, when things quiet down, we told him, he'd get a new passport and he could come back."

Suddenly Dougherty's big voice boomed across the floor. "Al, we got trouble!"

Dougherty was standing on the eastern edge looking down toward the entrance. I stood up and moved closer to the desk so I could see. The guards were standing outside the security booth with their hands in the air and a group of police cars was coming in through the open gate. There were about ten of them, their lights flashing in the late-afternoon light. Cops never looked so good.

Suddenly Norens was talking into his telephone. "Peter, Al Norens. Is he there?" His voice rang with anger.

The cars all stopped inside the gate and now the cops were getting out. Norens was talking again. "I don't care who is in his office! I need him now! This instant!" He leaned back and watched the cops gathering in a huddle. Then he spoke into the telephone. "John, I'm real sorry to bother you, but somebody's sent a mess of cops down here to the Hudson Harbor and they're crawling all over the place. I got a couple of money people here from Europe and the cops are making them nervous. I'm gonna lose the whole thing." He listened for a brief second. "No, I don't know what they want. Listen, John, you know me. Anytime, anywhere, anybody wants to talk to me, I'm game. But not now, for Christ's sake! John, I need you to get rid of these guys. Please!" His face suddenly broke into a smile. "That's what I need to hear. I owe you one. Bye."

He slammed the telephone down in triumph. "Okay, Eddie. Keep watching."

It was impossible to make out individuals from the distance, but some of the cops were in plainclothes. One of them would be Branby. The huddle broke up, and police started to fan out, walking through the muddy field. My heart sank. Even if the mayor or chief of police didn't call them off, they would never find us.

No sooner had they begun to spread out than a plainclothesman at the cars began to wave them all back. A giant pit opened up in my stomach as I watched them all stop and head back toward their cars. Norens watched too, until they were all back in their cars and heading out the gate.

"Bill told me right up front that the hardest part was going to be keeping it all quiet," Norens said, his voice suddenly lower and more serious. "But between him and me, we've got this town covered."

I watched the last of the cars disappear through the exit and felt a sickening anxiety as the guards closed the gate behind them. "We used separate banks," Norens was saying, "separate title companies, and separate lawyers for each deal. Bill took a lot of time picking them out and matching them up. Dorfman was our first problem. Lucky for us, he was dumb enough to call Pulaski and ask him what the hell was going on. I sent Mitch over to explain things to him, but

Mitch was never very good with words, if you know what I mean."

The cops were gone and I was on my own. "Mitch used to work for a union out in New Jersey, didn't he?"

Norens smiled. "Maybe he did, but he never talks about it. Then again, I never ask. Anyway, Fidel figures it out next and disappears on us before Mitch can get over there to explain it to him. Bill's firm hires you guys to find Fidel, and we bust our asses trying to find the son of a bitch before you do. We took the Rolodex from his office and the address book from his apartment."

"You arranged for the fake cops?"

"You were riding my bird out to Jersey while they went through Fidel's apartment. Anyway, I'll tell you frankly, we were having a hard time, and we were starting to get scared, and then Bill calls me and tells me you're in Fort Lauderdale. Mitch was down there in a few hours, and you led him to that ex-con, who led him straight to Fidel. Only we missed him."

"Then you came back here and had to be a pain in the ass by staying on the case. That Pinder girl called Bryant after you talked to Barry Fried, so we had a feeling you might be on to us."

"So you tried to push me under the Number Six."

Norens turned and faced the river, and I heard the roar of the helicopter as it suddenly came lifting up over the side of the building. It hung for a moment, level with our floor, and I tried to look for Pulaski and Fields in the back seat, but it was too far away. Norens waved and then the helicopter headed away from the building, out over the Hudson River. As I watched it shrink against the New Jersey sky, I realized that I was not looking at the Spitfire Taurus that Norens had taken me in. This was the old Hiller, the one he didn't know what to do with. The one he had said might come in handy.

Norens winked at me as he sat down behind his desk. "We've all got to go sometime."

I stared at his devilish grin and suddenly I understood.

I turned back to look at the helicopter just as the sky exploded into a violent ball of red and orange fire, rocking me in my seat and making me feel sick. One instant the helicopter was there, and the next instant it was gone. I watched a piece of the tail fly up out of the flames and then suddenly drop, spinning as it fell and burning until it hit the water.

CHAPTER
——28——

I watched the black smoke from the explosion slowly dissipate over the Hudson River. I felt the wind ripping through me. Mitch Dougherty had made a complete trip around the periphery and now stood near Norens. He turned to me and smiled, and I felt the air rush out of me, leaving me like a flat tire. As he took his first step toward me, the floor and the sky began to spin. Norens was talking, his voice a thousand miles away, saying something about trespassers and the assumption of risks. I should have been listening. I should have been talking. I had to tell them that Raymond Fidel knew everything and that he would be calling Murphy. I had to do something, but I could not move.

Dougherty grabbed my left arm and lifted me out of the seat. I had no energy to fight. He twisted the arm up behind my back, and suddenly I felt his big rough hand wrap around my index finger. Slowly he pushed it backward toward the outer side of my hand until it began to hurt. I could not believe this was happening.

"No, Mitch," Norens said calmly. "Not the fingers."

Mitch stopped, and I could hear him breathing behind me, his hand still anxiously holding my finger.

"Don't you understand, Mitch?" Norens was saying. "If they find him with broken fingers, they're gonna nail you."

Mitch grunted and let go of the finger. He still held me by my arm, just below the shoulder, and he began to pull me toward the edge. My knees gave way and my body collapsed, but Dougherty held me up and dragged me, my shoes scraping across the floor.

He held me at the edge of the floor, my feet somehow standing on their own, my arm beginning to ache from his grip. The sky over New Jersey had darkened into a purple smoldering gray, and I could already see the lights coming on in the apartment buildings by the river. People led their lives in ordinary ways. They went to work, they came home, they took vacations. There was no grand scheme of how it was all supposed to be. Life was nothing more than the warm twinkling lights in somebody's home after a hard day at the office. I looked at the silver and brown waters of the Hudson River, feeling its wisdom and its power. Dougherty pushed me right up to the edge, and I knew I was about to go over.

"Come on, Mitch," Norens said, with obvious aggravation. "Stop fooling around. You know we can't do it here. Not with the helicopter mess."

I felt myself pulled backward away from the edge and I sucked in a lungful of air. I had not been breathing. Dougherty laughed and led me back to my seat, this time, my feet moving slowly in cooperation. I was breathing and walking. He let go of my arm, and I literally fell into the chair, my legs shaking uncontrollably.

"What's the matter, Eddie? Don't you like heights?" Norens asked.

I couldn't answer.

"Don't worry about it," Norens was saying. "Mitch is gonna find you a nice deep swamp to sleep in."

"Raymond Fidel knows everything," I said, the words rushing out. "So does Alice Pinder."

Norens shook his head in disbelief. "So what, smart guy? They can know whatever they want, but the only guy they have evidence against just took a swim in the Hudson. Ocron is being dissolved as we speak."

The elevator doors suddenly closed with a loud metallic bang. Norens and Dougherty exchanged looks. Norens picked up the rifle and then snapped his fingers and pointed over the edge for Dougherty to take a look.

"The cars are all gone," Dougherty said. "I can't see anything."

Norens handed the rifle to Dougherty and pointed at the door. "I don't care who it is," he said, his voice solemn and low. "Kill him."

Dougherty let me go and grabbed the rifle. Planting his feet firmly on the floor, he held the rifle by his side, the nozzle pointed dead smack at the middle of the elevator doors. Norens stood behind his desk, and he winked at me and smiled. "You're gonna love this, Eddie," he said.

Whoever it was would be dead unless I did something. Norens stood defenselessly behind his desk. He was not a problem. Mitch Dougherty was the problem. He stood, like the monster he was, waiting to waste whoever stepped through the elevator doors. I didn't have much to work with, but I did have the chair I'd been sitting on. I had to be ready to move the instant the doors opened. My legs tensed and my fingers grabbed the seat.

With the first crack in the doors I leaped up and hurled

my chair at Dougherty's head. He held the rifle out to block it and tried to duck, but the chair hit him squarely. I turned to the elevator for help. There was no one there. I turned back and saw Dougherty, knocked off balance, but not down, and I watched with horror as the chair bounced once and then rolled over the edge of the building.

"Nice work!" I heard Norens say, and then I heard the shot. Dougherty stumbled slightly, the rifle falling from his hands onto the hard floor. He looked at me with a strange expression of confusion. Then there was another shot, and he pitched backward and then forward. He looked at me again and then slumped to the floor.

Branby stood outside the elevator doors, his gun still trained on Dougherty. When it was clear that Dougherty was down, he turned his gun toward Norens and started walking toward us.

Norens was standing behind his desk, grinning like a child. "What can I do for you, sir? I think you just shot my foreman," he called out to Branby.

"You can put your hands in the air and stay where you are," Branby called back as he approached.

Norens waited calmly behind his desk until Branby approached. "I think you're going to have some explaining to do," Norens said.

"The mayor's not gonna be able to help you out of this one, Norens."

Norens was still smiling. "And I'm afraid I don't know what you're talking about."

"You're under arrest, Mr. Norens," Branby said, and then he smiled.

Sam Pulaski stumbled out of the elevator with his hands cuffed behind his back. Murphy stepped out behind him and gave him a push across the floor.

The smile disappeared from Norens's face and he instinctively turned and looked out over the Hudson River where the helicopter had gone down. He stepped back from the desk, just inches away from the edge of the building.

"Fields and the chauffeur are downstairs," Branby said. "It was a nice try."

Norens suddenly regained his composure as Murphy and Pulaski approached the desk. "So, who *was* in the bird?" Norens said.

"Just the pilot," said Branby. "We let it go so you wouldn't get suspicious, although obviously we had no idea how low you would stoop."

Pulaski's face was contorted with rage. "Norens, I'm gonna see your fuckin' ass in hell."

Norens was smiling again. "For once you're right, Pulaski, you asshole." He stood staring at all of us. His smile was too big, and suddenly I knew that he would have the last laugh.

I screamed, "No!"

But Norens took the last step backward and as he went over the edge he erupted into wild hysterics. We stood helplessly, listening to his screaming laughter fade as he fell.

EPILOGUE

Alice Pinder said that neither of us was ready to get involved in a relationship, and I guessed that she was right. I was feeling crazy enough just being back in New York and adjusting to my new job. She had just ended a four-year affair with some guy who decided to marry someone else; she didn't even know he had been seeing her. We agreed to be friends, and so it was with this in mind that I had accepted her invitation for a lunchtime stroll.

It was a cold December afternoon, but there was plenty of sun, and we walked to the little park along the East River by the United Nations. We stood leaning against the railing watching the sea gulls glide and dip over the murky waters of the East River. Alice was wearing a dark wool coat, buttoned up to the neck, and her pretty red scarf matched her wool gloves.

We talked about our jobs. I told her about the new cases Murphy had assigned me to, and she talked about what the real estate department was like at Fenner, Covington & Pine without Bill Bryant. Bryant had been forced to resign because of his arrest, and now, without him and without Raymond Fidel, the department was even busier than usual. It left Alice even less time for herself.

It was a pleasant hour, strolling in the December sun and talking about our jobs and our lives. And yet, as we left the park and headed back toward our offices, I was overcome by feelings of uneasiness and anxiety. I felt as if the whole walk had been for some secret purpose that was being concealed from me, and I began to wonder if this was a friendship that I had any real interest in pursuing.

As we stepped out of the park onto First Avenue, Alice gently slipped her hand into mine, and the deep longing I had felt that night with her suddenly came back to me. I found myself staring at her. Her eyes were clear blue and her cheeks were bright red. I could see the steam from her breath in the cold December air. I wanted to say something. I wanted to tell her all that I was feeling, but my brain was not working, and my voice was gone. I squeezed her hand in frustration and then let go and we walked back to our jobs in silence.